WHO SH
JACKSON BRODIE?

NICKI THORNTON

CHIMNEYS
PUBLISHING

CHIMNEYS PUBLISHING

www.chimneyspublishing.co.uk

First edition by Chimneys Publishing 2026

Paperback 978-1-068-27002-4

Printed and bound by
CPI Group (UK) Ltd, Croydon, CR0 4YY

Cover design by Holly Astle

"Cozy crime & an Indy bookshop, a match made in book heaven! Perfectly plotted, buckets of humour, littered with red herrings & satisfying twists big & small. A must read for all fans of cozy crime & Indy bookshops!"—Sally Poyton

"I thoroughly enjoyed being in Nicki Thornton's murderous world of a seemingly innocent bookshop. A wonderful new voice in cosy crime fiction."—Kate Wells

"Thornton keeps the twists coming… I can heartily recommend this book."—AnnaBookBel

"The Little Bookshop of Murders is a LOT of fun, and highly recommended for cosy crime fans"—Nairn Books

"A very readable page-turner with a protagonist I care about, an intriguing plot and interesting side characters!"—Sammysbookhaven

ACKNOWLEDGEMENTS

As Keera Munroe would tell you, there are many people who go to making a book a success. So thank you so much to everyone who champions my books at every stage and contributes to making them better books, or helps get them into the hands of readers.

Thank you to my incredible team at Chimneys Publishing and to everyone who has reviewed my books or contacted me to say lovely things about them. It means so much.

I am a huge supporter of independent booksellers who constantly matchmake and place books into the hands of readers. So I want to mention some booksellers who have been wonderful, championing the first book of the Little Bookshop of Murders mystery series, including B for Butterfly in Manchester, Bodies in the Bookshop in Cambridge, Booka Bookshop in Oswestry, The Book Corner in Saltburn, Hungerford Bookshop in Berkshire, Wantage Bookshop in Oxfordshire, The Little Bookshop in Cookham, Nairn Books in the Highlands of Scotland, North Books in Hay-on-Wye, Red Lion Bookshop in Colchester, and Tea Leaves and Reads in Andover.

I know many other indie bookshops have stocked, sold and championed this series. Thank You! Keera would be thrilled.

To Sandra and Geoff, for all your hard work
on this book, which is very much appreciated, as is
everything you do

1

Keera

From the second he walked into my bookshop I knew what he was.

Tall. Late fifties. Greying hair clipped short. Upright. Muscles less from pressing weights, more pressing faces to the pavement. Mint-coloured polo (ironed) paired with black jeans even in this weather (and ironed). A poor attempt to look casual. Black shoes (too shiny) that squeak as he crosses the tiny space between the door and where I'm hiding behind the counter with a fixed, tense smile.

One of the many downsides of running a bookshop is that you cannot choose who's going to walk in your door.

'Hello Keera. Lovely shop,' he says. 'It is Keera isn't it?'

How does he know my name?

And what has brought police into my lovely bookshop?

Not to kick-start a reading interest in romantasy. Too much to hope he's here to buy a book at all. Easier to imagine he's the front man, the distraction, making sure I'm in place as a SWAT team descends on all sides to drag me into an underground room for questioning.

All my past misdemeanours rise up from my memory and he slides a slim briefcase onto the counter; unclips it with two unnaturally loud metallic clicks. His hands go inside his briefcase. I hold my breath.

He slides a printed dossier of A4 pages across the counter.

Refusing to Remain Silent *the unvarnished truth of forty years a copper* by *former DCI Mitch Ravenscroft.*

'You're an author! Wow, did not see that coming.' My shoulders drop and I resume breathing.

His wolfish smile I see less as predatory, more nerves. Mitch, I guess. So even hardened coppers get the jitters going into a bookshop to ask for help trying to find readers for what they've written. I guess it's why he's here.

'You've a book coming out!' I say. 'That's why you're looking shifty! Well, it's not often I get to feel intimidating, especially not to police. I'm a bookseller. You're with Ripper Press. Small publisher, but love the name. Do you want to tell me about it?'

Mitch clears his throat. I get a whiff that he went for a coffee before coming here and hope he supported one of our nice local, indie cafes.

'None of the big publishers could see making millions from a memoir by an ex-Met officer who didn't deal in any high profile crimes,' he says, more relaxed now he's got the difficult reveal out of the way. 'I'd love to prove those big publishers wrong. I'd love at least to cover my very small advance. Would you be interested in helping? Would you be kind enough to stock it?'

I'm more in the habit of asking tricky questions than answering them. I'd like to ask why an ex-Met copper would trail into my tiny, wholesome village bookshop, Between the Lines, to ask for support. He feels a long way from home. But Mitch is waiting and still I hesitate. Because Mitch is about to discover a brutal truth. Brutal truths might be commonplace in the police, but the one in publishing is that there are millions of books out there, tens of thousands of authors – and only a few hundred bookshops and nowhere near enough shelf space.

'Opening my bookshop opened my eyes to a lot. Like I never knew how many people are writing books,' I begin. 'My shop probably has less shelf space than my biggest-reading, well-heeled Crossways customers. Deciding what to stock—nothing but a total nightmare!'

The door opens to admit Verity Anderson, granddaughter of one of my bookgroup members; here for the summer under rumoured cloudy circumstances that have got Crossways gossiping, although it doesn't take much. Verity's a recent English student, a big reader. Would Verity be up for London-based true crime?

'Hi!' I say. She smiles back at me.

Verity's volunteering next door for the new Eliza's Deli. Owner Eliza Somers wears floaty summer dresses and chats effortlessly while serving salads and small cakes. Verity sports unobtrusive straight brown hair, long, grey skirt and top in the same, shadowy colour. I could more easily believe she's auditioning for an undercover agent than enjoys selling olives.

Her arrival gives me a moment to consider how I tell Mitch his book is not the greatest fit to fly off my shelves.

'Things all good with you?' I ask as Verity goes straight to my popular nature-writing section.

If Mitch was pitching a book about the joys of sheep farming, my customers would be more easily sold.

'Hi Verity.' Mitch greets her. 'It is Verity isn't it?'

Verity looks as pained as you might expect if an obvious police officer (even ex) knew your name when you'd only been in town a few weeks. We share a worried glance. *How does he know both our names?*

'I hardly ever sell true crime,' I admit. There, I've said it.

How will Mitch react? It's me who's nervy now. Many authors argue. Quite a few get angry, as if shouting at me will encourage me to support them. Another of the mysteries of bookselling.

Mitch smiles and shrugs. 'A tough crowd, I get it!' Which makes me warm to him.

'Now I have books to save!' I say. 'I need to move into kick-ass superhero bookseller mode and save the books in my window. It's been so unseasonably hot the covers are beginning to curl in all this bright sunshine. But I got distracted by a crime thriller about stolen birds eggs.'

'Reading on the job? I'm sure it happens,' says Mitch.

'Rather too much, I'm afraid. Although being distracted by bird eggs was unexpected. The Impossible Thing, brilliant read. If you're looking for a recommendation.'

'I can't think why I haven't been in here before, this is a lovely shop,' says Mitch. 'Busy writing this book I guess! Many start writing, but few ever finish. I'm not surprised now I know the unbelievable amount of time involved. I can imagine selling books is challenging. Particularly selling a memoir of a copper no one's heard of.'

Mitch gives a wry chuckle. 'But when your very small publisher drops hints that any publicity is down to you, my first strategy was making friends of my three local bookshops. And they are all lovely! One of the things I'm liking about your book world is how incredibly kind booksellers are.

Kindness is something people are generally short on when talking to police.'

'You're local?'

'I am now. Tom over at Lindford Books has very kindly asked me to give a talk.' Mitch crooks an enquiring eyebrow at me. 'Not too much blood. Unless your tough crowd could do with a bit of blood? Bit of excitement?'

We both unobtrusively slide looks towards where Verity's happily browsing. Not much blood in nature writing, although perhaps there should be.

Mitch's hand hovers over the manuscript on the counter between us. 'I got into the writing game through a side hustle offering authors insider tips on crime authenticity. A few big names, actually. One of the things I love about the book trade over police work is the shiny glitter that surrounds authors. In the force it's never glitter you get covered with. I really want to make this work.'

Could I make this work? Can I help Mitch?

I'm not sure, but I find I'm asking myself: *what would Liv Trent do*? One of the unexpected benefits of my fresh start and new life and opening a bookshop has been how many customers have become friends, particularly Liv Trent, who is exhaustingly full of smart ideas. Author events being one.

My definition of a good time is finding people the right book to read. Liv's is going for the evening crowd: celebrity authors, interviews with sassy questions over wine. Her plan is to get me organising, filling venues and hosting. It fills me with more terror than my previous life. And that involved a lot of police and blood.

'Armchair detectives used to mean people who read crime fiction,' says Mitch. 'Now its podcasts and online chats and people trying to solve real-life cases of murderers who got away with it. I'm told true crime is quite the hot ticket. Just keep me in mind for a talk. The author you get when you can't get a famous author. My plan in moving here was to take an easier path. Only partly worked. But it's my patch now.'

Mitch is not alone in hoping Crossways offers a door to a simpler life. I know about needing to take a step back from the worst side of life. Even demure Verity, frowning at a tough choice between two popular nature books, came to wholesome Crossways for a fresh start. If the rumours are true, which they very probably aren't. Crossways is big on chatter, low on facts.

I came here for a fresh start, despite my family, friends and particularly Supportive Mum, being keen to point out I knew nothing about bookselling. Or retail. Or small businesses. Or events. Or villages. She gave my wild and risky bookshop plan a year. *'No, two, because you never know when to give up, Keera, so you'll stick it out long after you should have given it up. And then you'll end up with debts as well as regrets over abandoning a promising career.'*

But I am still here. Am I getting any better at bookselling? Mostly, I thank my lucky stars I have Liv. Liv is actually good at all of it and so full of boundless enthusiasm and ideas I have started to feel she's my boss. I know she's right about events. Mitch is right here…

'Maybe a crime writing workshop might suit your tough crowd?' he offers. Can he tell I'm wavering? 'My book's not all murders. There are some fun bits.' Mitch twinkles at me. 'There's one case where a girlfriend gave a watertight alibi and then her boyfriend made the tactical error of going off with her best friend, then she was singing like a canary. I haven't actually said the singing like a canary bit in the book. I have tried to avoid some cliches.'

I smile and wonder if this is the moment I stop trying to resist Liv's mission and go along with her tactic for success in life, which is to turn everything into a party.

Imagine showing off to Liv Trent that I've booked an author event without any help.

But true crime? Will anyone turn out for that? Or a crime writing workshop? Is anyone around here writing their own book? It seems unlikely.

'How do you even choose which of your cases to write about?' I pick up the manuscript sitting on the counter between us.

'There are always cases that stay with you,' Mitch says. 'Too many, sadly.'

'Because the cases were so shocking? Too much blood? Or because you feel you're responsible for the wrong guy languishing behind bars for years?'

We both throw another discreet glance at Verity, embroiled in the battle of the nature writers.

Mitch rubs his chin where his skin looks a little raw from a close shave.

'Obviously there was one I had to include, the one I'd most love to get a new lead on. My hope is the book will spark some chatter. Something new will come of it. And that keeps my deluded hopes alive that it will become a surprise bestseller.'

'Surprise bestseller? That's not a myth publishers like to dangle, a bit like children and Santa Claus for ensuring good behaviour? So. What would you most like a lead on?'

'Well. Moving here was supposed to be a soft curve down to retirement. Instead, I walked into one of the worst cases of my career. Just imagine. If we could get a new lead on the Crossways Killings. That would be something.'

The world feels as if it's tilted and there's a rush of blood to my head.

'Your book features an unsolved murder in *Crossways*?'

I turn, thinking I heard Verity take a sharp breath. But she's very absorbed with Merlin Sheldrake and Guy Shrubsole and who will win the nature-writing war.

'Not just one murder, two,' Mitch says quietly. 'Ah, you're new here. What they call a media sensation. Interest faded when there wasn't enough for journalists to get their teeth into. I have a feeling it's a Crossways shameful secret brushed under the carpet. Maybe I'm just too addicted to checking under carpets,' says Mitch. 'Or an expensive rug, this is Crossways. An impossible crime. I'd like to prove that wrong too.'

'You hope your book will get people talking about an impossible crime that happened right here?'

'It was a tough one. The victims weren't local. No witnesses. One of those random crimes. But a small village where everyone knows everyone and no one saw anything…? Sometimes all it takes is for things to get stirred up, a reminder that it hasn't been forgotten. One tiny new lead, something overlooked at the time. That's how lots of old cases get solved. Where's the harm? Because the Crossways Killings is the very definition of a case that will only crack if someone decides to talk.'

'When someone starts singing like a canary?'

'Because they always do sing.' Mitch nods. 'Eventually.'

2

Verity

An about-to-be published book that no one had read yet, containing potentially explosive insider facts. Just sitting there on the dumb bookseller's counter. It took all Verity's focus to remain calm.

Verity knew about the Crossways Killings, of course she did (unlike the dumb bookseller). Surely anyone planning to move to a new place did basic research into Anything Even Remotely Interesting About Crossways.

Verity had had zero hope of anything but boredom while staying with her grandmother in her summer of shame. But here, in this tiny, untidy bookshop, Verity had never felt more filled with the surge of clarity and purpose while she feigned interest in a book on fungi.

An impossible crime. Words to make you tingle.

She'd accepted this fresh-start offer from Grandma after her parents hinted they weren't keen for her to move back into her old room (as if she was keen on that option). Grandma's wasn't so much her best offer as her only offer.

This was her lot. What you got for being twenty-one, with your biggest skill being your ability to write essays about books. Nearly three years of university brought to an abrupt end with all the accompanying debt, but no degree. Living with your Grandma and volunteering dishing up olives in a dull village. But all the community positivity, all the chocolate-box niceness, had to be concealing something slitheringly dark and properly poisonous. Verity wouldn't have been surprised if Crossways was ruled by mind-control aliens, a cult, or werewolves.

But of course, Crossways' secret was a shockingly brutal murder.

And in an unexpected twist, fate had been with her all along. She'd been on a date with destiny and was now close to a huge, unparalleled opportunity. An actual real-life cold case presented to her, along with someone with a plan to solve it.

But she'd have to tread carefully.

'This must be a lovely job,' Mitch chattered. Chat had gone all boring once Keera had offered to help him sell his book. 'Books are so wholesome.'

But were they? In books Verity saw war, oppression, murder, obsession. And that was just the kids' section.

She needed to find a way to get Mitch to involve her in his quest to finally unmask the Crossways Killer. But how? Without jeopardising the terms by which she got a roof over her head this summer?

Grandma gave her a daily reminder Verity had been put on the naughty step.

'Being interested in people is not the same as obsessively poking your nose into their lives and digging into their secrets. What you won't accept, Verity, is that you can do more harm than good.' Grandma had said in what were becoming feature breakfast lectures (not Verity's best time).

Verity had finished the dregs of cereal chocolate milk with a spoon rather than tipping it up and drinking it, because Verity was on best behaviour. And even a breakfast lecture meant Grandma switched off her jaunty Tidal playlist. Eighties was a bit much in the morning. So a point to Verity. But nowhere near the score she'd get if she could find answers to the biggest mystery in Crossways.

Then Verity would prove everyone, including Grandma, wrong. She'd make Grandma see it wasn't *causing* trouble that Verity relished – it was noticing it. But where to start?

From listening to a lot of true-crime podcasts, Verity knew you were lucky if you started with much more than a sliver of new intel. Mitch was right and fresh eyes might produce the tiniest lead, the beginnings of a crack. So what slivers had Mitch revealed in his book about the deaths of those two incomers, who had apparently done nothing wrong other than moving to Crossways?

And how could Verity get to read that manuscript?

'What I want for you this summer is to find a way to use your skills and imagination for something less obsessive; something valuable and productive,' Grandma had said only this morning.

Valuable. Productive. This from the person who was, unironically, making her work for the summer for no pay. And considering what a forensic sort of a person Grandma was (and she was a chemist), you'd think she'd be careful about how she used terms. Like *obsessive.*

'You really don't need to come to bookgroup tonight.' Keera unexpectedly brought Verity into the conversation.

'Oh I don't mind,' said Verity quickly. In truth, bookgroup was essential to making her summer of shame bearable, because Verity already had a few small cases to solve.

Embarrassingly small. Revealing the true secret of David Purkiss's shed or Isha Cheema's winter holiday exposé weren't going to get anyone's pulse racing, but this was Crossways. And solving something was how she'd impress Grandma, even though she knew she had her work cut out as Grandma Smollett was nothing if not stubborn and used to winning all her arguments.

'I can have a word with your grandma,' offered Keera.

'No! I mean, please don't worry. It'll be fine.'

This would be a disaster. Not least because Keera had a terrible reputation for blundering in and always saying completely the wrong thing.

'Grandma made me follow her up and down Crossways high street in my lunch break and she spent a small fortune on artisanal cheeses,' Verity said. 'Apparently that makes it a proper Crossways party tonight. How could I miss that?'

Keera grinned. 'Bookgroup is full of people who like their cheese.'

Bookgroup was full of people who prided themselves on being crucial to Crossways, a bit like those fungal cordyceps with far-reaching underground bonds: tug on one and you never know where the networks would end.

What could be more perfect to find out secrets than where people felt chatty, rather than under scrutiny? Verity was grateful to her earlier self for starting her *I am not going to bookgroup, no way, campaign* early, drawing battlelines over the breakfast table. Bookgroup was a secret weapon, a way to move forward without Grandma knowing what she was doing. Because Verity could quiz them right under Grandma's nose. And she was going to have to be at her slipperiest and best to conceal her covert case-cracking. Until she could amaze and impress everyone with the big reveal. And now there was a chance she could expose someone, very possibly living right now, quietly among the very good and very dull people of Crossways.

A murderer.

What could be more useful and productive than that?

3

Verity

'Goodbye Verity. Lovely to meet you. See you soon.' Mitch was leaving before he'd said anything useful.

Verity flinched when Mitch opened the door as it let in the sharp retort of a crow-scarer, bringing the raw of the countryside into the soft silence and papery aroma of the bookshop.

He'd left his manuscript on the counter.

Mitch's departure also let in a ferociously ugly tabby who greeted Verity with his famously over-loud miaow.

'Hey Jackson Brodie!' said Verity, stroking his fur.

Jackson was a roamer cat with a lot of untidy brown fur. A dark patch on his right eye looked like he'd been punched in a brawl, and he carried a world-weary air, as if he'd come off worst in too many fights. His pale paws were dark with dirt and he was constantly cleaning them.

'Eliza says she's never known a cat to be such a digger,' Verity said. 'She can't believe he found anywhere to dig as it's been so dry lately. Terrible what's happened to his tail. Dinner time again, Jackson?'

'We're both feeding him, aren't we?' sighed Keera, going to find a cat bowl in a crammed side room in desperate need of a clear out. 'What about his tail?'

'Lots of people feed him,' said Verity. 'You'd think that means everyone loves Jackson Brodie. But he must have an arch enemy, mustn't he?'

'Do cats have arch enemies?'

'Well Jackson must. Eliza's determined to get to the bottom of it. She quizzes everyone. See how his tail's not straight? Someone's taken a shot at him.'

'Jackson Brodie was shot?' said Keera, pausing in shaking out cat food. 'Good for Eliza to try to find out what happened.'

'Everywhere has its dark side I guess.'

'She means by accident I hope,' said Keera, fussing the cat as he ate. 'Who would shoot you?'

'Crossways is surprisingly full of guns,' said Verity. 'But not awash with things that need shooting. More sheep than zombies. Not that guns work well against the undead. Everyone deserves justice, don't they. Even cats.'

'Absolutely. What is everyone saying?'

'Eliza says Crossways rumours are notoriously unreliable, but that doesn't stop them spreading. She's looking for evidence about who shot Jackson.'

'Although it can be informative to listen to the gossip.'

Verity wasn't as interested in rumours about the cat as she was in her boss, as one of her cases was: Who Would Harm Eliza Somers and Why? Eliza took a keen interest in the lives of all her customers, not just the furry one. Her caring attitude was probably part of the reason the deli had been such an instant success, because she definitely over-priced her olives. But Verity was curious. Why would a single woman, only in her thirties, choose to move to a village backwater to set up a business selling a range of salty continental cold meats and sugary small cakes?

Verity had squeezed little out of Eliza above that she'd been a teacher and had worked in all sorts of remote places, but got tired of travelling.

'Talking of rumours,' said Verity, seizing the opportunity to move along her caseload. 'What do you think of the story that Eliza's here hiding out from a violent ex-lover? Jackson's not the only one who looks like he's been in a fight.'

'If anyone can get to the bottom of that,' said Keera, 'it would be you.'

This was true. Grandma had volunteered Verity to step in after Eliza had appeared one day with a black eye, bruising to her leg, difficulty moving and suspected cracked ribs and was struggling to run the deli on her own. Naturally, with injuries like that, Verity asked herself if someone was out to deliberately harm friendly, community-positive, olive-selling Eliza?

Verity was on the inside track, but so far she'd found only one excuse to go upstairs to Eliza's flat above the shop, where there must be clues to Who Would Harm Eliza Somers and Why?

There had been too-little time to do more than observe the furniture was big for such a small space, as if Eliza had left somewhere in a hurry. And no time to look properly at what was all over the big dining room table: what appeared to be a detailed research project.

Verity had no chance to do more than glance at it, be intrigued and curse herself for not having her phone with her so she could take photos and look properly later. She'd be more prepared next time.

Sometimes all you needed was a sliver to find a crack and split a case wide open. But Verity was only here for the summer. Now in her caseload she had: Who Did the Crossways Killings and Why? Priorities.

'Eliza's lucky to have you helping,' said Keera. 'And if you want a hint for a successful bookgroup evening, I'd say don't put the cheese anywhere near Grant Michaels. Especially if it's expensive cheese.'

'Noted.' Although Verity had her own plans for what would make for a successful evening. 'Guess I'll see you later.'

To think that for a while, Verity had been worried her biggest summer entertainment was going to be investigating Who Shot Jackson Brodie?

4

Keera

End of day customers are often the worst dawdlers, and the worst buyers. So when my door opens just when I'm rushing to finish urgent tasks I should have finished ages ago, all I can find is a tired welcome.

I'm relieved it's Liv Trent as I am *very* behind with my urgent tasks.

'It's that time of day when customers have lost the chance to buy any more books to get them through the night.' Liv turns my sign to *closed* with a flourish.

She drifts in on a wave of expensive Dior with her always perfect hair, discreetly expensive jewellery, wearing a floral dress that's way too pretty for bookgroup, waving a bottle of wine that will be too good for bookgroup. I check the time and panic.

'It's a little early for closing, but I won't object,' I say.

'That means you're behind. Hopefully because you've been rushed off your feet with customers and made loads of sales and not because you got distracted.'

'I may not be behind. Looks like you've got everything you need for bookgroup, so give me a sec,' I say as Liv plonks the wine on my counter where my tea normally sits. 'Is bookgroup now officially part of your mission to turn everything into a party? And I may have exciting news.'

'Only you seriously believe they come only to talk about books.'

'But everyone loves talking about books.'

'Possibly not as much as they enjoy the chance to not feel behind on the gossip. Exciting news?' Liv crooks an eyebrow at me.

'Wait. I need to despatch my customer orders or Dahlia Figgis won't get the Skandar book she promised for her grandson tomorrow and I'll be toast. Or unicorn food.'

'I almost brought two bottles of wine, but it's so hot I thought everyone might be on water.'

'Bookgroup? Not a chance.'

'Margot will bring a nice bottle anyway. I remember when Margot was made redundant and had to rent out rooms to make ends meet. Do say if I'm distracting you.'

'You are distracting me.'

'Shall I sweep? Because either I'm the only one who ever sweeps, or your floor breeds dust balls.' Liv grabs a broom. Liv is the only one who sweeps.

'I'm sure yet another minibreak has to be a cover for house-hunting,' she says.

Liv helps me so much I don't mind putting up with her bottomless well of enthusiastic ideas of how I should be running my business. I am eager to hear what she says about Mitch, but she's busy on Margot and David gossip and I'm deciding if I'll sell another copy of Wintering now we're plunged into the hottest spring for years.

'I'm surprised it's taken them this long to move. Their house is tiny. You know David got rich from a business spin-off from his science research?'

'Margot can afford to bring expensive wine to bookgroup because David made a load of money?' I murmur, trying to concentrate on reordering from sales.

I try to keep up. Crossways is fuelled by gossip. So how did I miss there was a double murder here?

'I heard David made four million. I also heard he's still seething because the people he went into business with made more. I doubt it was anywhere near that, but he and Margot have retired in their fifties,' says Liv. 'You'd think that'd be enough for anyone. Can you see anyone as mild as David raging? Now if you stop gossiping and get your jobs done, we could grab a bite at Halfway. You won't have eaten, if you don't count a few spoonfuls of peanut butter straight from the jar.'

'That's healthy protein. And Ashley always does quality nibbles, so we don't need to drop in at Halfway. And I'm not the one gossiping. Can I ask your opinion?'

'Of course! Ask away!' Liv pauses in her sweeping. 'I cannot believe my opinions are not more eagerly sought by many more people.'

'It's that I still don't really get how people think around here. Crossways still feels like stepping into an alien world. Without you this bookshop would be the doomed idea my friends and family warned me about. My supportive mum would be crowing about being right that I have a history of making poor decisions. I'm sure people will be interested.'

'Everyone loves your bookshop! It's a fabulous success.' Liv crooks a single eyebrow at me. 'What's your latest dumb move? Or who have you been rude to this time? Or lost your temper with?'

'I want to ask your opinion on crime.'

'Hugely popular. Crime fiction you mean? If I see one more book described as *the twist you won't see coming* I may murder someone. Our bookgroup needs to branch out.'

'I was thinking more true-crime.'

Liv shudders. 'Best avoided. In Crossways, edgy is a bit of sad girl lit, not serial killers.' She pauses on the broom. 'What have you been doing? Or saying? Who exactly have you upset?'

'It's more who I might be about to upset. What about murder?'

'It's not Elliott is it?' Liv sweeps the dusty floor, making me feel guilty that she does so much for me. 'Has he been in here irritating you again?'

'Not recently.'

Elliott is Liv's son and in the local police. I can't help it if I'm someone who cannot walk away when I see injustice. I guess he can't help his views on people who stick their noses into police business. But does he have to share them with me quite so often? Not a great starting point for us to ever really get along.

Shame Liv's caught in the middle.

'Can you make a party out of true crime?' I ask.

'You are being cryptic and not a little spooky. Keera, please be specific. Real life crime is what you are trying to put behind you for very good reasons. I'm going to cash up. You are way too distracted.' Liv nudges me to one side at the till. 'You love to see yourself as the avenging fury who carries a flaming sword for truth and justice.'

'You have me so wrong. I just want to sell books, live quietly and not get involved. I'm just the bookseller. Even events are a bit too exciting for me.'

'Making a party of bookselling is sound business.'

'I can see arguments on both sides.'

'This version of you feels very unfamiliar. What happened to the plunge-in-ask-questions later Keera?'

'I'm not behind because I've been reading all the books I'm supposed to be selling. I started looking into the murder of two people in Crossways. How did the Crossways Killings never get solved?' It bursts out of me.

'What on earth made you do that?' says Liv. 'Have you really only taken two hundred pounds today?'

'Some days people just don't want books'

'All the more reason to crack on with events planning. If your plan is to cover your rent and your bills.'

'Newspaper reports barely got beyond: wealthy couple, recently retired, move to village where no one knows them. Burglary goes wrong.'

'And that is the reason, sadly, it never will be solved,' says Liv. 'Evidence and suspects were thin on the ground. The murdered couple weren't local, so no possible reason for anyone from around here to kill them. The police ended up landing on the unlikely theory they were followed from the airport in some burglary gone wrong. Lack of CCTV meant that only ever remained a theory. No better alternative came up. I guess it faded away with no new leads.'

'So what did everyone around here think really happened?

'People hate talking about it. It was a horribly painful part of Crossways past. And it was years ago.' Liv efficiently despatches my orders and starts to cash up.

'Not that many years. And everyone around here gossips about how broke Isha paid for a holiday and how much money David Purkiss made in that business buyout. You're telling me it wasn't raked over? That no one had a theory?'

'I was lucky enough to miss the worst of it. I was on a yoga retreat in Marrakesh.'

'Only you could have been on a yoga retreat in Marrakesh,' I mutter.

'Strictly, I was helping a friend to set up a yoga retreat. Why are you worrying about the Crossways Killings when you have so much else you should be worrying about? And who is Mitch?'

'But how can I ignore it now I know about it? The media called it an impossible crime. But Mitch is right. It's impossible no one knows anything in a small place. We should—'

'Leave it. Your instincts are yelling that you're near something that should come with an Approach with Caution warning. Don't go near the Crossways Killings.'

'I can see why it's a painful part of Crossways past. I can see people might not want it brought up again… I did have a qualm.'

'Keera Munroe had a qualm? That must have been a new feeling. I'm surprised you recognised it. This new, dithery Keera is worrying me. What exactly have you done?' Liv puts her stern face on.

'Mitch is an ex-Met officer. He's written a book and he's offered to give a talk. I thought how impressed you'd be with me for moving along the author event idea.'

Liv blinks at me. 'I thought you were leaving events to me. I've started putting out feelers.'

'And it would be a good thing if an unsolved murder could be finally solved, right? It will grow cold unless someone mixes things up, reminds people it's not over. In the gossipy place no one talks about it. Odd, right? And this is the case he'd most love to get solved in his retirement. He hopes writing about it will spark a new lead.'

Liv's eyes become round as she stares at me. 'He's not going to… Mitch hasn't… He's not put *that* in a book? And he's going around doing publicity and raking it up again? And you've invited him to give a talk about it? Here?' Liv looks around, as if Mitch might be hiding under one of the display tables.

'People talking about it again is the best way to a fresh lead. A couple with no connection to Crossways move in—and the night they arrive they are both shot dead. Mitch said it was one of the worst cases of his career. People will want it solved finally. Won't they? What if there is a killer in Crossways?'

Liv shudders. 'How could you possibly interpret all my advice about authors and events as meaning dragging up a horrible local piece of Crossways past that's best buried and forgotten? What were you thinking? Do not let yourself be the one bringing all that up. It was hard enough to live with before. Will the people here thank their new bookseller for joining forces with Mitch and dragging it all up again? Not bloody likely.'

Liv likes to disguise her super sharp brain and prefers to be known for organising parties. She doesn't miss much. I hardly ever hear her swear. I should listen to her warning.

'The answers don't lie here,' Liv says. 'It cannot get raked up again. It was one of those awful, random crimes and those are always the most impossible to solve. What exactly is Mitch's angle?'

'He wants to sell his book. I don't think he has a secret agenda.'

Liv crooks an eyebrow at me. 'Everyone has a secret agenda. Except me of course. True crime writers all want one thing.'

'To bring up a sensational new lead and solve old cases?'

'To stir up sensation about painful things because trouble sells books. Voila! He knows it'll never be solved. But that won't stop him stirring it all up. And Crossways gets all the pain. Everyone felt under scrutiny, everyone felt accused.'

'I can't believe you actually said voila! Mitch says two local bookshops are helping with publicity, so it's going to get talked about anyway.

'Two local booksellers who are happily not on the doorstep,' says Liv. 'You have a business right here. Do the sensible thing and show Mitch the door.'

Liv sees me hesitating and reads me too well. 'You've already said yes to him, haven't you? Because you think you're going to go full-on Zorro and solve the crime that the police gave up on. What happened to trying to leave your dark past behind?'

'It's being published. Is it all in the past really? Or just squashed down and threatening to erupt at any moment? Maybe talking about it will bring new evidence. Maybe kick-start a cold case? Maybe he's going to make some explosive reveal when his book comes out. Where's the harm in helping if we can? If there is a killer in Crossways.'

'Is this because of what happened before? When you were the only one who thought a death was suspicious and you plunged in to clear-up Crossways?'

'Well. I was right. That death was suspicious.'

Liv takes a deep breath. 'All right. Tonight you have the perfect opportunity with a great cross-section of Crossways. Test the water with bookgroup. Is this the risk you are ready for right now? Now, talking of risk, we need to get to bookgroup before Grant Michaels eats all the cheese and drinks all the wine.'

'What am I supposed to do? Drink wine and eat cheese now I know there's an unsolved murder on my doorstep? What about the poor couple who moved here and died? What about justice for them? I'm with Mitch. For someone to get away with a double murder, someone must be hiding something,' I say. 'Someone always knows.'

'We've had to live with the fact that there were no answers. Crossways has put all that behind us and moved on. You think you'll stir things up and miraculously you'll find answers the police failed to do when the trail wasn't cold? Ask yourself if it'll still be worth the harm if you and Merry Mitch go stirring it all up again and you end up with exactly the same result?'

'Not solved? Just dug over and re-buried you mean? Ok, yes, that could possibly go wrong.'

5

Verity

'One hour to bookgroup. Bong!' Verity announced to Grandma.

Verity delivered a mixed cheese platter to a low table in the cosy, clutter-free and recently hoovered front room (details you noticed, and bliss after gruelling house-shares where everyone pretended the mess belonged to someone else). In Verity's world looking like you haven't gone to a lot of bother (while being bothered) would be having two flavours of crisps *plus* twiglets.

Grandma had rinsed two types of grapes and was busy piling up salted pretzels into little bowls in the too-warm front room, heavy on plush velvet and sinkably big cushions you really didn't need in this weather. It smelled heavily of a huge vase of freshly cut lilies (covering up a body in the basement?). Grandma did cover things up. Like the shelves of serious reads downstairs and all the trashy novels on the landing.

'Is Keera Munroe any good at running a bookshop?' Verity felt it was safe to risk a few questions. She wanted all the dirt on bookgroup. And Grandma could call it taking an interest in people, but she was a terrible gossip. Not that Verity would rely solely on Grandma's gossip. You should never rely too heavily on a single source if you are interested in the truth.

'Keera's in charge of bookgroup, so why do they meet here, Grandma? Is Keera any good at running things?'

'Everyone's supposed to take a turn as the bookshop's too small. You don't have to keep calling me Grandma, you know. Call me Ashley.'

This wasn't the first time Grandma had tried to get Verity to call her by her first name, but it felt weird.

'I think we all know Between the Lines would be a shambles and probably have closed by now if it wasn't for Liv Trent stepping in,' said Grandma. 'Liv Trent's a force of nature. Lucky for all of us. Keera doesn't have much of a clue. I think Keera was a lawyer and all it's given her a taste for is asking intrusive questions. Also unfortunate.'

Verity was liking this rare moment of talking to Grandma other than the breakfast lectures she yawned her way through. Verity was getting early nights, but twigs scratching at her window in a disturbingly Wuthering Heights way kept her awake. Plus there was a loudly enthusiastic owl neighbour (an actual owl).

She was used to being lulled to sleep by the regular swoosh of passing traffic and soothing crashing around of the odd marauding student drunk.

'You love books Verity,' Grandma had said in yesterday's breakfast lecture, on her way to do something senior but part time at the nearby university.

Verity yawned and ate chocolate cereal as Grandma packed her ultra-slim laptop that went with her everywhere, as she was writing the popular science version of her particular field of insanely complex chemistry (good luck with that).

'I doubt bookgroup wants to learn how to write essays about them,' Verity had said. *'If you want me to meet people we should have an evening at the Waggon and Horses. They have live music.'*

There were young people in Crossways; young as in being pushed around by parents (who was anyone kidding – mums), who wheeled buggies into the deli and did a bad job of faking positivity that being embroiled in a whirl of overpriced coffees, YogaBabes and PTA was a patch on having a job that paid and getting evenings off.

Verity had identified a couple of people her age also stuck in Crossways for the summer: Cal Kinsky and Taylor Messenger. Verity already had a mini mystery about them in her growing case notes in her Doodles of an Evil Genius notebook – a present from a boyfriend (ex, obviously).

Living with Grandma had not been as Verity had pictured. No evenings being mothered with home-cooking, which would have been brilliant after almost three years of shared kitchens and pot noodle. She'd imagined sipping Grandma's expensive Sancerre, watching reruns of Happy Valley together.

The reality was breakfast lectures and contact mostly via a mini chalkboard on the fridge: *YogaGals tonight, Half a pasta in the fridge x*

There were few signs of the quiet life Verity's mum had predicted when Grandma Smollett downsized and moved into sleepy Crossways when Grandpa Smollett died four years ago. Ready for a slower pace (so Verity's mum said). Grandma had moved into one of the 'new estate' homes (1980s) hidden away at the car park end so as not to shamefully disrupt the aesthetic of quaint workers cottages in the high street. These were sought-after for their characterful Victorian features (the chocolate-box vision, not the damp, outside privies or the smallpox virus).

Verity observed Grandma was now a wearer of a new shade of lipstick (orange), even at breakfast, where she ate only slivers of mango. Verity could believe Grandma had been initiated into some secret Crossways cult.

She was about to put another question and voice a *'half an hour to bookgroup (bong!)'*, when a sharp knock on the door told her they were off early. Verity hadn't even had a chance to pass on Keera's tip about not putting the cheese too near Grant, let alone get the dirt on bookgroup.

Bland, suit-wearing estate agent, Grant Michaels, was here early, in a jumper with a squiggly pattern and more than a hint of the tank top about it, announcing it was predicted to be officially the warmest day of this early spring tomorrow.

'But you can never be too careful,' Grant said as he tucked his umbrella in Ashley's hatstand beneath her treasured members' hoodie from the golf club (another place Grandma was always found, according to the daily updates on the mini-chalkboard on the fridge).

Grandma had dished a little dirt on Grant earlier: Grant was a real asset to bookgroup, not because of his love of reading and insightful comments, but because no one wanted to be the last to hear any gossip and Grant was the biggest source and knew everything going on in Crossways.

Grant often popped into the deli to chirrup something like: *'meeting a lovely couple with unexpected triplets on the way and only last week they were after a two-bed!'*.

There was something so unremarkable about their bland-looking local estate agent that he'd make an ideal assassin. Or serial killer. All that going into other people's houses… If Grant popped his head in and said: *Just off to a new-build to get rid of an unwanted wife'* Verity and Eliza would very likely just nod.

But Grant was here first, so a fine first target for a sliver for her Doodles of an Evil Genius notebook.

Verity had an ambitious challenge. By the end of the evening she must have a snippet of intrigue about each member. It did not have to be big or exciting (this was Crossways). But a sliver for everyone. That was her rule. Because you had to start somewhere.

Grant rubbed his thin pale (serial killer?) hands together and grabbed a handful of crisps as Ashley passed. Grant was at the centre of who's selling and why, who's marriage was failing, who's moving up. Grant should be a great source.

'Let me at those delicious walnutty crackers,' said Grant, 'before everyone else arrives and pinches all the cheese. And a glass of red as usual for me, Ashley.'

Verity did not underestimate the challenge of solving a horrific unsolved murder and unmasking the Crossways Killer. She only had a few weeks. And Crossways was the unlikeliest place to be concealing a killer. Its folk tended towards the grey, embroiled in a thrilling whirlwind of overpriced coffee, golf, a committee (at least one), voluntary work for a worthy cause no one had ever heard of, YogaGals, and a comfy cardi even in the heat. This pretty much did checklist Grandma (although she fell short in the comfy cardi department).

'Margot and David are spending some of David's *little windfall*,' said Grant.

'You're hinting they're not just spending their money on weekends away? You can't mean they're away so much house-hunting?' Ashley sounded shocked. 'They want to spend money on a new house? And leave Crossways?'

'I thought no one could leave,' said Verity. 'Isn't Crossways a secret werewolf haunt and no one actually can ever leave once they discover the truth? Guess that doesn't look so great for me. Unless you're only here forever if you get bitten? I might still get away.'

'You've got Crossways quite wrong,' said Grant.

Verity didn't think so, but she was considering if it was playing by her own rules to include David's *little windfall* as a snippet in her notebook? Was it too well known? Plenty of Crossways gossip was about how much David had made from his business launch from some science discovery, which seemed very unlikely, until Grandma said plenty of university folk lived in Crossways and that you fell over world-renowned scientists buying broccoli in the Co-op every day. But David's story had a twist in the tale and might be worth exploring.

'No werewolves here.' Grant's face cracked into a wrinkly grin. 'Close—it's witches. Cult initiation and the never-leave spell takes place after you've been here six months. So you can still escape. Unless we persuade you to stay.' Grant's chuckle was a sound like dry leaves rustling.

'That sounds very sinister, but does explain why Grandma is annoyingly secretive about Crossways,' said Verity. 'She's always out on these unlikely activities. Golf and YogaGals? Has to be a cover, right? She never let on about the witches. Interesting. So who's chief worst witch?'

'I guess that'd be Belinda Messenger,' chuckled Grant.

'Belinda Messenger, she's head of the local swanky girls' school?' She's bound to have secrets? And Grant, you know I'm here to get to know everyone. Grandma says you know everything, so… What are the rumours? Embezzling PTA funds? I'm relying on you to tell me something interesting about all of them,' Verity said in a low voice, taking advantage of Grandma being in the kitchen, out of earshot finding the walnutty crackers.

'Sadly for you I think the school's low on scandal because it's near Crossways, thus so far from anywhere the girls don't even bother to break out,' said Grant taking off wire-framed glasses to give them a polish.

'Being unable to escape I'm sure makes all those teenage daughters enthusiastic about late-night cocoa and crossword puzzles for entertainment,' said Verity. 'I'm sure it doesn't suppress raging hormones and doesn't twist them into those delightful games of social torture that schoolgirls excel at,' said Verity. 'Or lead to experimenting with drugs and inappropriate sex the second they get away.'

Grant chuckled so much he choked on his wine. 'I thought there would be shock and outrage when it got out that Belinda was having a wild affair with the gym mistress. But they're married now with a daughter. I guess that's not the big deal it once was. You know Taylor Messenger? Our colourful bird of paradise in beige and grey Crossways.'

'I guess it's what you do,' Verity said, who was very aware of Taylor Messenger, 'if you're daughter of a headteacher at an elite school. Get piercings and a tattoo of a badass fairy on your left wrist and dye your hair blue.'

'What are you two gossiping about?' said Grandma, appearing from the kitchen and passing Grant the crackers.

'Grant's very kindly telling me who's in bookgroup. Grandma says Liv Trent really runs Between the Lines as Keera's terrible at it, has a temper and an unfortunate habit of speaking her mind. Has Keera had arguments with anyone interesting?'

'Verity!' said Grandma. 'Did I really say that?'

'It's what you meant.'

'Now there's a story,' said Grant. 'Keera had an argument with a customer who died the next day in suspicious circumstances.'

'I assume you are joking?' said Verity.

But he was unfortunately interrupted by another knock at the door. Verity felt sure there was more to be squeezed out of Grant. Because Verity had learned things from almost three years at university (brutally cut short). There were always secrets. No one behaved impeccably all the time. Everyone seemed to have a secret shame, something squashed down into guilt by society norms. And those who appeared the most impeccable often had the farthest to fall.

And Crossways was luckily full of those.

Verity felt suddenly buoyed with high hopes of bookgroup and getting her sliver of intrigue about everyone. She could do this, even though she was only here for a couple more months. On a deadline. Tick-tock.

But getting a sliver on everyone included the person who was going to be most challenging of all: What about Grandma?

6

Keera

Liv and I arrive at the same time as shy David Purkiss and posh but motherly Margot Latimer, with Margot in full-on rant to sharp-faced, sharp-haired head of the local girls' school, Belinda Messenger.

Margot's warning about a nearby town where developers are buying up back gardens to build housing. 'We must never let that happen in Crossways! The over-crowding.'

'We're surrounded by countryside and Crossways gardens are so long no one knows what to do with them,' says Belinda smoothly.

Belinda's tall and angular, with sharply cut, sleek blonde hair and an imposing presence. She lives in a vast home, beyond the church, on the outskirts where there's no danger of the end of her garden being targeted by developers.

Margot looks deeply shocked. 'We must stay vigilant!'

I meet Verity's eye. I bet Verity's dying inside.

First, her Grandma volunteers her to work for the summer in our new deli; she's had to come to bookgroup.

Now she's listening to Margot being outraged about typical Crossways woes. I still don't understand half of what gets people riled in Crossways and I've been here more than a year.

Margot turns with a sweet smile to Ashley. 'What can I do to help?' She hands Ashley a very nice bottle of wine. 'We can stay and help with clearing up at the end too.'

'Very kind, but it's all under control thanks to Verity's help,' smiles Ashley.

'Bless,' says Margot.

'I'm happy to take my turn, even though my house is probably the smallest,' Ashley adds, looking pointedly at Grant. He's forties, married, but there are rumours of some kind of domestic strife, so although he lives in a huge house, he never invites bookgroup. You cannot help but know everyone's business in a village.

'Your hair looks nice, Margot,' says Grant. 'Have you had it done?'

I reckon Margot attempts to tame her curly hair in a style that resembles sharp Belinda's smooth crop. I think Belinda has noticed that Margot tries to follow her style. I think it rather irritates Belinda. Motherly Margot's new red skirt suits her more than the shorts she strides around in daily. A walker in need of a dog I think. Her skirt is very similar to the one Belinda wore to last bookgroup.

'Yes, but I didn't have my hair done for bookgroup,' Margot insists as we go into Ashley's tiny kitchen at the back where doors are open into a welcoming summery garden smelling of newly mown grass. 'David has such a passion for visiting gardens.'

'Treating yourselves to more breaks?' says Ashley.

'You know you are fuelling speculation that it's a cover for house-hunting and you have secret plans to leave us,' says Grant, with one of his dry chuckles. 'Although Verity is a girl with wonderfully wild imaginings and she's already spotted Crossways is a cult and no one can ever leave.'

'People don't want to leave because we are so lucky to live here,' says Margot. 'Which is why Crossways should never change.'

But a look passes between Margot and David. And Grant has unfailingly correct instincts about these things. He probably is onto something that the pair might be trying to leave. It would be a shame, not least because I think we get points for having two men in our bookgroup, not that I'm convinced David Purkiss reads any more than Grant does. David mostly gives shy smiles and broods behind heavy framed glasses. He has longish dark hair and is mistakenly trying out a beard.

Everyone loads up on drinks and snacks and has to hear Margot's warnings. Bookgroup is full of the loveliest people in Crossways. Not only because they read and support my shop. They support lots of events in the village, even the dodgy or dull ones. But what about an iffy one where I've invited a copper to talk about his memoirs and dig into a Crossways shameful secret? Getting Liv's opinion has made me anxious. I feel hot even knowing I have the Refusing to Remain Silent manuscript shoved in my bag.

I should say no to Mitch. Liv's probably right that he doesn't seriously expect to solve the Crossways Killings and it's just cynical publicity for his book. I'm not surprised the police plumped for an explanation that involved an outsider following the unlucky couple from the airport and that nothing pointed to anyone in Crossways. It's too grim to bring up again. Certainly too grim for bookgroup.

Liv's right. I should learn to leave things alone. My priority is to sell enough books to pay the bills and honestly, that is challenging enough.

I wanted a fresh start and that means ingratiating myself with Crossways; coaxing a fledgling events programme into life. Not asking awkward questions. Not worry about that poor couple, shot the night they moved to Crossways.

But I can't stop thinking about it. Not now I know about it.

'Are we waiting for anyone else?' Margot asks Ashley.

'Shall we sit outside?' says Ashley as she counts on her fingers. Me, Verity, Keera, Liv, Belinda, Grant, David, Margot and Eliza—just Isha to come and she said she'd come straight from the allotment and might be late.'

'Let's hope she doesn't bring any more of her early cabbages to share,' says Margot with a shudder.

'But I love how everyone here swaps things from their gardens,' says a voice. Eliza Somers has joined us.

She jumped at my invitation to join bookgroup. Well it is the beating heart of Crossways and Eliza's chatty, friendly, keen to fit in. She wants people to support Eliza's Deli, where she offers olives and salads, imported sausages, bread (only on weekends as it's the only time a local baker could fit them in). Thursday's special is the little cupcakes Eliza makes. Eliza has no-doubt discovered running a shop in a small place means people come partly for shopping, mostly for chat. And she reads. So I'm doubly pleased to see Eliza this evening. I should really make it my mission to make more of a friend of her. She's only next door, we're both around the same age, both single women running small village businesses.

Both running away from something?

Opening a business in an idyllic village was my way to have a fresh start.

What about Eliza?

She has the pale serious look of someone who spends her time indoors serving olives and salads. Her impractically long and curly hair is tumbling loose and free this evening. It spends its days in the deli swept away in a high ponytail.

But since opening, Eliza has suffered a few unfortunate accidents.

No one expects the giant bruise on her face that's finally turning lettuce-green (even though she covers it carefully with make-up). Or the way she limps and moves her left arm only cautiously.

'I tripped and fell out of the back step. It's a very old building.' Eliza offers this same (not convincing) story to everyone. *'The shop is old and a bit of a deathtrap.'*

There's also a rumour of problems with her other neighbour, the Crossways Cafe, run by Benj Beresford. But then Crossways folk feel everything can be improved with a light sprinkling of drama. Is it over-dramatic to say Eliza is a little bit of a mystery? Am I getting sucked into the rumour machine that is the true life-blood of Crossways?

Thankfully, Margot's melodramatic 'Stay Vigilant' warning is running out of steam and there's agreement to break out to the relief of the cool garden.

We are just finishing loading up glasses and plates of cheese when Isha Cheema, our local poet, arrives and instantly objects to the garden, even though she and Grant are wearing jumpers. Isha's green v-neck matches the knitted beanie pulled down over her lush hair, dark but with the first sprinkling of grey. She feels the cold too badly, she says and everyone shuffles back into the stifling front room looking daggers at Isha.

'I wasn't expecting it to be about kids books,' says Grant, surprising everyone by kicking off talk about the book. 'I got bored and didn't finish it.' He helps himself to more red wine and leaves the bottle near him.

Sharp Belinda is at my elbow, asking quietly for a chat. My heart jolts, panicking she's heard about Mitch and wants to lodge an early objection. But she wants closer links between the bookshop and her school. An author event?

I need to focus. I need to sell enough books to pay the bills. I need to stick to my whole bookselling success plan. But right now I need to focus on getting everyone saying something about the book.

7

Verity

Verity had been hoping everyone had forgotten they were supposed to be discussing the book and everyone would get straight into the gossip and Keera would bring up the Crossways Killings. But no. Keera seemed determined they would all offer an opinion on the book.

'All the off-putting spelling mistakes. I'd have thought being a teacher you'd have hated that, Belinda. You too, Isha,' said Grant.

'I rather think that's the point—I thought it was original,' said Isha.

'It was an authentic part of the characterisation,' agreed Belinda. 'It read excitingly like one of those children-foiling-kidnappers and solving-clues stories, like a Malcolm Saville,' Belinda added, flexing the breadth of her literary knowledge by mentioning an author Verity had never heard of.

Verity told herself to be patient. But it wasn't easy. Four weeks in a tiny space, serving up freshly made salads, olives and ridiculous sounding crackers would have been as dull as a tin of value plum tomatoes if Verity had not had her imagination and her summer-saving case notes.

What did she have on Isha?

The biggest mystery about Isha was surely that Isha had escaped Crossways, but had come back again.

Why would anyone do that?

She'd been teaching (abroad, Verity had heard), but returned to care for her ailing father in a sadly dilapidated childhood home where he devoted invalid years waging war on the crows and rabbits in the garden until the day he died.

Instead of selling up and getting the hell back out, Isha had stayed to learn plumbing and DIY and fix up the house. Being left a rotting house and no money had led to Crossways speculation. But not about why Isha stayed, but about how Isha managed to afford a recent luxury long winter holiday. That was what everyone gossiped about.

But Verity had found a way to include Isha in her case notes. Did Isha need money badly enough to break into the home of a wealthy couple and steal some of their valuables?

Because somebody had. The bare bones of the Crossways Killings were that newly-retired Chris and Carrie Winter were burgled. But things had gone badly wrong when unfortunately the Winters had arrived earlier than expected. Cue surprise, gun, blood, brutal ends.

And Isha had been brought up watching her father ruthlessly killing things he considered in the way. Isha was no stranger to a gun. What happened to Isha's father's gun? Two slivers for Isha.

'I didn't like the main character at all, all that admitting to those terrible crimes,' shuddered posh but kindly Margot. 'I wish we didn't always read about these horrible crimes.'

'Wasn't there a question about whether any of those really happened?' asked Isha to a confused look from Margot who clearly hadn't reached the end, but everyone was too gentle with her to point this out.

'It hardly matters if what we read feels like utter tripe,' said Grant, balancing a large piece of smoked cheddar on the last walnut cracker. 'I've got a much better idea, but before you ask, I'm keeping it to myself until someone I know becomes a bestseller, then I'll let them know my idea, they can write it and we can split the profits.'

'Don't publishers take the profits?' said Isha.

'Maybe don't go around telling us you've got an idea worth killing for,' said Belinda with a sly smile. 'Wasn't there a film about someone who had such a brilliant idea for a book, a rival murdered them and pretended they wrote it?'

The hands on Grandma's ornate mantel clock were going very slowly. Secrets were not exactly tumbling out. Was Verity going to fail even in the challenge of one tiny snippet for everyone?

'I think many people believe they have a great idea, but isn't the skill turning an idea into a good read?' said Eliza gently.

'David will write under a name that's both bold and unusual,' said Margot. 'I've always liked Royston.'

'That's more like the hero in one of those bodice rippers,' said Isha. 'Are you writing one of those, David?'

But the fates were still on Verity's side. Verity hadn't missed the dumb bookseller had actually brought along that copy of Refusing to Remain Silent that Mitch Ravenscroft had dropped off. It was sitting in Keera's bag, which she had stupidly left in the hall, inviting anyone who happened to read it to find out in advance what sensational new facts Mitch was going to reveal. All Verity had to do was sneak out and photograph the relevant pages to read later. Was now a good time? She didn't want to miss any secrets.

'Shouldn't you have finished writing before you think of your pseudonym?' chuckled Grant. 'Tell you what, you become a bestseller, David—maybe I'll sell you my idea.'

'Imagine if you had a pseudonym and became famous and then everyone called you Royston. And inside you'd be crying out *but my name's David!*' shuddered Belinda.

'These days everyone's after ghostwriting work for celebrities,' said Isha, scratching under her beanie hat. 'No one's even sure who's actually written what.'

Verity slipped into the hall. Margot's voice carried after her, declaring that David would write a bestseller, make a fortune and they could retire and live somewhere they could swim in a warm sea every day. A collective sharp intake of breath followed. Because the couple already had the money to retire and take holidays? Or shock that anyone might attempt to break the Crossways spell and leave?

Verity slipped the manuscript from Keera's bag and asked herself again if she was counting David's windfall as a snippet? By the rate of progress, she would have to.

At least the whole of the story wasn't completely known, which is why it fuelled so much speculation.

Few people would look at David and think there was a scientist who made some discovery that got him a coveted-if-dull-sounding Guild of the Business of Science award and a shedload of money. People said David made a crucial science-y breakthrough, but the ones who took care of the business side made more cash, leaving David raging at the discovery that the people making the creative breakthroughs are seldom the ones really making the cash.

The story went how David was bruised (but now seriously minted) and remembered poor but kindly Margot from when he'd stayed with her on a trip to the university. Everyone knew Margot had been forced to turn extra cash renting out rooms after a badly timed redundancy. So David pitched up for some sympathy and to lick his wounds.

Verity would bet that when David arrived after his misfortune, Margot didn't abandon him to DIY salad in the fridge while she disappeared off to endless golf and YogaGals. They'd have watched the box-sets in the evening and drunk all the expensive wine together.

Verity took her phone and the manuscript into the downstairs bathroom, perching on the loo seat and turning pages to find a reference to Crossways, while trying not to breathe in too deeply of Grandma's mimosa air freshener.

Nothing. It was unlikely she'd be missed from bookgroup, but there was a high chance someone would need the bathroom after all that wine. Even so, she went through more slowly a second time and found reference to Michael Grant and Churchways. Grant Michaels, obviously. Mitch had made a poor attempt to disguise Crossways and real names. Because the case remained unsolved? And Grant came off badly. Interesting.

Verity identified what she needed, took photos and slipped the manuscript back into Keera's bag.

Back in the stifling lounge had she missed Keera bringing up her event with Mitch and finally getting everyone talking about the Crossways Killings?

No. The hands of the fancy gold clock on the mantelpiece were still moving so slowly it was as if time itself moved differently in Crossways. They were still talking about books.

'If you don't care about the characters, you don't care who did what to whom do you?' Isha was saying. 'Do we always have to read crime fiction?'

'We never agree what to read,' said Belinda, leaning forward from where she'd ended up in a dark corner.

'We could try poetry,' suggested Isha.

What were the chances of a sliver for most of these people? At this rate she'd be relying on her snippet of intrigue that needed solving for David. Because David's story didn't quite end with his happily ever after with Margot. There was a rumour.

David had built a fancy shed at the bottom of his garden, leading to speculation that David was secretly plotting another science breakthrough to rival the people who shafted him. Was Camp Secret Science Project correct? Or was his upmarket shed for some completely different reason, as rival Camp Secret Model Railway would have it, which was far more likely in Crossways. Verity had her own theory. If she was living with Margot she might have an escape shed.

'We could read one of those dark ones where the main character is a killer and gets right inside the criminal mind,' said Ashley.

So how about a sliver for Grandma? There had to be more to Ashley than an impressive academic job, healthy hobbies and a stash of expensive wine in the fridge. Verity would love to discover something to dent Grandma's perfect image.

'That sounds a very disturbing read,' shuddered Margot. 'Please let's not.'

'I'm sure killers are nothing like you read in books,' chortled Grant.

'Some authors are keen to get it right,' says Isha through a handful of grapes. 'If you want to write authentic crime you get tips.'

Now. Now was the moment Keera would bring up Mitch. And then onto the Crossways Killings. A perfect opening. But Keera didn't. Verity panicked. She had to risk saying something as the conversation was perilously close to moving on.

'Isn't that where experts like Mitch Ravenscroft step in?' Verity said. 'Isn't he a local police officer who knows about crime? Hasn't he just written a book?'

'Oh do some of you know Mitch?' said Liv. 'That's marvellous, because actually Keera has an announcement. Don't you, Keera?'

Now. Now Keera would bring up the Crossways Killings and get everyone talking about it.

8

Keera

'Well… Grant hasn't found a lot of our recent reads authentic,' I falter. 'So. Yes, I…'

'Weren't you going to sound-out bookgroup on an event idea?' Liv presses.

I came to this village longing for a fresh start. I never felt I'd fit in. Can I be the one to hurl in the news that Mitch has written about the Crossways Killings? Be supportive that it's all going to be brought up again? Yet I never thought I'd lose my commitment to truth and justice.

Maybe Crossways is having an effect; maybe Crossways changes people. Maybe all I do want is a quiet life and not upsetting people.

The room is stifling. Too many people in a too-small room. It's difficult to breathe. I can't look at Liv. She knew I was going to duck it. She threw the live grenade at me. And I'm sure Verity overheard every word of my conversation with Mitch and took everything in.

'Event idea?' says Margot eagerly. 'An author event?'

I totally bottle it.

'Mitch knows a lot of authors from giving professional detective advice,' I say, looking Liv right in the eye. 'Mitch is offering to bring a crime writing masterclass to Crossways. Liv and I disagreed if there will be enough interest…'

'That sounds a wonderful offer!' Ashley says excitedly. She rises to top up everyone's glasses. 'Margot wants David to write a bestseller. Grant has a brilliant idea. Inviting Mitch, what a wonderful opportunity. I'm up for a crime fiction workshop. Exciting! Anyone else in?'

There's a surprisingly positive murmur.

'Is that all Mitch is offering?' Liv presses me. 'What about this new book. Why don't you tell us about that?'

'I think we'll let Mitch do that, shall we?' I say. Smooth.

'Where would you start writing crime fiction?' Ashley says with a lot of relish and opening another bottle of wine. 'Let's say, how would anyone here commit a murder?'

'And get away with it,' says Eliza. 'Isn't that the difficult part?'

'I think killing someone would be the difficult part,' says Isha.

'I'd say killing someone is the easy bit,' says Belinda with an airy confidence. 'I'm with Eliza. Getting away with it would be hard. You've got the problem of what to do with a body. Forensics are so sophisticated.'

'What you need is for no one to find the body,' offers Grant. 'Be clever enough so no one even knows there's been a murder… And that's how you'd get away with it.'

'Easy around here. All this countryside to bury your bloodied corpse,' says Isha.

'Or is it,' says Grant with a twinkle. 'In this dry weather you wouldn't stand a chance of digging a big enough hole.

I'd say you'd be better somewhere like a cellar where you could take your time with it.'

'In your own home? Would that just be too gruesome.' Isha shivers. 'And what if you don't have a cellar?'

'You'd get creative.' Grant blinks at Ashley. 'I'd ask a chemist. All that expert knowledge. A chemist would have a very good chance of getting away with murder.'

'Funnily enough, I did just read a great body disposal method that really got me thinking,' Ashley says, with a surprising amount of enthusiasm. 'In this novel the murderer uses biological laundry detergent to disintegrate a corpse and I asked myself whether that would actually work? I mean, how much detergent would you need? What about somewhere to leave the body while it disintegrates? And you'd be left with the bones.'

'Is that going in the popular chemistry book you're writing?' Verity asks.

'Maybe murderers do use detergent to dissolve corpses. You just need readers to believe it's plausible,' says Grant, more than a little garrulous from the wine. 'Let's be honest, some real crimes don't sound plausible. Who knows better than us about impossible crimes and how truth can be stranger than fiction? If you put into a book about two people arriving somewhere no one knows them and getting murdered—would that go down as believable?'

There's a deathly silence that goes on way too long.

I'm not going to break it. I'm too keen to know what everyone's going to say.

'We had a very unfortunate thing happened a few years ago,' says Belinda carefully, addressing Verity.

'Unfortunate thing?' Verity says. Verity knows.

'This couple had valuables. They were followed from the airport. And killed,' says Belinda. 'Utterly tragic.'

'Of course no one believed that story,' says Grant, reaching for more olives. 'Police pestered us for weeks.'

'What did people believe?' Verity asks. The end of her nose has gone a little pink.

I suppose I can forgive her for finding a double murder interesting.

'No one had the faintest idea,' says Belinda. 'No one knew them. Killed the first night they moved here.'

'That didn't stop the police going around asking endless questions. It was horrible.' Margot shivers.

'Although not as horrible as it was for the poor couple,' says Eliza, leaning forwards and wincing as if her ribs hurt.

'Well, no of course!' says Margot. 'I was only…'

'But a burglary gone wrong… Doesn't that throw up a lot of questions?' says Verity. 'Why take a gun to burgle what's supposed to be an empty house? And people around here, well, they do have guns.'

How does Verity know the house was supposed to be empty? That girl has way too much curiosity. She's also right. Her point about the gun is a good one. I have a horrible feeling someone knowing the house was supposed to be empty might point to someone in Crossways.

But the police failed to find any connection.

'What everyone's too polite to say, Verity, is that the police suspected me of this terrible crime,' says Grant, swigging a large glug of red. 'I was the only one who knew them. Unfortunately it is still a complete mystery.'

'There must have been theories,' says Verity. 'Why did they come to Crossways? Did they know someone here?'

'Sadly, just one of those random crimes and those often do remain unsolved. The case was closed,' says Isha.

'No justice for that poor couple?' says Eliza.

'But cases like that aren't ever closed are they?' says Verity. 'It just takes things to get stirred up, a reminder that it hasn't been forgotten to get one tiny new lead. That's how lots of old cases get solved. Getting people to talk.'

That echoes almost exactly what Mitch said earlier. Almost down to the singing like a canary bit. Verity really was paying attention. And Verity's worse than me for asking unpopular questions. I suspect the rumour is true that Verity has a little previous for sticking her nose into awkward places. Maybe Verity did leave university under a cloud and with no degree because of causing some upset.

Before the conversation can continue, Ashley gets to her feet. 'I'm sorry, but I've a busy day tomorrow and I do have a little headache coming. I think it's the heat.'

She thanks us all for coming and for the great discussion.

'But we haven't even agreed which book we're going to read next,' protests Margot, but we find ourselves bundled towards the door.

9

Keera

I ducked it. I know. I completely avoided the chance to ask bookgroup. I cannot decide if I should help Mitch. Is Liv right and there's too slim a chance of a different outcome? Liv's probably right, things are best left alone.

Especially as his Crossways chapter doesn't hold out much hope.

For a true-crime biography I'd been expecting breathy, thrilling, with a side-order of unsubtle hints and sensation dolloped in. But some chapters are little more than: *it's as much about my colleagues, all great characters, as the perps we wrangled with.*

Not such great characters, unless you find police banter especially entertaining. I've re-read it several times and I can't see where Mitch feels a new lead is coming from. Is it really just talk to stir up publicity for his book?

Chapter 5 It's Dark and Mysterious in the countryside

I thought I'd seen most things. Might even have been bold enough to call myself unshockable. But

I learned a valuable lesson that crime can still take you by surprise when you least expect it, and I least expected it when I'd taken a move out of the city to the slower pace of the countryside. Or so I thought.

Until I walked straight into a case that would be one of the worst of my career. One that had defeated my new colleagues. I walked into a good team with low morale. Like the dumb, over-confident city guy that I was, I thought I was going to stroll in and show them how murder investigations are really done, confident I could bring all my expertise and teach them a thing or two.

The facts were pretty simple. How could something so simple end in what would become called an impossible crime?

The Davenports had successful lives and careers, Peter a scientist, his second wife, Angela, had been a teacher. One grown-up daughter of Angela's first marriage lived abroad, so nothing tied them to anywhere as they reached a time of change, opportunity, relaxation. But retirement approached too quickly. They didn't want to look backwards. Yet they struggled how to look forwards.

Would their ideal retirement be the countryside? The seaside? A city where they could visit the theatre and attend the music recitals and talks they loved? Should they consider starting a small business? They were comfortably off, well-educated, successful, with a happy marriage. Everyone said they had everything to look forward to. But Peter loved his work, it gave him purpose. The question of whether he could afford to retire wasn't what kept him awake at night. He knew he was lucky, but still felt he was being put out to grass way too early. Retirement terrified him.

He knew he would miss a job that gave him a sense of being part of something that mattered, a daily feeling of achievement. And I got it. Maybe one of the reasons I was so keen for a solve.

They had a buyer for their house. The plan was to down-size, so they decided to press on, sell up and put their belongings into storage and travel, be free and easy, then decide their next move.

They'd already visited a lot of places that might be the perfect place to call their new home, assured they had plenty of time to find the right place, the right new direction.

They could not have been more wrong.

It was driving back from an investigation of a seaside town that changed everything. It was a longer drive than they'd thought, the town had been disappointing. They stopped off for a break. And they were instantly charmed by the place they'd stopped.

A quaint high street, the independent shops, the riverside walks. It offered a little bit of everything, and was one of those halfway places, in the countryside, but near to a city. Not too far from anywhere in fact.

They thought fate had lent a hand. A lucky accident. They made a last-minute decision to stay the night, laughing that after all their research, they might simply have stumbled into the ideal place in Churchways.

All of this was pieced together because of what happened the next day when they continued their spirit of adventure and called in on local estate agent Michael Grant, who was delighted to help them when they told him their story. Their house sale was to go through imminently, so again it felt like fate when Michael said he had a small but delightful rural cottage just completing renovations to rent out. It would be ready the moment they returned from the long holiday they were taking to celebrate their retirement. Everything was perfect and they went abroad, congratulating themselves everything had fallen into place.

How could they have any notion their plans were going to be cut short in the most brutal way?

Michael Grant took charge of everything, supervising getting their new place ready, even getting their furniture out of storage. He promised that when they touched down again, they could go straight to their new home. But instead of a fresh start, they were both brutally slain.

Mitch does a good job of setting up the scene. But it's just repetition of what was widely known and reported in the press at the time. The next bit is where it starts to get more interesting.

Michael Grant thought he was calling in to check everything was ready.

Grant's statement said he had an inkling something was wrong when he was shocked to notice a bloody handprint on the door window. But his assumption was it must have been left by one of the many people in and out doing the renovations to make the place perfect. There had been people in the house right up to the last minute. His only thought was that it needed cleaning up.

The house was supposed to be empty. He unlocked the door and stepped inside to a vision of horror.

Grant had no idea the couple had arrived earlier than expected. But they were lying dead inside. They were lying in a pool of their own blood. They had both been dead for some hours. Both had been shot.

When Michael Grant called the police he believed he had walked in on a double suicide.

His thoughts went not to murder, certainly not in an idyllic, quiet place like Churchways. His thoughts had gone to Peter killing Angela and turning the gun on himself. Grant knew Peter had defined himself by his job. Friends said he had been depressed towards the end of his working life, never receiving a major honour. And that despite all their best efforts, retirement weighed heavily on Peter.

And the murder of a couple in a place where they weren't even known seemed so unlikely, particularly an idyllic village like Churchways, Grant never even considered it. To be killed the night they arrived, to both be shot? No. And the suicide theory almost worked.

Except for one major flaw – where was the gun?

The mystery was a media sensation.

Someone else must have been in the house.

The gun wasn't all that was missing.

Michael Grant had been overseeing the couple's possessions and had disagreed when Angela Davenport said she wasn't going to put her most valuable jewellery into storage. Grant had advised her to put it safely into a bank when she told him she planned to wear all her rings and a diamond necklace on holiday.

Robbery became the obvious motive.

The cottage was at the end of a rural lane, isolated except for a solitary neighbour who had been watching television with the volume turned up loud in the back room. He had heard or seen nothing – hadn't even known the couple had arrived early.

Michael Grant came under obvious scrutiny. He had a key. He'd known the couple had valuables. There was only his word that he hadn't known the couple had returned early. But if Grant had wanted valuables why mention them at all?

Nothing could be proved. Nothing was ever proved.

Grant could not be linked to any firearm. And it seemed dramatically out of character. No desperate need for finances could be identified.

Police turned their attention to a small spate of burglaries in the area. Was that linked? But none of them had involved any violence.

No mention of being able to trace the gun. Doesn't surprise me. The link to other burglaries feels like a stretch. Was more known about the gun or the burglaries that never made it into the public domain? Is that where Mitch is hoping to spark a new lead? I read on.

Every lead was chased down in an attempt to find any motive. The couple were very private, even their neighbours where they had lived for the fourteen years of their marriage could say little about this quiet unassuming pair.

A main theory developed and took hold as the crime seemed impossible to explain. Were the couple followed from the airport? The investigation could not rule this out. But nor could it prove it. Lack of leads soon saw the police investigation stall and media interest dwindle with no new information arising. It was put down as a burglary gone wrong.

No one likes an unsolved murder. In a patch where murder is incredibly rare the local station likes it even less.

It was a big case for the small community, but it would have been big anywhere. A double murder. It's a case that still haunts people. It felt like it should not have happened. What could be a safer place to retire to than peaceful, community-minded Churchways?

But that case file is most definitely still open. I have a couple of ideas. Long shots. Budgets are better spent on something more likely to lead to success.

You could say I took it personally. Maybe it was that connection to Peter and his worry about retirement. Churchways was where I chose to move to as I tried to take it easier on my own road to retirement. It felt like a sign. Had fate played her hand in dropping this case right in front of me? Will that become my own retirement project? Is this fate telling me this is what I should devote my time to doing when I finally have to give up work? Will this give me purpose?

Because someone always knows something. How can I find them and get them to talk?

That was it. Reading it again I didn't get any more from it. If Mitch has ideas I can't imagine what they can be. Unless there's something on that local burglary angle?

Getting the police to take an interest isn't going to

happen without some new evidence. And where's that going to come from? From talking to people. The police aren't going to do that. But that's what I do all day.

Sod not taking an interest. Where do I start?

I guess I need to persuade Mitch to start talking. Or singing like a canary.

10

Verity

What sounded like an angry door slam had woken Verity. Grandma had left for work before even delivering her usual breakfast lecture.

There was a new, but equally unlikely message on the chalkboard on the fridge.

Expected to pop my head in at a work summer social tonight (yawn). Cheese needs eating up and there's a tomato – make pizza?? xxx

Verity found it difficult to swallow the idea there was any cheese left after last night. And another summer social? Grandma had been out three nights in a row. Almost as if Grandma was avoiding her.

Verity would loved to have pressed Grandma on a couple of points. The most interesting part of bookgroup had been Grandma surprisingly revealing her unexpected knowledge about body disposal.

'A chemist would have a good chance of getting away with murder,' Grant had said.

It was a sliver. Grandma's behaviour was exactly the kind of small detail Verity needed. Someone looking or behaving suspiciously, or differently. Add to that Grandma's suspicious keenness to shut down conversation about the killings and Verity was close to finding a way to squeeze Grandma into her Doodles of an Evil Genius notebook.

Verity munched chocolate balls and examined her case notes, deciding how many points to award herself for her challenge of getting at least a hint of a secret for everyone at bookgroup. It now looked a terrible strategy. Way too slow.

Crossways was like a fog of secrets, but stupid secrets about the silliest things. She needed to take more risks if she was going to dig through to what mattered. Even though even small secrets had the power to fester and grow the minute you turned them into secrets.

But she was on a deadline and needed some new, fast-track approach. The easiest route was through Mitch. So how to persuade Mitch he needed her help? Did she have any sliver to offer?

Grant Michaels had opportunity, but the police knew that. If Grant had got away with it all those years ago and been laughing to himself ever since, Verity would need to find a motive. What might have the investigation missed?

She had two slivers for Isha. Isha watched her dad having fun with his gun (giving Isha the means to do the crime). What about this recent money for an expensive winter holiday? Had Isha been sitting on valuables all this time and finally felt safe turning it into cash? Mitch might be interested in that. Had Isha even been in Crossways at the time? Verity needed a timeline.

Verity turned her attention to the photograph that appeared in every newspaper after the deaths of Chris and Carrie Winter – the real names of the murdered couple that Mitch called Peter and Angela Davenport in his book.

Those happy snaps that appeared following a tragedy were always so poignant. Chris had a distinctive high domed head, just a hint of remaining black hair tufting around the sides. Carrie was shorter with a wild tumble of dark curls and a bigger smile. Was there any haunted premonition in their eyes? No. No one could look at this captured moment, those smiles, and know it would be seen by thousands following their brutal and still unexplained ends.

The headlines gave away how little journalists could find to write about.

Interviews with residents with nothing more to say other than describing the village as 'shocked' and 'usually very quiet'. Everything was just speculation or versions on Sleepy Village Shocked By Events. Nothing to keep journalists hanging around.

Verity rinsed the dregs of chocolate milk from her cereal bowl thinking it wasn't called an impossible crime for nothing. No one here knew the couple. Maybe someone following them here to kill them was a more likely story. Maybe there wasn't a Crossways Killer at all. Yet.

Everyone knew that statistic that nine out of ten victims know their killer. Had coming to Crossways thrown them into the path of their killer? If they knew someone in Crossways, it was someone who'd stayed under the radar. Finding a hidden connection could be the sliver that would crack the case wide open. Someone the police had missed talking to at the time. How could Verity find out? And four years after the murders? The killer had been clever enough to evade the police, even the late-to-the-party arrival of Met-sharpened Mitch Ravenscroft. And he was still mad about it. Verity sighed.

This case would only crack if people talked about it.

But what better place than working in a small shop to find that hidden connection?

If she was smart and a little slippery, she could put to good use all that time she was forced to chat to people about their dull Crossways lives. People weren't on their guard when chatting in a shop. All she needed was just a hint someone knew the couple, but had never come to the attention of the police… That would be more than a sliver. That would be a breakthrough.

All she needed was someone to give themselves away.

11

Verity

All her plans and positivity and her mission to be a new, chatty version of herself evaporated when Verity arrived at work and was greeted with a scene of devastation.

Keera and Eliza were chasing up paper, cartons, cardboard and plastic packaging making a bid for freedom down Crossways high street. An empty bin was sideways on the pavement. Verity murmured something about 'how unlucky' and joined in.

'It's not unlucky!' said Eliza, her face thunderous.

Eliza might have a point. Splinters of glass were mashed among disgusting pulpy food waste ground right into the pavement.

'The only thing that's unlucky is being next door to bloody Benj Beresford,' Eliza stormed. 'He moved his bins to right by my garden gate. Just the night they *happened* to go over.'

'You're saying Benj did this deliberately?' said Keera.

'Well who else?' said Eliza.

'Or did the bins go over just before a herd of something large, maybe elephants, trampled through Crossways last night?' Verity said, trying to keep it light, never having seen Eliza angry like this as they swept up paper and plastic packaging and smelly food waste.

Verity and Keera tried in vain to get Eliza to leave the clearing up to them. But Eliza resisted all their efforts, although she moved uncomfortably from her injuries.

Eliza was small, neat and chatty with her customers, offered local produce and people raved about her take-away salad. If this was deliberate, it was nasty and vindictive, and definitely evidence that there was more to Crossways than comfy cardis, rounds of golf and YogaGals.

But was it deliberate? And was it Benj Beresford?

Benj Beresford's Crossways Cafe stood the opposite side of the deli to the bookshop. It was already doing brisk business for the early breakfast bap crowd.

Trouble was, Verity didn't have anyone on her list for the case of Who Would Harm Eliza Somers and Why?

'That'll need bleach,' said Grant Michaels as he parked his huge car in its usual space and came to offer advice. 'Otherwise that is going to stink and attract flies in this hot weather and you don't want that right outside a deli.'

'Thanks Grant. A bucket of hot soapy water and it'll be fine,' said Keera.

'It's like cleaning a crime scene!' said Verity.

'Well it bloody well is a crime scene,' fumed Eliza.

'What makes you think it's down to Benj?' asked Keera.

'What makes you imagine a bin like that would go over by itself?' Eliza swabbed furiously with a mop.

'All I ever see of Benj is when he heads off on his ludicrously expensive bike in bright purple Lycra. Particularly on Tuesdays when the local cyclists all meet up,' said Keera. 'Why would he—'

'Benj wanted my shop, but I got there first,' said Eliza. 'Everyone knows he's got it in for me.'

'Isn't your shop too small for a cafe?' said Keera gently.

'The day I opened he came round, I thought to welcome me, but he just showed off about how successful his business is. He said he couldn't have predicted how it would take off. When he started he let out upstairs rooms, but he quickly changed to put more tables on the first floor and he lives in a box-room in the attic. Then he told me he's got nowhere left to expand and accused me of strangling his business because I won't let him use my garden. He wants it. We are right next door, but he lost out. I never realised how determined he'd be in trying to get me out. I should have confronted him before.'

'Before?' Keera asked.

'This isn't the first time I've had glass everywhere! I'd only been open a few weeks when I had a rock through my window,' said Eliza.

'A stone could have been thrown up by a passing lorry,' said Keera, doing her best to smooth things.

'Benj had another friendly suggestion,' said Eliza, hurling empty cans into the righted bin. 'Cutting down the hedge so he could get into my garden and put in tables.'

'What did you say to him?' Keera asked.

'I told him over my dead body.'

'Was that before or after you broke your ribs falling down the steps?' asked Verity.

The story Eliza told was she'd taken a heavy tumble down hard concrete steps out the back of her shop. Of course there was a Crossways rumour of Eliza being here to hide out from a violent ex-lover… Verity gathered up plastic wrapping thoughtfully and a cloud went across the sun. Verity shivered. It felt like a ghost had trailed its fingers down her back. From feeling it was almost impossible the Crossways Killings could happen here, she was finding she could believe this was exactly the place for a double murder. And the murderer totally getting away with it.

Nowhere could be as nice as Crossways appeared. It had to be concealing plenty that was slitheringly dark and properly poisonous beneath the surface.

There were steep, concrete steps out the back of the shop. Verity always liked to dig a little deeper, so she'd dug around (of course she had) and removed a new piece of grey, almost invisible nylon thread wrapped around a low branch of jasmine just outside the back door.

Sometimes all you got were slivers, but sometimes that was enough to crack a case wide open. Verity twiddled with evidence she carried around in her pocket.

At least, to Verity it was evidence. Evidence someone had tied a tripwire to make sure Eliza took that tumble down those concrete steps. Was that Benj Beresford?

'I'm going to go around and push some of this stinking mess right under his nose!' said Eliza, showing quite a different side to the one who sold little cakes and did good deeds like trying to persuade people to donate funds to fix Jackson Brodie's tail.

'You want to question the suspect, see how he reacts, I get that,' said Verity. 'But accusing him before you've got evidence? Is that going to get you anything except denials?'

'I'm with Verity,' said Keera. 'If you go around while you are this angry, it could make things worse.'

'How much worse do you think things could get?' Eliza dumped another wad of stinking newspaper in the bin.

'If you explode in there in this mood in front of his early customers enjoying a breakfast bap… there will no longer be a question of whether there is a war going on between you. He'll see he's got to you and think he's winning. And what if it's not Benj?'

'As I already said, who else?' said Eliza.

'You mean Crossways doesn't always take to newcomers?' Verity said to Keera.

'I meant—you didn't handily hear a noise in the night, look out the window and see something, anything?' said Keera.

'I sleep at the back.'

'No handy hidden camera?' Verity said. 'You probably didn't think you'd need one moving to Crossways. Well, if bad things are happening, best let Benj know he's suspected, otherwise he's never going to stop is he.'

'Actually, that's not a bad idea. Thank you Verity,' said Keera.

'I didn't mean…' Verity could only stare at Keera. 'You want *me* to tell Benj we know he's got a vendetta against Eliza and warn him off?'

'Sounds perfect,' said Keera.

'Great,' Verity muttered. 'When Grandma volunteered me to help Eliza this summer, I didn't know what was going to be involved.'

'But thanks to your grandma, you were brought in to help Eliza. Good. Also, it means there are two of you,' said Keera. 'Standing up to Benj might be the most important thing you do to help Eliza this summer. I wouldn't waste any time. I'd drop in any time this morning.'

12

Keera

Spring sunshine brings out roses, fluffy fledgling birds, and day trippers… And luckily for me book sales! Today's been lovely and busy. Remi Aubert brought me a tin of homemade flapjacks. Unnecessary, but very welcome. Also, she made them vegan. So lunch sorted. Result.

I'm dreading the moment Liv Trent arrives. Bursting with ideas of how I can do things better and how badly I did at bookgroup last night.

Unluckily, it goes quiet just as Liv rolls in on a wave of summery perfume and a flattering dress. And just when I've a mouthful of my fourth flapjack (they're only small). No customers I can pretend to be busy with, which makes it look like I've done nothing except eat flapjacks.

'Tea?' I offer, stuffing in the last bite and dusting my fingers. I dive into what might popularly be called a cupboard, but which I call my back office and laughably small stock room. 'You look lovely. I guess you're on your way to a nice late lunch?'

'Are you hoping I won't have time to stay long?'

My slow kettle goes reluctantly about its one job so noisily I get away with pretending not to hear any incoming lecture. I rummage for biscuits as I make Liv rooibos with a hint of Earl Grey. Usual builders with oat for me.

'I can't find biscuits,' I say, 'but Remi Aubert brought me flapjacks.'

'Are there any left?'

'You probably won't want any if you're on your way to a lunch. Been one of those days I count it so lucky Crossways is on a main road on the way to a lot more interesting places. And has a massive free car park. When you consider the number of people who actually live here is no more than a small smattering, it's been surprisingly busy. Which committee is urgently requiring you today? No, has to be a spring party in that dress, unless you have someone you really want to impress.'

'I was supposed to be on my way to a meadow wildflower count, but they will manage to start without me. So I will have a flapjack. And quit trying to keep me off the urgent subject.'

Liv has a lot of friends. I'm pretty sure she also dates, but she's a lot more coy about that. I do find myself envying her easy life. She is equally happy lunching, partying, or volunteering for countless committees and causes. Can I see myself spending afternoons nibbling canapes and hob-nobbing rather than not selling quite enough books?

'I suppose you've heard about Benj and the bins?' I ask, guilty of trying to distract her from the incoming lecture. 'Don't mess with that stack of Paddington Bear books. They're perfect for gift-buying foreign visitors. I've been waiting for people to do their Crossways thing, drop in here when anything interesting is happening. But all tourists so far today. Do you think Benj is waging some vendetta to get Eliza out?'

'You should have warned people Mitch is going to poke around in the Crossways Killings,' says Liv. 'What happened to our tough, no bullshit, straight-talking Keera? You could at least have warned poor Grant. Landed with being chief suspect. He came off so badly in the whole affair and he was only doing his best. As for being the one to find those bodies… He deserves to be able to put it all behind him.'

'Although the easiest way to get closure might be to find out what really happened.'

'Four years after the first investigation failed?'

'I know. I ducked it. Verity did her best. You know it's going to get dragged up no matter what we do?'

'It already feels unstoppable?' says Liv.

'Things can escalate quickly. I'm surprised it's all escalated between Benj and Eliza so quickly. All that food waste trampled into the pavement right outside the deli was disgusting, but a pretty sharp reminder Crossways is not all grumbling about gardens. Although in this case it is actually about gardens.'

'Does Eliza have any proof it's all Benj?'

'I asked Eliza that and she said, *who else*?'

'Eliza should have gone straight to the police,' says Liv.

'Not everyone has the same confidence as you that the police would take the slightest interest,' I say, pleased when a customer arrives as I really don't want to argue with Liv.

Another A Bear Called Paddington flies out the door, followed by a fancy clothbound classic of Rebecca, and a cheap edition of The Adventures of Sherlock Holmes. Foreign visitors passing through Crossways do love a nice clothbound classic, along with my expert intel on Crossways' best places for lunch. I'm currently avoiding sending them to Benj's Crossways Cafe and sending them way down the high street to Halfway.

Isha drops in and sighs, possibly because she's in my poetry section and my expertise on poetry is as thin as my stock selection.

'We have to warn people,' Liv says, once Isha's gone (no purchase). I track her out of the window to see if I'm right and she's visiting the estate agent again. Is everyone thinking of moving out of Crossways?

'If Mitch's book is going to kick it all back into life, we could talk to people. Talking to people is what we booksellers do best.'

'I know bookselling is too dull for you after your exciting past life.'

'Hardly my fault if Crossways has an unsolved double murder in its past—'

'And you prefer sticking your nose in to selling books.'

'It's not that I find bookselling too dull. Although you might be right about my being nosy. What's Mitch going to follow up? Where's the new angle? It would help to know what was looked at in the original investigation.'

And what was overlooked. It's a surprise to me to find I'm thinking of Liv's son, Elliott, because he's police and my history involves too much time spent in police stations while they take their time fitting people up on very spurious evidence. I will grudgingly admit on more than one occasion Elliott has proved himself just a bit trustworthy. But he has very unsound views on everything from amateur sleuths to reasonable grounds for breaking and entering.

Could Liv persuade Elliott to go take a quick look at the Crossways Killings?

Amazingly, at that moment, Elliott shuffles in, running a hand through untidy sandy brown hair with a guilty air.

'I hope you're here to buy a book and not to tell me off for something,' I say.

'I hope I'm interrupting one of your malice and tea at four-thirty meetings,' he says, glancing at Liv.

'It's way off being four-thirty,' I say.

'You two never wait until four-thirty.'

'And isn't the quote *scandal and tea*?' says Liv.

'Don't be fooled into thinking all I do is chat,' I say. 'I have many other tasks. And not just reading the stock.'

Liv checks my takings on the till and raises an eyebrow. 'Bookselling success!'

'And don't forget not everyone who comes in actively wants to buy a book,' I say. 'Trying to convert casual browsers into book sales is my daily challenge. Particularly when there's an expensive bakery just down the road. It's like fighting a battle between the instant gratification offered by a carrot cake with sticky icing and a paperback that will give you hours of entertainment and enjoyment.'

I'm gabbling. It's not the only battle I feel caught in. Elliott doesn't just drop in. Liv knew he was coming and I'm caught in a pincer action between these two. From the shifty way he's behaving, he's here to tell me something I'm not going to like. But then he usually is.

What makes me even more uncomfortable are my suspicions Liv would like to match-make, but luckily neither of us want that. Not that Elliott doesn't have things going for him. In a certain light he has blue eyes that make me think of those husky-wolf dogs. When he's not looking at me disapprovingly, which is most of the time.

But Elliott is police so will always look at me disapprovingly. Plus I am absolutely sworn off men after a history of bad decisions and worse relationships that was all part of what had me running away to the countryside to do something wholesome like bookselling. The jury (and the current state of my anaemic bank account) hang in the balance on whether bookselling was a big mistake too.

'If I can't help with a brilliant book recommendation,' I say. 'I cannot imagine what I can do for you.'

'I want to read what Mitch is saying in his book,' says Elliott.

'Well that's nice and direct, but not happening,' I say. I shoot daggers at Liv. 'You told Elliott already?'

'Mitch's book is stirring things up. I need to know what he's saying,' says Elliott quietly.

I could admit the Crossways chapter is bland and Mitch definitely ducked it. There are no sensational reveals. But I hate being ambushed. Not in my shop. Forget I was just thinking I should be nice to Elliott and ask him to look and see if there's anything interesting in the original case files.

'Mitch called it an impossible case,' I say. 'Where's the harm in him devoting his retirement to it? Has to be better than it never being looked at again. Why wouldn't you want the case reopened and the chance of justice for that poor couple?'

'I can't sanction an unofficial investigation,' says Elliott at his pompous worst.

'Well at least Mitch is doing something to get justice.'

I am saved from being ruder by the arrival of an elderly gent looking for a thriller to keep him occupied on his coach journey, asking if there are any new Mick Herrons.

I recommend him Nick Harkaway's Karla's Choice.

'You've got an early copy of Mitch's book. I need to know what he's saying,' says Elliott once the shop is quiet again. 'We could help each other.'

'Mitch might not want you to read it.'

'He's found a publisher. His aim is to get as many people as possible to read it,' says Elliott. 'Him wanting people to read it isn't in any doubt. Why are you making this so difficult?'

'Sorry, but I have work to do because that familiar tuneless whistling is one of my delivery drivers and more books are on their way.'

I glower as I sign for the books and then the shop is empty again, except us three and a pile of boxes that now need processing into my impenetrable bookshop software.

'Were you involved in the case?' I ask.

Elliott shakes his head. 'I only transferred back here a year or so ago.'

'But you have access to official files and everything Mitch knows anyway,' I say, fighting to keep control of my temper. 'Maybe we *can* do a trade. You go look at the case-file, drop me a little hint about anything you missed. Like those local burglaries.'

'There wasn't anything missed.'

'You sound very sure about that. That means you've gone and read about it already. So what's Mitch onto?'

'If Mitch reckons he has new leads, I cannot see where they're coming from,' admits Elliott. 'It's why I'm asking you to let me read the book.' He suddenly changes tack and looks at me with pleading puppy eyes. 'Please. It would really help.'

'You should really talk to Mitch.'

'I will. When I've read the chapter.'

Where is another customer when you want one?

Why am I making this so difficult? I need to calm down. I need to do what I should have done the moment Elliott walked in.

'Tea?' I offer.

13

Keera

Elliott's builder's tea like me and doesn't ever complain, even if I put in oat milk. The kettle begrudgingly gets to work again. This time I also need a ginger biscuit.

'Maybe if you help Elliott, he can keep an eye on Eliza and her cafe-owning neighbour with a grudge,' Liv suggests.

'We don't need to involve police yet, thank you,' I say stiffly. 'Verity's going to have a quiet word.'

'And Verity's the best person for the job?' asks Liv. 'I know she's smart, but she's also slippery. She's also a reader. You should have been quicker when Ashley was looking for a position to keep Verity out of mischief this summer.'

'She is possibly more suited to selling books than olives and small cakes,' I admit. 'And Elliott, you do have a point that soon everyone will be able to read Mitch's book. Liv, did you bring any biscuits? Otherwise I'm out. And you're right about Verity being slippery. Someone at bookgroup's also read the manuscript, which I unwisely left in my bag.'

'Verity?' says Liv. 'It wouldn't surprise me if, rather than Crossways being the perfect place to keep Verity out of mischief, Verity thinks it will be amusing to go after someone who killed two people four years ago.'

'If others are reading advance copies, it's even more important I read it,' says Elliott. 'And you're right that there were burglaries at the time that were never solved either.'

'Fine!' I go to retrieve the manuscript. 'There's not so much as a hint of a new lead. No sensational revelations. Zilch. No wonder Mitch found it difficult to land a publisher.'

'Mitch is a professional,' says Elliott dryly. 'If he had any new leads he'd have gone through the official channels.'

Elliott holds out his hand.

I hesitate just a fraction before handing over the manuscript. Elliott takes it quickly, as if worried I'll change my mind.

'Maybe Mitch has a point about where's the harm in stirring things up,' I say. 'Reminding people it's not over. Sometimes that really is how cold cases are finally solved.'

'A murderer thinks they safely got away with it for four years. There was no explanation. That means the killer may still be living here,' says Elliott. 'There's the harm.'

'That's even more reason to want justice for that poor couple. Someone always knows something. Sometimes they even have a reason for keeping quiet. At the time. Things change. Has to be worth going over things, talking to people. The chances of the case being officially reopened are zero.'

'The case was never closed,' says Elliott coolly. 'You really think you, Mitch and Verity can solve it?'

'My neighbour's been the victim of a few too many accidents and something Verity said got me thinking. Any other incidents of other incomers being attacked? Is that a lead that was ever followed?'

'You think it's not Benj Beresford attacking Eliza?' says Liv. 'But no one's ever targeted you.'

'Am I strictly an incomer though? Eliza lives right here in Crossways, above her shop. I live in a horrible flat in Harcourt. Is it the same? To someone who doesn't like incomers?'

'You're not trying to make things more complicated than they are?' says Liv.

'Possibly. It very probably is Benj after her shop.'

A customer comes in wanting advice on something for her bookgroup 'to get their teeth into'.

Liv steps in, reaching for a Matt Haig and Liane Moriarty, giving me no choice than to deal with Elliott, who tucks away the manuscript, leaving me with the feeling he's leaving and the win is all on his side.

'You have been as forthcoming as ever,' I say. 'I do just have one more stupid question.'

'You know I can't discuss—'

'Ongoing cases, yes you've always made that quite clear. But this is hardly an ongoing case. Even by your own rules, you could talk about this one.'

'I'm worried about the consequences. Getting everyone talking may not give the outcome everyone's hoping.'

'Painful truths will be re-examined and the case still won't be solved?'

'If you understand that, why are you so keen to…'

'Stick my nose in? You can say it. I know what you're thinking. Because if gets people talking, where do they go to talk about it? Here. Between the Lines. Everyone who comes in here will be talking about it. I can't avoid it. Being in the bookshop means I hear everything. I could be useful.'

'And that is exactly the point,' says Elliott. ' You are exactly the sort who refuses to listen to good advice, goes to poke the hornet's nest, then seems surprised at the consequences.'

'Well. I guess someone has to.'

'No! Absolutely not! The sensible thing to do is steer clear of someone who until now feels safe that they have got away with killing two people. This is a bookshop, not somewhere the police turn to when they want gossip. If it was up to me there would be one rule around here—no amateur detectives.'

'Are you trying to call me out for being one of those true crime obsessives who tramples over evidence? You could be useful. Did you ever trace the stolen jewellery? What about the gun? What about DNA in the cottage? All of that is worth going over again. That's how cold cases might get solved.'

'It's not a cold case,' insists Elliott.

'It's not exactly a hot one.'

'And *might*? Is it worth the risk?' Elliott's angry now and heading for the door, clutching my copy of Mitch's manuscript. 'There's one rule—leave it to the experts.'

'That's two rules you've given me now.'

'No it isn't. It's the same rule.'

'You're talking about those same experts that failed?'

He's gone. The bored bookgroup customer has scuttled off. I was so busy arguing with Elliott I missed if she bought anything. It's just me and Liv.

'Elliott is right,' she says.

'Don't you start. He's not. Elliott is quite wrong. There's no way I'm ignoring this. It's the wrong thing to do.'

'The police will never reopen it. It's as good as closed. Mitch doesn't have any new leads. We've got nothing.'

'You've read the chapter? When did you do that?'

'Perhaps you shouldn't leave highly sensitive material about.'

'I'm pretty sure Verity's read it too. The way she lit up like a Christmas tree when the Crossways Killings came up tells me she won't listen if she's warned there was a killer in Crossways four years ago who might still be here.'

'She's young, has a lot to prove and she's another with a habit of asking intrusive questions,' says Liv. 'She's in the best place to help Eliza. The Crossways Killings are already getting talked about. You're right we can't avoid it.'

'You mean... You're admitting you were wrong? No improving lecture? We shouldn't ignore an unsolved murder?'

'Mitch is all talk and motivated by selling his book. It would take Elliott ages to go through official channels. But it is all going to get raked up again. And the best chances of it being solved do not lie with Elliott and Mitch Ravenscroft.'

'You think I can get answers for a horrible, impossible crime that the police gave up on years ago?'

'Not exactly. I'm saying you cannot do it without my help. You do everything better with my help.'

This was the last thing I was expecting.

'You and me?'

'It needs to be solved and quickly. Before kicking it all up again means something bad happens. Crossways can move on. And we have the unique skill-set to ensure it doesn't all just resettle with no different outcome.'

'I'm not so sure about the unique skill-set.'

'You know how to ask the right questions, especially the awkward ones. And you don't mind upsetting people.'

'I'm not sure those are my—'

'Everyone will be reminded of that horrible time, everyone will be talking about it and the truth is always in the details. Not the dramatic ones, the tiny ones. The overlooked ones. The clue everyone walks past because they're too busy looking where they expect the answer to be. That's where someone in a community is much better at solving crimes than the police.'

'Where do we start?'

'Where we always start. Tea.'

14

Verity

Eliza had been clear that Verity was never to buy lunch from the Crossways Cafe, her arch nemesis.

Which, of course meant Verity had dropped in right away to see what the deal was. And discovered a very good reason to keep dropping in there. Ensuring she kept it undercover from Eliza, of course.

Verity discovered Cal Kinsky. With his impressive big mop of dark, springy hair, kind eyes and soft brown skin, she could watch Cal Kinsky effortlessly doing his expert barista thing all day. She still thought of that first time with embarrassment. She'd had a hard time not simply staring.

Bad enough that she had been almost struck dumb in the face of so much gorgeousness. Then Cal asked how she was finding Crossways and Verity blurted out the honest answer she was finding it a bit dull, her mouth completely running away and somehow admitting how she was resorting to investigating the mystery of Who Shot Jackson Brodie for entertainment.

Cal looked amused. 'You're finding it a bit dull? You're investigating the cat shooting?' Cal tipped his head sideways sympathetically, his fingers deft as he ground beans and set the coffee machine hissing. 'Well, you just wait until the bodies start piling up.'

And she had known they we were going to get along.

And that was before he started smuggling her free broken shortbread along with her coffee every morning.

Verity was usually careful to get her timing right so Cal wasn't too busy to chat. And avoid arriving at the same time as Taylor Messenger (head-teacher Belinda Messenger's grungy-goth daughter) who also did daily visits to the Crossways Cafe. Suspicious, as she worked in a cafe herself. Was Cal giving her free shortbread as well?

Cal had the reputation as the local 'teenage tearaway' and Verity would love to know more, like why he was back for the summer from med school and not off somewhere (anywhere) more interesting. As long as it wasn't just about Taylor Messenger, who sashayed up and down the high street in sophisticated black even in the hottest spring anyone remembered and had a tattoo of a bad fairy on her wrist. Never before had Verity considered that maybe she should get her hair bleached with blue ends. Or a tattoo.

Verity had subtly probed Grandma and found out Cal was the son of the head of a local pharmaceutical company, big-reading Mrs Kinsky. There was animosity between small, cultivated Mrs Kinsky and tall, bossy, bottle blonde head-teacher Belinda. Grandma said it was because Cal Kinsky and Taylor Messenger had a 'thing' a few years back (Grandma's fusty way of saying they had teenage sex). Taylor didn't even get knocked up. That was Crossways for you.

The incident with the bins had thrown the day out, so there was already a queue of day-trippers off the coaches.

Cal was working with only one other person and queue grumblings had reached the theatrical checking of watches stage. Benj Bereford's success was no mystery. The Crossways was closest to the free car park and the first place offering a cup of tea and a bun to anyone released from being stuck in a coach for hours.

The air was full of the smell of toasted panini as well as grumbling and the aroma of the ever-popular all-day breakfast bap and coffee. Sort of the perfect British day out, along with nerve-shredding tension about the queue being so long there was danger of missing the coach.

There was little Verity could do except join the queue and observe it was sunny outside; packed and hot inside and feel butterflies about challenging the cafe owner and cross-examining of the suspect.

Where was Benj? Shouldn't he be here helping?

'Usual?' grinned Cal, spotting Verity and ignoring heads turning and silent queue-jumping daggers being thrown.

Verity nodded and grinned shyly.

At least Benj Beresford was a welcome new addition to her case notes. A vendetta against Eliza was better than a sliver, it was a brilliant starting point. Someone behaving very badly. Verity needed to find out more. She knew his cafe had been instantly successful and Benj had quickly pivoted, expanding his cafe into where he'd started out offering rooms. But when had that happened? When had he opened? And could Benj feature on her timeline, more a Venn diagram actually, of people who'd been here at the time of the Crossways Killings and were behaving badly and/or suspiciously. Moving to Crossways might also mean he could have known the Winters from before. Yes, she was very interested in Benj.

Verity was so distracted with her thoughts and mesmerised watching Cal, she almost missed the familiar flash of purple. Benj had arrived, but not to provide much-needed back-up. He was sweeping effortlessly on through, ignoring the queue. Verity had to grab him by his purple Lycra top in a way he couldn't ignore. He probably thought she was a complaining customer. She was, but not in the way he might think.

'Eliza's got a bad leg and broken ribs in an accident that requires a lot of explaining and she shouldn't be swabbing pavements because your bins have gone over,' said Verity. 'I've moved your bins back to where they should be. I am watching out for her. That means I am watching you.'

It had sounded better when she practised it in her head. The truth was, if you want to put the frighteners on – don't send someone who feels they look and dress like a librarian and serves olives and small cakes. She was expecting denial and probably bluster.

Benj had his bike helmet on, turned, looking startled, his grey eyebrows lost under the helmet. But mostly, Benj looked puzzled. 'Er, er… Something happened to the bins?'

'They're your bins, they moved, they went over, it didn't happen by accident. We know you want Eliza out, we know you want her garden. So just stop, because we know what you're doing, ok. Let's not turn this into bin-mageddon, alright?'

Queuing customers had little to do except listen to him being accused. The popular grumbling vibe turned into complete silence and Verity felt she should push home this small advantage. But how? Benj wasn't just going to admit it. If the police had plenty of suspicion, but no proof, they could resort to interrogations in dank underground rooms. Verity didn't have one of those.

'It wasn't just bins going over, there was disgusting food waste trampled into the pavement. It took forever to clean it up. I know Crossways is far from the cosy, bland place it appears. Bad things happen here. So we're looking out for Eliza.'

'I can't imagine why the bins got moved or how they went over,' said Benj. 'How terrible. I'll talk to my staff. You should have come straight to me.' Benj turned to Cal. 'Give Verity and Eliza coffees on the house.'

'Oh, well yes, that sounds very nice. Thank you,' said Verity.

Very nice thank you. Wowser she was such a pushover. As far as questioning the suspect went, she was awarding herself zero points. She had got nothing, well, except a free coffee. Benj was already off and heading for the door.

'And I have my suspicions about Eliza's accident too,' Verity called after him.

Verity thought that was it. But at the last second Benj turned. The chatter had risen again, as if someone had turned the volume back up.

'Eliza's accident, yes,' he said, and this time no one else appeared to be listening. She is just so very *unlucky*, isn't she.' Benj flashed Verity a horrible smile. 'So sad if she feels very unwelcome here. Such a shame if it all makes her decide to move on again quickly.'

And then Benj was gone. Verity's skin felt cool even in the heated atmosphere of the packed cafe.

Cal passed her order above the heads of the queue. Verity hoped it would contain the usual – not just coffee but a free broken biscuit. That would make her feel better, partly because Verity had theories that Cal might not be above a little subterfuge – because were there really that many broken shortbread in the cafe?

She had to move to the front of the queue to grab them and she asked Cal what he thought.

'Did you hear? Did that sound like a threat to you? Was that kind of an admission?'

'You said before Eliza reckons he's in some vendetta, but I don't know.' Cal managed to keep up a rhythm of making a cappuccino while chatting and not making eye contact with the disgruntled queuers. 'I did ask him for you.'

Verity couldn't disguise her happiness. 'You did?'

'Benj reckons she's got a ruthless streak cos of how she swooped in right under his nose to get that shop. But that wasn't so much Eliza being ruthless as a Grant Michaels screw-up.'

'Grant Michaels,' repeated Verity. 'His name crops up in anything to do with Crossways. How did he screw up?'

'Guess you could ask him?'

'Thanks Cal.'

'No trouble. I know how bored you are and how you like investigating. Got anywhere with who shot the cat?'

'Not yet.'

Cal flashed his irresistible smile. 'And I know you asked about finding out the truth about David's shed.'

'Did I?' Verity couldn't quite believe she'd spilled it to Cal that she wanted to find out if David's shed was the seat of planning a secret science comeback revenge project, or if Camp Model Railway was right all along.

'David and Margot are away this weekend.' Cal said it with a crooked grin, as if the queue of thirsty grumbling coach travellers had disappeared and it was just the two of them, with an illicit broken shortbread. And a secret.

'You think…' Verity thought how this summer would be way more interesting if they ended up tearing up Crossways together.

'I think this weekend would be perfect. And if you need help, I'm in. If… Operation Workshop is on?'

Just a boy standing in front of a girl and asking if there was a plan to do a little light breaking and entering on a Saturday night. All in the name of investigating of course.

He'd even given the Saturday night operation a name.

Sometimes things did fall into place like jigsaw pieces.

'Operation Workshop is on Saturday night,' said Verity.

It was very possible they were soulmates.

15

Keera

Crossways Estates, the biggest, most impressive space on the high street, is right across the road. Makes me wonder how Grant got away with planning permission for all that plate glass, but then Grant knows everyone in Crossways.

'Need me to mind the shop while you go and ruffle feathers?' says Liv, joining me staring at the window. 'Whose feathers are we starting with? Ah yes, Grant. Wise choice. His SUV's parked in its usual place, so he's in. It's only fair to warn him about Mitch's book.'

'Grant was the only suspect in the Crossways Killings. Although, can you see Grant killing two people?'

'Trouble is I can't see anyone killing two people. I also can't fathom why the Winter couple needed to die at all.'

'A case of mistaken identity?' I suggest.

'Mistaken for whom? There must be a reason. We need to find it. With our unique skill-set,' says Liv. 'Time to start getting people talking. I will leave asking all the awkward questions to you.

I almost bump into poet Isha coming out of Crossways Estates. Again. Tugging down her ever-present green beanie hat over her long dark hair streaked with grey, as if she thinks a hat will stop me spotting her.

'Hi Isha how are all the repairs and DIY going? All done and visiting the estate agent? Thinking of selling up and trying to leave Crossways? You've been chatting to Grant a lot lately.'

'You are incredibly nosy, Keera.'

She hurries off. Certainly before I can put the next intrusive question. How about the rumour that her father left her nothing but debts and a house he'd not touched with so much as a paintbrush for forty years? In a village fuelled by gossip, everyone's chattering about how she paid for a long winter holiday. And so I ask myself when exactly did she come back to Crossways? Did her money troubles coincide with the time someone robbed a wealthy couple? And those other burglaries? Someone desperate enough for cash to break into empty homes? Poet Isha?

And there you have exactly why no one talks about the Crossways Killings. It makes you see something suspicious in every move your neighbours make. Liv's right. If it's getting dragged up again, we have to solve it before it does more serious damage.

A woman in a dark suit is chattering away on the phone, advising someone to hire a gardener and improve something she calls kerb appeal. Guess she's not a reader as I don't recognise her.

'Hello Keera, lovely to see you,' says Grant, rising from his big desk right at the back. 'Too much to hope I owe the pleasure of this visit to the fact that Crossways has grabbed hold and you want your move here to be permanent?' Grant rubs his thin white hands together and flaps at me to take a seat. 'Yes Crossways does get people in a stranglehold.'

'I'm not actually a resident. I live in a horrible flat in Harcourt. So I've no way of becoming permanent.'

'Yes, of course you do. Terrible those bins going over in the night,' says Grant. 'How is Eliza?'

'Eliza doesn't think it was an accident and that trampled food mess was disgusting. Nasty, vindictive things happen even in the loveliest of places.'

An air-conditioning unit whirrs in the corner. Grant's jacket's slung over the back of his chair. He's wearing a pressed short-sleeved shirt and a narrow red-knitted tie and an eager expression.

'Sadly, I suspect unpleasant things happen everywhere. But so many people come here, love it and stay,' chatters Grant. 'You're in a low price rental, driving in every day from Harcourt and you're launching an evening events programme. You'll have a lot of late nights.'

'No surprise you are very well informed.'

'I love the events idea!' He clears his throat. 'So is the bookshop doing well? Because, you know, for a rental, the market just doesn't give the same yield on larger properties.'

'That's it, you've just exhausted my ability to do estate-agent talk. Are you asking how much I can afford?'

I'm not here to look for a new place to live. I'm here partly to warn Grant, but also to find out what he really thinks. And knows. Were the quiet, unobtrusive, recently retired Winters murdered by some random burglar?

'There maybe something characterful coming up right in the high street. But don't press me on it.' He raises his eyebrows as if pressing him on it is exactly what he expects me to do.

'Would it be a cheap flat?'

'It might be one of the more-affordable, two-bed cottages.'

'I'd need *very* affordable.'

It's not what I'm here for, but Grant saying that makes me realise how much I've been yearning to move out of my horrible damp and smelly flat.

But it's impossible. Moving to a lovely, pretty desirable village with astronomical property prices was exactly the terrible move Supportive Mum warned me about. I barely sell enough books to keep Between the Lines open. Having a home in Crossways is never going to happen.

'There's always a chance my mum might help me out.' Such a lie. I don't even know why I say it.

Even if Mum had surplus funds sloshing around in a forgotten bank account, she's of the view that people should stand on their own two feet and that no one should ever step in to offer a helping hand. But I can dream. Just for a moment.

'Ah a little help from the bank of mum and dad,' says Grant. 'Some think multiple buyers fighting gets a good price. That rarely happens. What you want is one serious buyer and to say goodbye to all that traipsing people around your home. I can put in a good word.'

Buying anything is a complete fiction, so it's tempting to up my game. Even a flat is a castle in the air. So how about a new pony-riding ambition and a need for easy access to bridle paths? If I drag Liv into snooping around mansions, I'd better throw in a wine cellar and outbuildings where we can set up a gin distillery on the side.

'We'll run financials and then we'll know what we're dealing with,' says Grant.

'Running financials won't help. I need you to produce a miracle and the cheapest thing you've possibly got. Eliza said you worked a miracle for her,' I say.

Grant removes his glasses to polish them and gives a dry chuckle that sounds like leaves crunching. 'One option to move more locally is a room. In Harcourt you have a whole flat. What do you think?'

'I think it sounds like a house share.'

'Exactly like a house share.'

Shared kitchen and bathroom. Like being a student again. Like slipping back in time and losing a whole decade of my life. But then Mum and people from my old life already think I've taken a backward step in taking up the gentle and not very well paid art of country bookselling. But I kept it quiet just how bad my options were at the time.

'Benj's cafe was an instant success and he's been looking for a way to expand ever since,' I say. 'Yet Eliza got that property. How did that happen?'

'Eliza happened to be here when the landlord was in.' Grant puts up his hands defensively. 'Out of my control. It did rather put me in the bad books with Benj.' He gives his hollow, mirthless chuckle again. 'I'm working on that.'

So not surprising there's a thick splinter of animosity between Eliza and her cafe neighbour. Do I believe this story of an accidental meeting?

'Property is what gets people very angry and fighting around here,' I say. 'Why did you favour Eliza over Benj?'

'Now nobody said that.' He pinches the bridge of his nose. 'Anyway, people don't really fight in Crossways.'

'Grant, you know better than anyone that they absolutely do. You saw that mess outside Eliza's.' It's now or never and I plunge right on. 'Two people got murdered. How did that happen? In Crossways.'

He blinks at me. His adam's apple bobs uncomfortably.

'You helped them too. And you found their bodies. That must have been awful. Beyond awful.'

'You shouldn't…' Grant fiddles uncomfortably with a pen on his desk. Then his collar.

'You can't believe it was just random. You know there can be a nasty side to anywhere. What was it really about?'

'Burglaries happen. I know sometimes it's just kids.' Grant swallows so uncomfortably, as if he's having trouble breathing. 'She refused to put jewellery into safekeeping.'

'People have theories about everything, even why David Purkiss has a shed. People must have talked about it.'

'Believe me, people were too stunned to talk about it.'

'People didn't discuss who killed them? Who knew them or what brought them here? Really?'

'They chanced on Crossways. They said it felt like it was in the stars.''

'They got shot and murdered. It makes no sense.'

'An impossible crime.'

'No such thing. It just means we don't have the answer yet. Also, it makes me a little nervous about Crossways. Maybe it's time we stop being too stunned to talk about it. Maybe the time has come to find answers.'

'Ah, yes, well.'

'Because I'm sorry to say I'm here to warn you about Mitch Ravenscroft. He doesn't just offer advice about police procedure and authenticity for crime writers. He's written his memoirs. He means to find a new lead to get the Crossways Killings reopened. You are the go-to person. Tell me what you know. And suspect.'

Grant takes another deep breath. He pinches the bridge of his nose, closes his eyes and his face drains of the little colour it has. He's sitting in front of the air conditioning unit, but Grant Michaels is starting to sweat. But he does start talking.

'This house was being renovated for rental. One elderly neighbour. Beautiful countryside views. Outskirts of Crossways, a rural location, but only a short level footpath to a very well served village, two pubs—one undergoing extensive refurbishment.' Grant scratches at the collar of his shirt as if it's grown too tight for him.

'I didn't mean the sales details. You were the only one in Crossways who even talked to them. What did they say?'

Grant wheezes. 'That's not quite true, because he was doing rooms back then. People forget. We didn't speak much. They went off on a long holiday and communications were difficult.' Suddenly, it's as if Grant's being strangled; he's fighting for breath.

'Are you all right?' The stupid question you ask even if someone is clearly very much not all right.

His colleague is still offering advice about hanging baskets and painting the front door. I get to my feet, uncertain what to do. Grant keeps on talking with difficulty.

'I—I walked in. I found them.' Grant's eyes bulge as he fights for a gasp of air. He's gulping, like a fish out of water.

'Do you need an ambulance?'

'There was nothing...' Grant is now fighting to breathe, still trying to get words out, his voice strangled like he's forcing words from his throat. He's bright red.

'Grant. You aren't going to die on me.'

I rush around to his side of the desk, thump him on the back. 'I'm calling an ambulance.'

'There was nothing,' Grant carries on, wheezing noisily. 'Nothing even left of his head.'

16

Verity

Someone slipped in from the shadow of a doorway and spoke in a low, threatening voice right in her ear, 'We know what you're really up to.'

Verity jumped and turned. Then she frowned.

'What are *you* up to Margot?' How had she let herself be ambushed by Margot Latimer?

'Emergency meeting in five.'

'I'm sorry, what?'

Margot gave an eye roll as if Verity was being spectacularly slow, rather than Margot being opaquely mysterious. 'Halfway in five. We heard about the bins.'

'What d'you mean you know what I'm really up to?' Verity couldn't stop herself flushing guiltily about Operation Workshop. 'What meeting?'

'In Crossways, we look out for each other. We Stay Vigilant. We aren't going to just sit back and let it happen.'

'I have to go back to work. And who's *we*?'

'Bookgroup. We want in.'

Verity stared. 'What are you on about? What do you mean you want in?'

'We've rumbled how Ashley sneaked you in undercover for the summer. You can tell us everything in Halfway in five minutes.'

Verity hadn't seen this coming.

It sounded horribly as if Margot, and others, wanted to be Watson to her Sherlock; Hastings to her Poirot. Verity, who prided herself on keeping all her investigations under the radar, *had* to keep it all from reaching Grandma's ears, had been rumbled by bookgroup. Being wrong-footed by Margot Latimer was not a good look.

'We can't let Eliza be a victim like this,' said Margot. 'Who is targeting her and why? What will she think of Crossways? Of us? She might leave. The shop might go back to what it was before. It sold baby clothes.'

How was involving bookgroup not going to be awkward? Members of bookgroup were part of her many investigations, Particularly Operation Workshop.

'Belinda sent me to get you.'

That made more sense. Verity could see Belinda being sharp enough to sniff out that Verity had covert plans.

'So it's more an order, or a royal command than a request?' said Verity. 'You mean I can't say no. Guess it's how things are when you're a headteacher of a swanky, successful girls' school.'

'It has to be now because YogaGals starts in less than an hour in the village hall.'

Verity could have guessed that. Margot was head to toe in Lycra.

Verity was conflicted. She was being presented with an opportunity to work on the inside and this could be a chance to covertly investigate bookgroup. Bookgroup were well-connected and knew things and people and could help with her cases. But that was serious undercover work. A challenge, more than a challenge. It would take someone extremely slippery and clever to walk a tightrope like that and pull it off. But slippery and clever were things Verity thought she could manage. This could be a case of keeping your enemies close.

Also, Verity's next step had been to quiz the key person in the Crossways Killings case, only the annoying bookseller had just gone into the estate agent.

Grandma had brought her here to help Eliza. If bookgroup wanted to help Eliza… it would leave Verity more time to devote to the Crossways Killings. Priorities.

'Fine. Eliza's always trying to get me to take longer breaks. Let me tell her I'll be back soon. Halfway in five.'

Margot strode off to report back success.

Five minutes to prepare what might be the trickiest challenge of Verity's life.

She stuck her head in Eliza's Deli, handed in Benj's free coffees, said she had nothing conclusive to report and that she had something else she wanted to do. As she headed for Halfway, Jackson Brodie unexpectedly appeared. He rubbed around her legs, as if offering cat-wisdom and comfort and joined her as she walked at the cat's pace.

'I thought I'd have nothing more interesting than solving who shot you, but I'm afraid now I'm just too busy. Sorry about that Jackson. But I'm on a deadline. I need to get people talking. But how exactly do I involve bookgroup without them knowing I'm also investigating them?'

A saunter along Crossways' long high street at a cat's pace gave an opportunity to enjoy the quirkiness of businesses and homes being side by side, so you were tempted by luxury baked goods one moment and seeing the flicker of daytime television the next. Then Verity was eyeball to eyeball with a small dog, paws on the windowsill, on vigil for anyone passing worth savaging or saving. The dog started yapping at Jackson, who was completely not bothered.

'Involving bookgroup is smart, because bookgroup is full of the sort of people who probably, collectively, have more answers than they know. The answer to the Crossways Killings has to be here. So can I leave protecting Eliza to them? Because ever since I found evidence of a tripwire, the question I've wanted to ask Eliza is: *is someone trying to kill you?*'

In her pocket, Verity played with that straggly end of the strong piece of almost invisible fishing line she'd recovered from the bottom of a jasmine by the back door.

'A tripwire sent her flying down lethal concrete steps. She was lucky not to break her neck. Someone meant her serious harm. Was that Benj, Jackson?'

Jackson answered by looking up at Verity, releasing one of his famously loud miaows. She bent to stroke the cat behind his torn ears.

'Would Benj Beresford actually want her dead over an argument about a garden? Is it safe to leave that case to Bookgroup Investigates? Eliza is definitely a mystery. And there's more. Eliza had all this paperwork spread out in her flat, like a research project. And me with no camera to take a single picture. All I had time to do was skim an article about some dull business awards gala dinner. Why would Eliza be interested in that? I have to face it, I have too many questions and not enough time.'

Verity was getting strange looks, but talking to the cat was helping. She had to be on top of her game if she had any chance of manipulating Belinda Messenger to her will.

'Everyone needs their Watson, Jackson.'

Jackson had accompanied her all the way to Halfway and miaowed again. Hinting and hoping a reward was due?

'I have to find a way to involve Bookgroup Investigates without them knowing they are being used, because they know everyone and the theory I'm working on is that the victim usually knows their killer. Did the Winters know their killer? Was the burglary a cover?'

Jackson answered again with another of his over-loud miaows. Although he could have been protesting lack of treats. Seeing none on offer, he scooted away down a side alley.

'Thanks Jackson,' said Verity, watching him disappear. 'Talking to you was very useful.'

17

Keera

I thought Grant was going to die right in front of me.

But he flaps a hand in the direction of a glass of water, which I pass to him. He glugs it down gratefully.

My thoughts of calling for an ambulance recede along with the brick red of his complexion and his struggles for air.

He takes one final cough and another drink while his colleague rambles on, still finding more to say about lawns and hanging baskets.

'So sorry about that, Keera.'

'It's me that's sorry for making you relive that,' I say.

The Crossways Killings doesn't feel in the least like a cold case. It's in the room with us now. The horror of unexpectedly stepping into the aftermath of carnage of two brutal murders.

'Worst moment of my life. I still dream about it. Sorry. Probably shouldn't have said that—about his head. Don't want to give you nightmares too. But the blood, the bodies. The smell,' he says in a whisper. 'Have you ever been inside an old fashioned butcher's shop? I haven't eaten meat since.'

I think we both need a moment after that.

Grant's colleague finally finishes on the phone and says she's off to buy a prawn sandwich.

Grant leans forward. 'I needed therapy for a year. Quite a lot of hypnosis. It was interfering with my work. Every time I went into a house I just imagined… Well I had these pictures in my head that I was going to find two dead bodies all over again, realise my feet were in a pool of blood. Sorry, sorry, I've said too much.' He waves his pale hands.

'Not sure even after hypnosis I could carry on walking into empty houses like you do. You've been brave.'

He takes a moment, closing his eyes tightly as if trying to drive the image from his mind. I wonder what techniques his therapists taught him because I feel he's using them now. Dust is in a slow dance in a strong beam of sunlight. The sound is him glugging more water over his dry throat and the white-noise whirr of the air conditioner.

'Are you really all right, Grant? And I mean seriously… I think I'd move away—'

'A fresh start? No. I couldn't. I love my job. Everything I need is right here.' Grant shakes his head. 'Crossways is a lovely place. You get the odd bit of random unpleasantness anywhere.'

'I think we both know you cannot describe the Crossways Killings as random unpleasantness. Crossways looks so lovely, but sometimes it just reminds me that when people yearn for nostalgia, they never mean the reality. Things people crave about the past is often just our memories filtering out the bad stuff. People often yearn for things to be cosy and simple. But you keep going back in time and of course they never were. The reality is the old days were brutal, raw, full of short lives, illness, superstition and self-appointed justice.'

Grant manages one of his wry chuckles and I'm pleased to see he's breathing normally.

'Crossways probably had bloodthirsty rituals and a callous attitude to anyone different or who didn't fit in,' I say. 'Nothing is ever as idyllic as it seems.'

'Verity Anderson said she wouldn't be surprised if Crossways reveals itself to be some cult and everyone is secretly witches or werewolves where you get initiated if you last the first six months. Then you never leave,' says Grant. 'Is Mitch really trying to reopen the case?'

'Part of his publicity plan is to stir things up in the hope it'll bring a new lead. My worry is it'll just churn up a lot of buried horror and still end with the same, failed, result. I'd love the buried horror to get some closure.'

Grant shakes his head like he's given up on that ever happening. 'We have to accept it was just one of those awful random crimes.' He folds his hands in front of him. 'Are you taking an interest, Keera, after all that business before… You're gathering a little reputation.'

'True this is not the first suspicious death I've encountered in Crossways. You'd think I wouldn't be so shocked learning about a double murder in the past. I'd hate to be thought of as one of those sofa Sherlocks, joining forums, trying to solve cases I've no connection with. This is here, it's happening. We've far more chance of getting a decent outcome if everyone collectively pools what they know. I've made you relive a buried horror. So can we make the most of it and please tell me everything you remember. Was it true about the bloody handprint on the window?'

Grant takes another glug of water. 'It's true. I guess I did know something was wrong. I went along to check everything was ready so they'd have a great start. I simply thought how I must clean it off. A horrible first impression.'

'Any other incidents of Crossways not being very welcoming to incomers?'

'Verity might make jokes about a secret cult, but this is a lovely place. People come to Crossways and never leave,' says Grant. 'And not because of a blood ritual. But you mean Eliza. She's been very unfortunate. I'm sure it's not Crossways taking against incomers that led to those deaths.'

'How can you be sure when we don't know the answer? No one bought that theory they were followed from the airport. What are the other ideas? In a place where everyone knows everyone else's business it strikes me as strange and I'm getting the feeling the Crossways Killings weren't solved because no one talks about it. Everyone knows Margot and David are away this weekend. Everyone would have known the Winters' house would be empty. So what can you tell me about the other burglaries?'

Grant clears his throat. 'Petty thefts. Quite different. I wish we could stop Mitch. I've resigned myself that we will never know.'

'Isn't it worth a little risk to get some closure? I know it's painful. But then everyone keeps saying how no one knew them and gossip about everything else. Does no one want the truth? It's almost as if everyone is afraid of the answer. Or covering.'

'It was painful, Keera. Now, start a serious talk with your parents about those financials. I have an appointment with a downsize after a wife playing away from home.'

'You see, you know everything that goes on, Grant.'

'People aren't always smart about not getting caught,' says Grant. 'And I end up trying to help people with the consequences.'

'Exactly. Please think.'

'Please leave it alone. I don't think anyone believes we'll ever get answers, so why go through the pain of bringing it all up again?'

'Unfortunately, if there's one thing I can't do is leave things alone. I'm terrible at it. Actually, add to that I'm not exactly great at being told what to do. Is whoever was behind the Crossways Killings still here, in Crossways, having got away with it for nearly four years?' I turn to Grant as I go. 'How is that possible?

But Grant's already taking a call.

18

Verity

Sharp-haired and sharp-faced Belinda Messenger and poet Isha Cheema were sitting with Margot Latimer around a table in Halfway, the bistro-cafe at the other end of the high street to Benj's Crossways Cafe.

One chair was empty, like a bad interview pretending to be a friendly chat. At least there was relief it wasn't actually the whole of bookgroup there to greet her.

They were all in Lycra (topped off with the ever-present beanie hat in Isha's case). Lycra was positively an epidemic, even worse than the comfy cardis. Posh Margot was looking glamorous and actually pretty cool in a matching black and pink Lycra ensemble that was very similar to Belinda's.

In front of them they all had identical green Rise-and-Align frothy smoothies that Halfway specialised in, the ones with spinach and very probably kale.

If Belinda ordered a green energy drink, the others doubtless felt obliged to do the same. It's what you called leadership quality.

In front of the empty chair was an unhealthy caramel shortbread and frothy cappuccino complete with sprinkles.

Verity's favourites. (How did they know?). Verity felt very exposed and slid into the chair with as much relish as if she was about to be tied to it by the ankles.

Isha looked enviously at Verity's coffee and cake.

'So has someone got it in for Eliza and doesn't want her here?' Belinda asked directly. 'Trying to drive her out?'

Verity could admire the head-teachery way she got down to business.

Being summoned here by head witch (according to Grant) was pretty disturbing. There was something about those bubbling green drinks, the Lycra and YogaGals that brought up that cult idea again. Vampires? Were those Rise-and-Align drinks a magical blood-substitution that also solved the problem of going out in daylight? Or a mortality elixir?

Isha took a sip with a very envious glare at Verity's caffeine and sugar. With Belinda in charge they all probably had a resting heart rate in the low fifties and were destined to live forever anyway.

Verity took a bite of her cake with a great deal of relish.

'The terrible mess was mashed into the pavement and only outside Eliza's shop,' said Isha, addressing Verity's chocolate covered shortbread.

'A targeted attack,' said Belinda. 'I presume you made sure you took photographic evidence?'

Belinda looked disappointed in her when Verity said she hadn't thought to take photographs.

'We don't want Eliza to leave,' wailed Margot. 'What can we do? How can we help?'

Verity busied herself sipping her coffee, playing for time, reminding herself that she had to play a clever game here. Between Verity, bookgroup and Mitch, there was a chance they would have the Crossways Killings solved, the perp tied up and the dirt on Benj Beresford to prove what he was up to by the end of the summer.

Verity needed a new piece of evidence, something to flag up, someone behaving out of character, or caught out in a lie. Any sliver that could be a potential lead to present to Mitch to get her on that inside track. Someone to throw under the bus, basically, or at least at Mitch Ravenscroft.

Her mission (should she choose to accept it), and looking at the intent faces of Belinda, Isha and Margot, she had a feeling refusal was not an option, was to get Bookgroup Investigates letting slip insider intel about the Crossways Killings, while taking responsibility for looking after Eliza.

It was a clever strategy, but tricky. Easy if it was just Margot and beanie-wearing poet Isha. Headteacher Belinda was a whole different ball game. Nothing much would get past her.

'What no Grandma here to help?' Verity joked.

'Ashley's sadly been neglecting her health,' said Belinda, not even trying to hide the judgmental tone.

'Hasn't been to YogaGals for ages,' said Margot sadly.

But Grandma was very much going to YogaGals. There were many messages on the mini-chalkboard on the fridge about YogaGals. This was disappointing. Bookgroup Investigates falling at the first hurdle of being well-informed.

Forget Grandma. Grandma was a distraction. Forget the vampires too.

'You're looking to me for answers,' Verity said carefully. 'But Crossways is like landing in alien territory to me. Whereas you three know everyone, all the gossip. Who's said anything nasty about Eliza?'

Belinda nodded. 'I understand what you're saying. Arriving here would be like trying to understand someone else's family dynamic. And gossip is very often bitchiness disguised as concern. You don't know what's behind the arguments about small things that suddenly explode.'

Somehow, Belinda had managed to make Crossways sound even more sinister.

'You're saying we need to help you understand what provokes people to lash out with a claw,' said Isha, poetically and with more than a smidge of relish. 'Reach the soft, vulnerable underbelly of Crossways and protect Eliza.'

'Put it however you like. You have all the intel. It's understanding the gossip as much as hearing it. People obsess about things that don't feel important. Like how an expensive holiday was paid for,' said Verity.

Verity had guessed right that this would land well.

Everyone turned to Isha, who immediately coloured up under her beanie hat. She turned from shooting avaricious glances towards a small but tempting display of cakes to looking at the table and biting her lip. 'Are people really speculating about how I paid for my holiday? That is no one's business. Why do people think I can't have saved up like everyone else?'

'Bless,' said Margot, taking another valiant sip of her drink with a sour wince that told Verity she'd rather be having a latte. 'How can you have saved up when you always moan how expensive it was to fix the roof and get that expert in for the rewiring? If you just came out and told people about how you suddenly got money…'

But Isha Cheema said nothing, leading Verity to wonder what she might have done so she could spend the winter somewhere warm and get a break from DIY in a dilapidated house?

Burglary? Blackmail? Steal some valuable jewellery after shooting a recently retired couple dead?

Definitely a sliver she could pass to Mitch. She still needed to confirm if Isha was even here at the time.

'Isha, you write the local history books. You were brought up here. I heard you went abroad to teach and came back when your father got sick. But he died soon after you returned—'

Isha spluttered. 'Are people saying I'm somehow to blame that my father died soon after I came back?'

'Of course not,' said Belinda soothingly.

'I meant you were a teacher,' said Verity. She needed people to talk, not create seething resentment and a wall of silence. 'And that's Eliza's background too isn't it? It's a connection, so I'm hoping you chatted to her about it and she might have told you something about what brought her to Crossways? When did you come back?'

'I've never talked to Eliza about it,' said Isha, annoyingly not answering the direct question. 'How about you, Belinda?'

'Technically, she's a head,' said Margot.

'I understand the existential dread of the job,' said Belinda, smoothing her hair. 'And why Eliza might want a fresh start. The kids are fine. It's the parents with too-high expectation, wanting transformational magic performed on their kids. The level of vindictiveness directed towards teachers... I've had teachers accused of ruining lives. Some parents you wouldn't want to bump into outside school.'

'That's pretty dark,' Verity said. 'You think an ex-parent might have it in for Eliza?'

'Things blow up because parents do not behave rationally where their children are concerned. Even over small things, like classroom seating,' went on Belinda.

'You get complaints about seating?' asked Margot.

'Emails, phone calls and urgent requests for meetings.'

'You've got first-hand experience dealing with a bunch of humans driven to the edge,' said Isha. 'But you think a disgruntled parent might have tipped over Eliza's bins? She didn't even teach around here, did she?'

'One of the unique aspects of Crossways, is that it is full of people passing through,' Belinda went on. 'I've bumped into the most random people here on my days off.'

'No wonder you're addicted to those true crime podcasts,' said Isha.

'I'm not addicted to true crime,' protested Belinda.

Finally, an interesting secret about Belinda. With secrets so far being Isha's winter holiday and David Purkiss's shed, the teaching angle counted as a sliver. All that about vindictive parents was interesting, but a workable theory? Not without a mass of police resources. But interesting how many teachers, or ex-teachers, like Eliza, have rocked up to Crossways. Almost as popular as being a scientist.

'You do too love those podcasts. Do you believe anyone can turn nasty, be a killer?' asked Isha.

'A vindictive parent driven to distraction?' said Margot, pushing aside her half-finished drink. 'That's your theory? Would you like a sandwich, Verity dear?'

'No thank you. Has there ever been a podcast about the Crossways Killings?' Verity wanted to know.

'Never enough material,' said Margot, shaking her head sadly. 'I think everyone has accepted it will never be solved. Those random crimes are difficult.'

'Hardly any CCTV around here doesn't help, not with so many people passing through,' said Belinda.

'Don't people in Crossways think it had to be a crime closer to home?' asked Verity.

'But who on earth would shoot dead a couple on their first night arriving in Crossways?' asked Isha. 'The answer obviously lies outside of our village.'

'Although,' said Verity. 'Their stuff was just brought out of storage. They were loaded. The house was supposed to be empty. Does it feel like someone knew all that?'

'Makes more sense that someone at the airport spotted they had valuable jewellery and followed them,' said Margot.

'Weren't there other unsolved burglaries?' Verity said.

'Very minor,' said Belinda. 'The sort the police don't bother to investigate.'

'Crossways doesn't really have troubles,' said Margot. 'Apart from people wanting to sell up their gardens. If we're talking crimes in Crossways, look no further than people wanting to make ready cash from their gardens with no care to how it changes the aesthetic of the place. I have heard,' she dropped her voice, 'that Jaxx and Maya who own this place, have very ambitious expansion plans.'

Please not the gardens hijacking the conversation again.

'Jaxx and Maya weren't involved in the Crossways Killings, they weren't around,' said Isha.

'How do you know?' said Verity. 'Were you here then?'

'Actually Jaxx and Maya were,' said Belinda. 'That's when their renovations started to modernise Halfway.'

'You have such a good memory,' Margot said admiringly.

'And what about Benj? Was he here when the Crossways Killings happened?' asked Verity.

'Benj Beresford? Yes.' said Isha decisively. 'I remember because he moved here same time as Ashley and Ashley joined in with everything and we just knew she'd fit right in. But Benj didn't.'

At least that confirmed Isha was here. But her memory wasn't that reliable, because Verity had once risked bringing up the Crossways Killings with Grandma, who had shut down that conversation saying it happened before she'd moved here.

'When the horrible thing happened I hoped it wouldn't put Ashley off,' said Margot, 'because we were so pleased she'd moved here. Unlike Benj, you're right, he's never joined in with anything, not interested in the parish council.'

'Not a committee or even a fundraiser,' agreed Isha.

This was disturbing, because it looked like Grandma had been caught out in a lie. Sadly, this was exactly the kind of suspicious behaviour Verity was looking for to present to Mitch. Lying about not even being here would definitely be marked as behaving suspiciously. If it wasn't Grandma.

Annoying. And there was that little misunderstanding about Grandma no longer going to YogaGals. Another mistake, because Grandma was definitely still going. Although the three witches didn't seem to think so.

Rather unfortunate that the most interesting sliver had once again been about Grandma. A bit like the best reveal at bookgroup being Grandmas expert chemistry knowledge and an interest in disposing of dead bodies, and shutting down any chat about the Crossways Killings.

Verity needed to try harder.

It wasn't supposed to be Grandma who needed to sing like a canary, or be thrown under the Mitch Ravenscroft bus.

Time to move forward, test these waters, see how useful (or not) Bookgroup Investigates were going to be.

'What I want to know,' said Verity, 'is if we are committed to getting this case with Eliza solved…' Three heads inched forward. 'How far are you three prepared to go?'

19

Verity

'You want us to interrogate someone?' Rather than reluctant, Margot sounded all too ready if she might be required to tie someone to a chair in a place no one would hear you scream.

'We can sit here all day and come up with theories,' said Verity. 'What we need is evidence. What would you say if I said I need you involved in a covert surveillance operation?'

If Verity had planned to drop it in for a big gasp-effect, it could not have landed better. Margot's mouth opened. Belinda's eyes positively lit up, making Verity think there was truth in the rumour she was a true-crime enthusiast.

'If you mean like a round-the-clock surveillance,' said Isha, drawing in air noisily through her teeth. 'My allotment is very busy. It's murder with all this dry weather.'

'Is this how we catch Benj?' Margot asks.

Verity felt a bit played that they'd only just mentioned they all thought it was Benj.

'I think the idea is we gather evidence and keep an open mind,' said Verity.

Once again, there was a serious lack of theories being put forward. If Verity was right and Eliza's injuries were caused by a carefully placed tripwire, then Benj was guilty of more than just a vendetta so he could take over Eliza's garden. Would Benj actually try to kill Eliza? But then who would? And who would kill a lovely, wealthy, retired couple when they just moved to Crossways? So here was a new idea. Was it possible Benj was involved in both crimes? What might that scenario look like? Was there anything that linked things together?

'Oh yes, wouldn't it be dull if it turned out to be the most-obvious person,' sighed Isha.

'Having only one genuine suspect is the opposite to intriguing or even fun,' agreed Belinda.

Belatedly, Verity was aware of someone paying far too much attention to their conversation.

Taylor Messenger, Belinda's grungy goth daughter was wiping the crumbs from the next table in a surly manner into a customer's lap. At work, Taylor wore a demure black skirt and white blouse rather than the lace and shorts combo she usually favoured. She'd removed her piercings too and blended in. It was the tattoo of a bad fairy on her wrist that gave her away. Verity was annoyed it took so long to clock her and wondered how long she had been there.

But why listen in? What possible interest could Taylor have in their covert surveillance on Eliza? Could Verity treat Taylor's interest as a sliver? She'd quite like to get something on Taylor.

Belinda and Taylor did no more than acknowledge each other with a nod. Verity stared pointedly at Taylor until she tossed her head and left.

'How do we catch Benj in the act? I may have a way to gather the evidence we need,' said Verity.

She needed to be smart and a step ahead, like Poirot, the bit where he dropped in cryptic clues and sent not-too-smart Hastings off gathering intel he didn't understand. She needed to regain the upper hand.

'But I have one big restriction if we are going to do this.'

They all leaned in closer.

'Even this conversation is in direct contravention of the rules by which I get a roof over my head this summer.'

'You mean keep it a secret from Ashley?' said Belinda. 'I don't understand. She brought you in to help Eliza.'

'You think Grandma's got me on some undercover mission. But the truth is the opposite. I am steering clear of intrigue on pain of death—well not death, but similar. If you want my help in this, we must keep it a secret from Grandma. Understood? Grandma might even disapprove of my helping Bookgroup Investigates set up a hidden camera.'

'Bookgroup Investigates? Is that us?' said Margot, sounding thrilled. 'Are we setting up a hidden camera?'

'Evidence first. Let's see what we're dealing with before telling anyone, even Eliza,' said Verity.

'Ah yes, intel,' said Belinda. 'See what we're dealing with. Don't tell Ashley. Understood.'

'We won't blab to Eliza,' promised Margot. 'Or Ashley.'

'Well that'll be pretty easy,' said Isha.

'Where does she go these days? First not YogaGals, now not even golf!' said Margot with a hint of a wail.

'She resigned from our golf committee when she gave up her lessons,' explained Isha with an annoyed puff. 'We hardly see her.'

'Makes us suspect she's holding out on us. Making a bid to leave.' Belinda's eyes drilled right into Verity's. 'Is she?'

'I didn't think anyone could escape the cult,' said Verity with a poor attempt at a chuckle.

The very last thing Verity needed was to learn another uncomfortable truth that indicated the person she lived with might be keeping secrets, lying even.

Golf lessons had definitely been mentioned on the mini-chalkboard and Grandma's golf club hoodie was on the hatstand in the hall as if she used it all the time.

Why did Grandma have to display suspicious behaviour just when Verity was on the look out for it? Far worse than lying to the three witches about where she was and what she was really up to, why had Grandma needed to lie to Verity?

She needed something to offer as a trade to Mitch. She had to find someone, now anyone apart from Grandma, who'd been caught out lying. Not to Verity's face, because Verity hardly saw her either. Verity was beginning to feel lucky she at least had Benj Beresford to investigate.

'What's Ashley up to?' said Isha darkly.

'Maybe we should do a little surveillance number on Ashley,' joked Margot.

'She's keeping a lot of secrets from us,' said Belinda. 'Won't tell us what she's up to. We felt sure you'd know.'

Verity could not believe she'd let herself be ambushed twice in one day. And by Bookgroup Investigates. She thought she was the one with the covert plan and the upper hand. She felt both played and wrong-footed at the same time, because Bookgroup Investigates thought Grandma had a secret life and finding out what Ashley was up to was at least part of why they invited her here.

Verity forced out an excuse. 'She's busy mothering me. I take a lot of looking after.'

This was the opposite of true. Grandma was barely home. None of the expected home-cooked meals, box-sets and wine had arrived. It was all messages on the mini chalkboard on the fridge. Even tonight Verity would have no chance to quiz her.

Visiting dignitary I'm expected to wine and dine. Staying overnight at room in uni. Have been shopping. The pop and ping lasagne tastes better than it sounds x

Grandma wasn't even coming home. Was she even at the university? Was it just lies? Certainly Verity thought she was probably lying about the lasagne being tasty.

When had Grandma become such an expert liar? Why had Verity, who prided herself on noticing things, suspected nothing?

And Grandma had forbidden Verity from investigating anything. Was that because Grandma had her own secrets?

Getting some surveillance on Eliza's Deli was urgent. The tripwire pointed to someone meaning her serious harm.

Verity had already suggested setting up a camera and collecting evidence. As long as no more evidence pointed at Grandma.

New priority: find someone who was keeping more secrets and behaving more suspiciously than Grandma.

And find out what Grandma was really up to.

20

Keera

'I don't know what they serve up in those police canteens. You don't have to be standing there dangling a pair of handcuffs to look like you want to make an arrest. You're spooking my customers,' I say to Mitch, who has been hovering, pretending to be considering buying the latest Janice Hallet for at least half an hour.

'People won't think that,' says Mitch. 'I'm retired.'

'Don't put it back,' I say as Mitch tries to replace The Killer Question. 'You should buy that, it's as brilliant as all her others.'

'I suppose I should buy something.'

'You won't find me arguing with that.'

'I've been waiting for ages for you to not have any customers so we can talk about promoting my book. I thought someone said the bookshop's not that busy.'

'Don't be fooled by everyone coming in actually buying something,' I say. 'You know one thing I sometimes miss about office life is how people made appointments. Very few people just turned up to chat.' I look daggers at Mitch as he puts the book back on the shelf.

But right now, I do want them to come in and chat. I've been waiting for them to share their gossip, but one look at Mitch and they've been scuttling out quickly.

'Tea?' says Mitch, as the shop is now empty. 'Have you a kettle hidden around here somewhere?'

'Shouldn't that be my line?' I do want to get rid of Mitch, but maybe I'll talk to him first. 'Fine.'

Mitch points. 'This cubbyhole?'

'You mean my kitchen and back office and repository for books I ordered but can't sell. Returns are complicated and take a lot of paperwork and I hate paperwork. Be warned the fridge is on its way out, so please check any milk products. You may have to wash up some mugs,' I call over the sound of my very ancient kettle making so much effort it sounds as if it's expecting a round of applause.

Verity's talking to shy David Purkiss just outside and I can't hear what they've found to talk about. It's a surprise when David opens the door. Not a huge book-buyer.

'Are you two both wanting a book?' I say cheerily.

'I am,' says David, beating my adopted bookshop cat, Jackson Brodie, through the door by a whisker. 'But I don't think the cat's learned to read yet.'

'He spends enough time in here he should learn,' says Verity, hesitating by the door. 'I should go back to work.' But she steps in and starts breathing in deeply. 'But I love that new book smell. I can't resist.'

'Something to do with the chemicals used in the paper making process?' says Mitch, arriving with tea.

'The inks for printing the jacket, and there's the glue to bind the pages too,' says Verity. 'One of the strongest smells is vinyl acetate ethylene if you are interested.'

'I am interested and I did not know that,' I say.

'Well, the manufacture requires many chemicals at several stages, so books are just little clusters of hundreds of ongoing chemical reactions really,' says Verity. 'Book and paper production changes, so you can tell the age of books by the chemicals. The smell of old books is the pages slowly decomposing from exposure to light and oxygen.'

'That sounds rather sad,' says David.

'You sound like you know more about chemistry than David,' Mitch chuckles.

'You do like to go into details about things,' I say

'I really do.'

'I have turned my back on chemistry,' says David.

'You went and looked it all up,' I say to Verity.

'What I find difficult to understand is why everyone doesn't go and find out more about subjects that interest them.'

'If Eliza stops needing you, you could come and help out here,' I tell her. 'A good researcher and a good memory comes in handy if you're a bookseller. Actually, sometimes I feel the most useful bookseller skill would be second sight. I had an enquiry this morning about a book I was supposed to recognise from the clues that a customer read it as a child and it featured caves and unusual pets. I said it was probably out of print. She was disbelieving that books don't stay in print forever.'

'And left without buying anything?' Mitch asks.

'You are quickly understanding my business.'

'I think yours might be the ugliest cat I've ever seen,' says Mitch, bending to stroke Jackson under his chin as I shake cat food into a bowl. 'What happened to his tail? And his ear?'

I peer more closely. 'I think he's lost a bit more of his ear. I think he must have been in another fight.'

'A fight or just more digging? Such an exciting life,' Verity says, stroking him. 'What tales you could tell.'

I sweep up all the mud crumbs Jackson's deposited on the floor.

'I never knew a cat that loved digging, but perhaps he can't climb with a broken tail,' says Verity, showing Mitch. 'See how Jackson's tail no longer goes straight up, but bends halfway like a crooked finger? Eliza thinks someone took a shot at him and he's got some sort of pellet lodged there. She asks everyone if they know anything. It doesn't seem to bother him, but she's thinking of starting a fundraiser to get it looked at. Who Shot Jackson Brodie? Another Crossways case that will never be solved?'

'Maybe you should add that to your retirement caseload,' I suggest to Mitch.

'Talking about things to investigate, any update on the Crossways Killings?' says Verity, way too eagerly. 'Any new leads? Because I really need to get back to Eliza.'

Mitch murmurs that he cannot possibly comment.

I have my suspicions that Liv is right (as usual) and Mitch's main concern is publicity. I also think Liv's right and Verity's far too nosy and always ready with an intrusive question. I don't agree when Liv says Verity's my twin.

'How hopeful are you of a new lead after all this time? What about those burglaries?' Verity probes. 'And did the police look for a motive for killing them from someone outside of Crossways?'

'Yes Mitch,' I say. 'All what Verity just said.'

'Someone's memory might be jogged after reading my book,' says Mitch. 'Something small they didn't share because they didn't think it was important at the time. People do speak up about cases even if they've kept quiet for years.'

'A sliver,' nods Verity. 'Can often crack a case wide open.'

'And I was just here for any books on writing tips,' chuckles David.

'Ah well, there I can help. I'll be recommending some, if we can fix a date for my course,' says Mitch, glancing at me. 'Have you heard of Save the Cat?'

David shows impressive knowledge about story beats. Definitely more chatty when he's not with Margot. Is he really secretly writing a crime novel?

'I'll make sure any classes aren't on a weekend,' Mitch says with a sly look. 'You should come along.'

David gives a shy laugh. 'Am I surprised everyone in Crossways has noticed we've taken a lot of breaks lately?'

'The gossip is that you're house-hunting and want to escape Crossways,' says Verity. 'Away again this weekend?'

David pushes his glasses up his nose. 'Yes, but not house-hunting. Please do your workshop any time, Mitch. It'll give me an excuse to miss another stately home that will look like every other stately home. Don't tell Margot I said that.'

'You prefer the gardens?' I say.

'I can't bear gardens either. Margot loves all of it. Makes me feel an idiot for having no appreciation. Margot also has a terrible habit of choosing the absolutely worst places to stay. I don't know if she leaves booking until the last minute, but she has a proper knack for finding horrors.'

'I'm about to do something unprofessional,' I say. 'Can I leave you discussing writing and in charge of my shop?'

'Not me,' says Verity. 'I've hardly helped Eliza today. I can't even remember what I came in here for.'

'You came in, rather charmingly, to smell the books,' says Mitch. 'Off somewhere very suddenly, Keera?'

'I just thought of something that should have clicked earlier. Like you say, get people talking about the Crossways Killings and suddenly you think of something. It was when David mentioned awful places to stay.'

When I was talking to Grant, before he turned purple and started fighting for breath, I missed it. The significance of what he said has only just struck me. I'm getting slow.

21

Keera

It's not easy to wander into someone's cafe while they're drinking a milky coffee and tucking into toasted cheese after a bike ride and ask them if they murdered two people. Even for me. And I know I have a little reputation for blundering in and asking awkward questions.

Is that what I'm going to ask Benj Beresford? Is that what I really think? I have to keep reminding myself someone pulled that trigger. Someone must know more than they are telling. Is Benj Beresford the person we need to start singing like a canary?

My flash of inspiration came about the time a flash of purple told me Benj had just returned from a cycle ride. So good timing. My shop will be fine for a few minutes.

I catch him in the cafe – not serving customers, he's sitting eating a panini and ignoring that his staff could do with a little help.

Luckily he's squashed in a corner and there's an empty chair opposite, so I slide in knowing he'll have difficulty sliding out. Just in case he doesn't like what I'm going to ask. I begin with a polite opener.

'Hi there Benj, business is good. Can you send a few customers my way?'

He chews a mouthful of panini slowly. Benj looks smaller without his bike helmet on, although he also looks more startled as he has huge tufty grey eyebrows.

'What do you want, Keera?' he says.

'You say that as if I have never dropped in for a chat before and have a reputation for sticking my nose in and not always being polite about it. True, but I'm still genuinely impressed you've hit pay-dirt. I'd love a few tips on how you've achieved what I've completely failed to do.'

'All right, I'll bite,' says Benj, wiping a dribble of grease with a napkin. 'What have I done that's so impressed you?'

'I imagined running my own bookshop would mean discussing books, ringing endless sales through the till, maybe running a popular bookclub. Going home, reading and congratulating myself on having a marvellously fun, rewarding life with low stress and enough income.'

'Please get to the point.' He wipes his greasy fingers on another napkin. 'Please tell me there is a point.'

'This place is rammed. You must be coining it. You can afford staff to do all the actual work while you drift around going on cycle rides. And you don't even do what people expect successful Crossways folk should do, like joining the parish council or the village hall committee fundraising for a new roof. You run a profitable business and live in a small village and remain gloriously aloof. How?'

'That's your question?' His grey busy eyebrows make it difficult to tell if he's genuinely taken by surprise as he looks constantly startled.

'Only partly. What did you do before? What brought you to Crossways?'

'I cannot believe any of that's any interest to you.'

'You'd be surprised. All right, you're not in a chatty mood, so let me guess. Early retirement? Generous lump sum? You've probably always fancied running your own business, be your own boss, go out cycling whenever you like. I know with these long, light evenings you go out twice a day sometimes. You thought a cafe would be a good way to achieve all that. And you've not been wrong.'

'I'm still waiting for the point.'

'The point is you're a bit under the radar. But I want to change all that, get you involved. I want to get everyone talking about a double murder that remains unsolved, because collectively, we might find an answer. And I've just worked out you were here. From something Grant said. And you spoke to them. When hardly anyone else did.'

He really does have the most incredible eyebrows. They come into their own when his eyes widen in sham innocence. I know it's sham, because I've worked out he has a connection to the Winters.

Which is why I've come around here in an impulse move that I realise I could have thought through better.

But is Benj the guy, the one under the radar, the one we need to start singing like a canary for the Crossways Killings to be solved? Can I get him to sing?

'There's a new chance to get justice for that couple,' I say. 'And we all want that, right? I mean it's only an impossible crime because no one's talking isn't it. So you're bound to want to stop being under the radar and to help. You'd like to help to bring justice and closure, right?'

Benj has finished his greasy panini and I'm glad I took the chair that pinned him in the corner as he's fidgeting and looking to end this conversation. But I'm not moving.

'Waste of time,' he says. 'The media circus called it an impossible crime because two random outsiders were followed from the airport because they were silly enough to take valuable jewellery with them. I've nothing to offer.'

'But you have! Think back. Sometimes thinking back you remember things differently.'

'I'm sure that's a bad thing, when you're talking of evidence.'

'Evidence isn't as fixed as you might think. You hold a piece of the puzzle, Benj. What I want to know is how big a piece. So start talking.'

'Why do you think I'm holding any piece?'

'It was called an impossible crime because no one here knew them. Hardly anyone even spoke to them. But you did.'

'You've made a mistake. Apparently you're famous for them.'

'At least tell me what you told the police at the time.'

'What makes you think I talked to the police?'

'Because the Winters stayed with you. Not the time they arrived back from their holiday and went straight to their house and got killed. Everyone says how they were killed their first night in Crossways, but that's not strictly true, inflamed by the media to make a bigger story. They first stumbled on Crossways by accident, liked the place, went to talk to Grant the next morning. So they must have found a place to stay the night. I almost missed it. The night they were killed was the *second* time they were in Crossways. Halfway was undergoing renovations. So the first time, they must've stayed with you.'

I think Benj is going to deny it.

I almost missed this when I was talking to Grant.

'I barely spoke to them,' says Benj eventually.

I leap in and seize the moment. 'Barely is a lot more than anyone else in Crossways. Did you know them from before? Is that why they came here?'

'You really do get things completely muddled.'

'Well you must have done a good sales pitch because they loved Crossways so much they wanted to move here. So, what did you talk about?'

'Just because I was offering rooms when I first opened doesn't mean I talked to my guests very much.'

'But I don't believe you didn't speak at all. And you do want justice for that poor couple? Did you know them?'

'It was years ago, you cannot expect me to remember.'

'I cannot expect you'd forget. They died a few weeks later. And they'd stayed with you.'

I tell myself not to get stressed. Don't be rude. Don't say out loud what I'm thinking right now, which is that I'm going to get an answer out of Benj even if I have to drag it out of him in unpleasant ways.

I'm here hoping he holds crucial evidence. But I'm also asking myself: do I think he killed them?

'You're right that Halfway was undergoing a major refurbishment when I moved here,' Benj says, finally. 'When they reopened they swiped the lion's share of the evening meal and rooms market. But I fought back. I worked out turning the rooms to cafe tables would bring an easier profit anyway. As you so kindly point out, I am very good at running a cafe. I live in a tiny room in the attic and don't have to talk to anyone. It suits me.'

'Benj it's great that you're all chatty about your business model. I get Halfway didn't so much as swipe customers from you as you were terrible at it anyway—'

'I wasn't terrible. I expanded the cafe to upstairs.'

'But what do you remember about the Winters?'

'You may be right that hospitality is hardly my thing. You know what those bed and breakfast guests are like—small talk and giving the same advice on the best places to visit. I used to switch off, all right. I don't remember any of what anyone said.'

'I do mostly see you in a blur of purple, but you don't only cycle alone. You head towards Harcourt on a Saturday evening where that cycle group meets. So I don't believe you never speak to anyone. You are one of only a couple of people who might actually have answers. So think.'

Even this is a long shot. What could have come up in that banal bed and breakfast conversation that would give me answers? Or even more unlikely, meant Benj had to kill them? Unless they knew Benj from before? Then I remember how awful he's been to Eliza and that Benj has a very nasty streak.

'Is that it?' Benj says.

'Not quite. What is going on with you and Eliza?'

'You mean the bins going over and making a mess outside Eliza's shop? But you can't blame me.'

'They were your bins. And you want Eliza's shop cos it's got that great garden out back.'

Benj gives me a stare that makes me feel glad to be surrounded by a lot of customers enjoying a cream tea.

'You are so confused. Are you here to accuse me of keeping back vital information from the police? Making some sort of deliberate attacks on Eliza. Or maybe you suspect me of killing my B&B guests? Are we done?'

'I don't know Benj. Maybe I'm giving you a friendly warning that we all want Eliza to stay and are looking out for her, and the police are looking into the case again. And we are all working together to get justice for that couple. Have a think. Anything the Winters said. Any reason why they landed in Crossways would be a start.'

'Didn't Grant say they felt it was fate? And it would be such a tragedy if Eliza felt Crossways wasn't for her,' he says nastily. 'But again, nothing to do with me.'

'I'm trying to persuade you to help, get involved for once. I believe in justice. And people trying really hard to think before I come back with more questions. Which I will do.'

'Oh don't you long to be our avenging angel responsible for clearing up everything bad happening in Crossways,' Benj says in his slow drawl and with a malicious smile. 'You've accused me of all sorts of things, but you're barking up the wrong tree and wasting your time. Leave me alone.'

'Which tree should I be barking up?'

'Have you had a conversation like this with Grant?'

I try not to show any reaction. Grant was the only suspect at the time. Is that all he means?

'I am talking to everyone. If you hint there's something I should know, it means you could tell me a whole lot more,' I say slowly.

'I won't deny that hearing Eliza's had some bad luck wouldn't please me a little. She stole that property that was rightfully mine. But here's the thing—I don't need to mess about with bins to get her out. Think carefully before you all want Eliza to stay. If anyone's keeping secrets, it's not me.'

I have to admit, this floors me. 'It sounds like you've something you're dying to share. Get it off your chest.'

'Why? Because Crossways becomes dangerous if you know too many secrets?' says Benj.

'No, I meant, because if you can help, why not?'

'Of course, dear Keera, you know all I only ever want to do is help.' Benj gives a horrible smile. 'So I'll say this. If you want to talk to someone who's lying and keeping secrets, I'd say the person you should be asking is the one who's gone to the bother of getting a business started when they'll be gone within a year. Is that help enough for you?'

He's talking about Eliza. I can't work out if he means he will drive her out within a year. Or something else. Is he throwing shade at Eliza to divert me from talking to him? Or does he really know something? I have no clue.

I guess I need to find out.

'Have all the fun you like running around trying to solve that Winter case,' Benj says. 'But don't waste your time looking at me to solve anything.'

'But I am looking at you. Think harder. Anything you gossiped about—any seemingly small or random thing. Because I don't really back down. And I will be back.'

'Oh good! You're right of course. Bad things do happen in Crossways. And the last thing we want is for you to have all that nasty broken glass to deal with when a rock goes through the window of your utterly delightful bookshop.'

22

Keera

Liv has two customers and is selling one of my favourite uplifting reads, The Hometown Bookshop by Jenna Warren, and greets me with a quizzical raise of an eyebrow as the customer leaves, clutching the book.

'You're here and my chalkboard outside is advertising a crime fiction writing workshop,' I say.

'It's not that difficult to arrange author events if you're properly committed.'

'You arranged that while I popped next door? Tea? Although I think I need a long shower after talking to Benj. And one of your Ox Gins.'

'Things go well with interrogating Benj? Yes, I have organised a workshop and sold books, even to this lovely lady who came in asking about the best place for a sandwich.'

The woman smiles as Liv rings her sale through the till, a bestseller from a while ago that made it onto telly. One of the few books I sell regularly about chemistry. Lessons in Chemistry by Bonnie Garmus.

'Are we charging?' I say when I bring through tea.

'For the workshop, or for interrogations?' says Liv. 'Yes

we are charging for the workshop. Mitch and David were here and I seized the moment. It's all done and sorted.'

'You had more luck than me. The only thing I got out of Benj Beresford is that I think he just threatened me.'

'Are you counting that as progress? Did you accuse him of killing two people?'

'Not really. I was polite and friendly. Ish.'

'Do you think he killed two people? What did you say that upset Benj so much he threatened you?'

'I told him I'd be back.'

'Very polite and friendly. Not at all Terminator-like.'

There's more on the chalkboard behind the till and my jaw drops at the unbelievable detail.

'Mitch is starting the crime fiction writing workshop *tomorrow* evening? How on earth are we going to have enough time to get enough people by *tomorrow* evening?'

Liv's sceptical raised eyebrow returns. 'Have you not learned that in Crossways news spreads? It's how I knew you were next door confronting Benj. Everybody knew.'

'Confronting!' I say. 'You know how good I am at getting people to open up with a friendly chat.'

'I do know. Anyway, David Purkiss signed up immediately. Isha and Margot were hanging around, and not in a way that suggested they were shopping, so goodness knows what they are up to. Something with Verity, and that means nothing good. But I signed them up and I sent Belinda along to see Jaxx at Halfway to double check we can have the back room tomorrow and for the next six weeks. It's only small so we can't sell many tickets anyway.'

'You're charging that much?' I say. 'We're really doing a crime writing workshop for six weeks!'

'Mitch suggested twelve. Jaxx is hoping people will buy drinks, so your only cost is paying Mitch. This is a new world of how we make your business pay, so we don't lose our bookshop and we don't lose you, Keera. I want to pay Mitch for his time, even though we know Mitch is mainly motivated by promoting his book. You must have had a sudden idea to leave Mitch and David in charge. So tell all about interrogating Benj, before we get customers.'

The last bit Liv says in an undertone because a customer in shorts has just walked in to look at the local walking guides. They've said they just want to browse.

Luckily, as well as her brilliant business brain and her can-do attitude, Liv has also turned up with Hobnobs. The non-chocolate variety obviously as they are the best. So I can forgive her for being so bossy. Also she's charged way more than I'd have done for tickets, so how can I say anything against suddenly being in charge of a crime writing workshop? I just sip my tea and take a bite of Hobnob.

'You know how the narrative goes that Grant Michaels was the only person who even spoke to the dead couple. It's why everyone calls it an impossible crime.'

Liv nods and tidies. Someone must have brought in young kids recently and I hadn't even noticed things out of place.

'The Winters were travelling back late, were passing through Crossways and decided to stay, fell in love with the place, went to see Grant Michaels in the morning.'

'Ah! So who did they stay with the first time? That's what sent you scampering to intimidate Benj. Very smart, Keera, and interesting. Because Benj offered rooms when he started. Halfway was being renovated wasn't it. He must have only just set up the Crossways Cafe.'

'Benj didn't deny they stayed with him, but he claims he never spoke to the couple above a bit of small talk. He was only too happy to turn his upstairs rooms into more cafe space and lives in the attic. I asked him to try to remember what they talked about. I wondered if he knew them.'

'Everyone bought into the narrative that fate brought them to Crossways. You think it might have been to see Benj Beresford? The hidden connection we're missing?' Liv puts down her tea and tries to open a window at the back of the shop that is definitely painted shut. The air is very still.

'It got me stressed that he didn't seem bothered at all. If two people stayed in my rooms and were killed the next time they set foot in Crossways… wouldn't you be bothered?' I say, ignoring the curious expression of the grey-haired walker in shorts, because he's definitely listening in. 'How unbothered he is seems suspicious. Being threatened is good too. I think you're right. Progress.'

Liv waits until our customer in shorts departs after shuffling through all the guides, but not buying anything. Liv arranges the maps back properly on the shelf. 'Keera, being threatened is never good.'

'Not even a little bit threatened? And doesn't being threatened confirm Benj is definitely the most likely suspect for those nasty incidents against Eliza?'

'Plan A is working. Don't get impatient and ruffle too many feathers. We get everyone talking, someone may say or remember something new. It was a case that defied answers four years ago. If we're stirring it up because we think the answer lies locally, then someone capable of killing two people is going to get to hear about it. Please don't be too reckless about how you go about things.'

'You sound so much like Elliott. Luckily I am the model of subtlety when it comes to poking my nose in.'

'If only that were true. Benj is not a nice man. Do just please tread a little bit carefully, Keera.'

I nibble on a third Hobnob and hear a couple outside seeing my sign and talking about the crime fiction workshop.

'Well, Benj annoyed me. I'd love to know exactly how much of a suspect he was,' I say. 'With the police.'

'Benj didn't feature in Mitch's chapter,' says Liv. 'But the police would have talked to everyone.'

'There will be a lot of useful dirt in the police files. But it'll be years since Mitch Ravenscroft read any of it. If only we could find out what was in his statement,' I say, with no hope, because whenever *police* are mentioned, I can't help but think of Liv's son, Elliott and how he's a total waste of time when it comes to sharing potential leads or any insider information. 'Is a fourth biscuit unwise? And do you think Elliott's likely to take an interest?'

'Is Keera Munroe saying we need police help? Is this you grudgingly admitting if Elliott takes an interest there's far more chance of a positive outcome than leaving things to Mitch, who I fear is only concerned for the outcome of his writing career.'

'Elliott could easily look things up.'

'Maybe you could work on changing the way you go about asking for favours,' says Liv.

'You mean anything that involves me and a charm offensive doesn't go according to plan?'

'It's always good to be learning new skills.'

'What else can we do other than nudge folk to remember something. Or wait for Benj to crack. The idea was to get this solved, save it causing any more damage in Crossways. What next? We're stuck.'

'The police failed when the trail was hot. Now it's stone cold—'

'Do you think we need a Plan B? Do we have one?'

'Absolutely. We always have a Plan B, but you're not going to like it.'

Liv raises an eyebrow at me and I turn at the sound of the bell signalling my door's been opened. Elliott walks in.

'Oh please tell me this isn't our Plan B.'

23

Keera

Liv and Elliott exchange a glance that lets me know I'm being ambushed.

'Tell me Elliott isn't your Plan B?'

'I'm not anyone's Plan B,' says Elliott stiffly.

'Actually, you are,' says Liv. 'A great Plan B. And Keera's keen to practice being charming. It's perfect.'

'The one who pompously tells me he can't possibly tell me anything useful and always tells me off about something?'

'I'd say that's not the greatest start for being charming,' says Liv.

'And I'd appreciate it if you stopped talking about me as if I'm not here,' says Elliott. 'And if you're trying to involve me in sharing anything that's a police matter, the answer's no.'

'See. Pompous,' I say.

'And unhelpful,' adds Liv. 'Although what Elliott means is that of course he always appreciates our help. And what Keera means is that she doesn't want to be rude, but she's stressed about a lot of unpleasant things that we would really appreciate your help with. So let's work together. I thought you two might have a walk and a chat.'

'Then you won't want tea?' I say.

'Actually, I'd love a tea.'

'Are there any of Remy Aubert's flapjacks left?' Liv asks.

'No. I can't imagine what happened to them,' I say. 'A chat sounds ominous.'

'It's just a walk.'

'And a chat. What would we be chatting about? Or is it more a lecture?'

'You know me, always chatty.' It's not only Elliott's grin that's unconvincing as I go to make tea.

'If you're here to reassure me the police have this all in hand and not to go around upsetting everyone by interrogating them, you can save your breath. And you're in a suit. I can't tell if I'm some kind of break from work, or if I've become actual work now.'

'Have I caught you at a bad moment?' Elliott asks.

'Keera has a wonderful habit of turning a lot of situations into bad moments,' says Liv, taking over from me and washing up mugs. 'Sure you want tea? I'll mind things here. There's nowhere I need to be.'

'There's no chance that's true,' I say. 'You can't convince me this is the one day you're not invited to a bajillion parties.'

I hope for an unexpected customer, particularly an awkward one who I then amaze with my bookselling skills and they are so wowed they buy at least a dozen books. Needless to say, that doesn't happen. Or has ever happened.

'What happened to the charm offensive?' says Liv

'I'm looking around for biscuits,' I say. 'Is that enough?'

If he's even thinking of reopening the case, I don't have a charm offensive big enough to get him to talk to me. I don't even have biscuits. Liv pushing for a chat is the worst of all possible outcomes, because Elliott will probably insist I have to share anything I learn or he'll throw me in jail for obstructing the police. But he won't share anything.

'Elliott, why don't you tell me what you thought of Mitch's chapter I very kindly shared with you?' I say, taking in Liv's pointed look.

'It's terrible,' says Elliott.

'At last! Something we can all agree on,' says Liv.

'It was just a rehash of what I've read online. Nothing new. But accurate?' I ask Elliott. 'Cos I'm only measuring it against media reports.'

'Why are you even supporting Mitch?' says Elliott. 'He's just stirring up a painful crime to sell his book.'

'Keera thought a true-crime biography that raked up the most terrible and notorious part of Crossways' recent history would be a boom for business,' says Liv.

'Although look at how quickly the tickets for Mitch's crime writing workshop have sold. But yes, I made a bad call. I'm famous for them, but that means I can see when I'm partly responsible that things are getting dredged up now. So I have to take responsibility for sorting things out.'

'You do know that is absolutely not true,' says Elliott over the familiar sound of my ancient kettle considering if it can be bothered to do it's one job.

'Mitch's chapter told me the police never got close to why that couple were killed the moment they set foot in Crossways,' says Liv.

'Apart from the being followed from the airport idea,' I say, not quite able to believe we really ate all the Hobnobs. 'I've been thinking about it, obviously. I have ended up with a load of questions. You could just say yes or no if I ask a few questions,' I plead, trying this charm offensive. 'That isn't breaking your strict police code of conduct.'

I fish around under the counter and find a secret stash of ginger nuts. My personal favourites.

'I'm calling a truce between you two,' says Liv, bringing forth tea. I swear she even manages to get my kettle to boil faster than I do. 'We all want the same thing.'

'How closely did the police look into Benj Beresford at the time?' I ask.

'I thought we were going for yes or no answers,' says Elliott.

'All right, did the police look at him closely?'

Elliott accepts a ginger biscuit delicately, as if even accepting a biscuit might compromise him in having to offer something in exchange.

Mitch is heading past, so I step to the door and watch where he's off to. I see him disappear into the Crossways Cafe. After one of the famous breakfast baps? Or following the lead I worked out? You cannot even trust ex-police.

Liv tells Elliott how the popular narrative was that the Winters were killed on the first night in Crossways. 'It makes for a good headline,' she says. 'But Keera worked out it's not strictly true. They stayed at the Crossways Cafe first, run by a nasty piece of work. So what did you have on him?'

We haven't agreed at all to bring Elliott into this, as Liv goes over what Eliza's had to put up with. We definitely did not agree to share this and Eliza said she didn't want to involve police. Liv doesn't see that Elliott's someone who goes by the rules. You can't trust anyone. It's lucky that a customer drops in wanting a read for a bright eight year old's birthday. I need to calm down.

'What about any trace on the gun?' Liv asks, once the coast is clear of customers again.

Elliott does not endear himself to me by munching the last ginger biscuit in the pack.

'That one is a simple yes or no answer,' I point out.

'And what about the burglaries?' Liv presses on, still hopeful of getting somewhere. 'I mean the local ones, not this idea of them being followed from the airport by professional criminals. Those break-ins point to someone in Crossways being pretty desperate for cash. Is that a lead Mitch could follow up on?'

'The burglaries were small stuff, pinched from empty houses with open windows. The popular theory was that it was probably kids,' says Elliott with a shrug.

'Because there are so many kids in Crossways,' I say. 'Is that what led to the followed-from-the-airport theory? Or was that something to do with the gun?'

Elliott looks uncomfortable. Am I onto something?

'None of the media coverage says anything about the gun, so we've assumed a shotgun, because you get those around here. But that wouldn't square with them being followed and robbed by professional criminals.'

'Yes the gun hardly features in any media reports. So it was significant because the police didn't share,' says Liv. 'Was it something more like an air rifle? Because some of those are super powerful and you don't even need a licence.'

I know little about guns, but are air rifles powerful enough to kill in that gruesome way Grant described? I haven't passed on those details to Liv.

'Or was it more the sort you'd find at a shooting range. Is there one near here?' she asks Elliott.

'If it was, it was probably obtained illegally,' I say.

'Someone from their previous life coming here, bringing a gun to shoot them? But a motive like that, the police would have found it, surely,' says Liv. 'The media portrayed them as a mild, unassuming couple. And they *were* robbed? Jewellery was stolen, wasn't it?'

'What happened to the yes or no answers?' says Elliott.

'Come on,' says Liv. 'These are good questions. We've worked out a lot. Help us out here.'

'You've reached theories, based on very little.'

'Very little is all we have,' says Liv. 'What you mean is well done, you're smarter than I realised, sorry I underestimated you. Let's work together and get this thing solved.'

'That's not what I mean.'

I know all Elliott wants to do is stop us. But won't he see we're not going to do that? And listening to Liv tells me we are working things out. Getting closer?

A couple I've never seen before drop in and start browsing. Liv gives them a friendly greeting and asks them if they're just visiting Crossways.

Everyone's dismissed the police theory about the couple being followed from the airport. But if that is where the answer lies, we're never going to get an answer, no matter how hard Liv and I try to get people talking.

'Shall we go on this walk?' says Elliott.

I turn to him, surprised.

'We are still doing this walk? The chat too? You know how chatty you always are. Then let's go. I'm already looking forward to hearing everything you're going to chatter on and tell me.'

24

Keera

Elliott strides ahead, taking a route along the high street and then diving off, following one of the footpaths signed by a wooden fingerpost.

Is this less a chat than a walk where we're heading somewhere?

Because he's moving quickly. Even in a suit, Elliott wins by having a pair of chunky boots that are more appropriate than my tired trainers. I can feel every rut and stone through worn-out soles as the path quickly becomes a standard Crossways dirt track across a field, mud all baked hard, smell of manure and the sporadic retort of the crow scarer interrupting the heady chorus of birdsong. There must be many little creatures hiding in the trees.

'Did you want to see some of the local countryside? Liv's in charge and she'll sell more books than me. Last time I went out to interrogate someone, when I got back she'd organised an entire programme of writing workshops and got people to sign up and pay for them. So no hurry.'

He says nothing and I'm determined not to fill the silence.

Something shuffles low in the green unfurling of new undergrowth.

Am I going to spot a hedgehog or a deer (small one)? I carry on watching and a blackbird hops out.

'Didn't you promise to be chatty?' I say, hurrying to keep up.

Elliott turns and grins. 'Who were you interrogating?' His eyes flash with a surprising blue in this sunshine. Sometimes he really does remind me of a husky.

'Benj Beresford. I'm not telling you anything more cos I know that game and you're not getting me to talk when you said you'd do all the talking.'

'I'm surprised you believed me,' says Elliott, smirking. 'That I'd be chatty. I always had you down as someone quite smart who can see through the BS and the lies.'

'Then what's this walk for? I can give you something to be chatty about?'

'Does it involve you asking me to give you insider police-sensitive information?'

'Only a little. Just a hint to save me wasting my time on the wrong person.'

'You're asking how much did Benj Beresford feature in the Crossways Killings? Even though you pretty much talked yourself into thinking the most likely answer is an outsider?' says Elliott. 'You could stop wasting your time.'

'I'm only doing that because you refuse to help.'

Crows squawk overhead in a black line. We've only been walking maybe ten minutes. Already there's no one around.

'I'd be happier if you didn't spend your time interrogating someone you suspect of shooting two people in cold blood,' says Elliott.

'Why are you worried if you truly believe the answer doesn't lie in Crossways? So did you eliminate Benj as a suspect? And I cannot believe this is just a pleasant country walk, but I don't get out much, so I've no clue where we are. What are we doing?'

'Making the most and getting out more,' says Elliott. 'Drinking in the fresh country air that definitely has a whiff of the manure about it.'

'A bit like your answers.'

'I'm sure it's not news to you that you have a nasty suspicious mind,' says Elliott.

'Takes one to know one.'

I can see the end of the field we're walking through. Ahead of us I was expecting a farm building, but it's a house, right in the middle of nowhere. Well, nowhere but still only a ten minute walk from Crossways high street. As we get closer, actually it's two homes. Semi-detached cottages in a mirror image of each other.

Each has a front door towards the middle and a window on each side. Probably built for farm workers past, now what Grant Michaels would no doubt call authentically rural with charming original features. But that's where the mirror image ends as only the near one got the estate agent memo about hanging baskets, a newly painted front door and kerb appeal.

A dog starts barking. The deep, loud bark of a big dog. There's movement in one of the front rooms.

'Someone or something is looking out of the downstairs window.' I say. 'I think it might be a very hairy monster? I really hope it's a monster. I've always wanted to see a monster in real life.'

'It's a lurcher,' says Elliott.

'It could easily be a wolf. Or a husky.'

'Not with those ears.'

'How do you know the breed of dog that lives here? Are you a dog person? Is this why you are suddenly chatty?'

'He's called Leonard and technically, Charles lives here,' says Elliott. 'Leonard just lives with him.'

'So you know the dog's name and the owner's.'

'Charles is not known for being neighbourly.'

'The big barking wolf-dog and the grime on the windows weren't giving neighbourly vibes. I don't think the greenery's ever been told it can't take over. The hand-written Keep Out sign is also a big clue.'

'Leonard's loud barking and Charles's poor hearing is why he heard nothing and didn't so much as take a neighbourly look out of the window,' says Elliott.

Then I get it.

'You mean on the night the Winters were killed. This is where the murders happened?' I give an involuntary shiver.

I take it all in. The two cottages are surrounded by farmers' fields. There's less of a road, more a track that peters out at a copse just past the pair of isolated homes. Yet we're not far from the bustling high street.

'If you were looking for the perfect setting for an impossible crime with no witnesses, you could hardly choose better,' I say.

The cottage on the left has the look of where something grim happened. But my attention slides to the pristine adjoining house.

'The Winters had a late flight and planned to stay at an airport hotel,' says Elliott. 'Grant had left keys in a keysafe just in case. They arrived by taxi. Charles was watching television in the back room and didn't even hear the taxi.'

'Shame you can't ask what the dog saw.'

'Leonard barks at foxes, so Charles takes no notice. Whoever killed them could have arrived by car.'

'You tracked down the taxi driver?'

Elliott gives a short nod.

Leonard finally decides we aren't a threat and stops barking.

'It's easy to imagine the Winters are in there, right now,' I say. 'Just returned from a long holiday to celebrate their retirement. Settling in their new home. The big decision made, the fresh start, it all begins here. Grant Michaels has supervised renovations, redecoration and the arrival of furniture from storage. How long had they been in before it happened? How closely did you track their movements?'

'Couldn't be exact. And you're right about all the renovations. Played havoc with any DNA,' says Elliott.

'Are we here because you're trying to reassure me the police investigated fully? Or to show me that I'm involved in stirring up not simply some cold case from Mitch's book, but with real people? I'm really not one of those sofa Sherlocks who cannot see the humans behind the puzzle. Being here just makes me long for justice for the couple even more. Time even seems to move differently here. It feels like this could have happened yesterday.'

'I know what you mean,' says Elliott. 'I know you always want to see me as deliberately obstructive. But despite chasing down what they could, the team was faced with very little. Mitch got that right in his book.'

We stand in a field, staring at the cute country cottage. Scene of a horrific double murder.

'Looks like someone's living in it now. Think they know their hallway was the scene of a notorious double killing?' I say. 'It was described as isolated. But actually, it's much closer to the high street than I imagined. Does it make you feel you might've just walked in the footsteps of whoever killed Chris and Carrie? Cos I'm getting uncomfortable prickles on the back of my neck.' I actually shiver, suddenly cold in this baking hot, glorious day; birds overhead, bright green catching my eye from the copse at the end of the lane.

It makes me feel unbearably sad and long to be home. By home I mean sitting behind the counter in Between the Lines.

'He was killed first,' says Elliott. 'It looked like Chris answered the door and was shot right in the hallway. His bloody handprint was on the window.'

I want to let him talk, surprised at Elliott sharing this much. But I can't help but comment. 'Chris was shot when he opened the door?'

'Carrie was found further back in the hall, so we guess she was presumably startled by the noise and came to see what was happening. I doubt Chris and Carrie Winter knew much about what happened. They'd both have died quickly,' Elliott says. He knows my imagination is flaring.

In my head, I can almost hear the screaming. But there wouldn't have been screaming, not if they didn't get a chance to work out what was happening. So there was no burglar surprised inside the house.

I can easily imagine footsteps coming silently across this little-trodden path approaching the cottage? A shadowy figure with a gun and a determination to end two lives. Elliott's letting me know that the police definitely kept it quiet how quick and efficient it was.

I burn with the injustice that such a thing happened at all. No one has paid for their deaths. It's still a mystery.

'Someone came here and wanted to kill them,' I say.

'Someone could easily have come across this field from Crossways. Do you get the feeling the case was never solved because there was always someone you missed? You never talked to the right person who knew something.'

'Mum's right when she says if we had the reason why, we'd know who,' says Elliott.

'Who needed to kill a pleasant couple who never seemed to have harmed anyone? I think I will forever be haunted by what Grant said about finding the bodies.'

'What did Grant say?'

'There was nothing even left of his head.'

'Must have been grim being the one to find them.'

'Also something about the smell and never having eaten meat since.'

'Ok, yes, that's grim.'

'He needed therapy to keep doing his job as it involves walking into countless empty homes.'

'Murders always have far more victims than just the dead,' says Elliott.

'You really don't believe stirring things up now will bring a different outcome?'

'I want you to stop. Yes.'

'But I can't help but feel that's because you think bad things will happen if it gets stirred up again. And that means you think there's a chance I'm right and answers lie here.'

'We can't rule it out.'

'It has to be worth a shot, sorry, poor choice of word. Trouble is, you've shown me it'd be pretty easy to do what we've just done and walk across the fields, follow the footpath from Crossways high street with no one seeing you. Standing here just makes me believe this is a local crime. The answer lies in Crossways, I feel sure of it.'

'Then the obvious sensible thing to do is definitely leave it alone.'

'Yes, sensible is exactly the word that springs to most people's minds when they think about me. Also, that thing about leaving things alone.'

'It was thoroughly investigated.'

'I know you've brought me as a warning. I'm getting the message it's dangerous to poke my nose in. But sorry, Elliott. You're also giving me a signal that if you think digging is dangerous, it just confirms you have the exact same sense as me, this is not a cold case. Someone right here, right now, knows something. So we can get answers.'

'Then I'm giving the wrong message.'

'Getting everyone talking about it again, thinking about it, stirring things up, reminding people it's not over. There has to be a chance we'll finally find out what happened.'

'Not the message I'm trying to convey at all.'

'And you've really got me thinking now about if we can crack the motive, we'll have cracked the case. Who in Crossways could possibly have wanted a nice, recently retired couple dead so badly they'd just walk right up here and shoot them? Particularly as, so far, we've only identified two people who even spoke to them. You still haven't said if the police talked to Benj Beresford. He's not someone who was overlooked, is he?'

'You're making out solving an impossible crime is a puzzle you have to crack. But two lives were ended horribly and the killer got away with it. There's a chance they might still be living here quietly under the radar. Someone ruthless. Someone who until now, thinks they're safe.'

'Stirring it up is dangerous, I get it. But not a reason to stop. If a ruthless killer who murdered two people lives in Crossways, of course I want to keep digging. Of course I want it solved. So help me. Stop me blundering about more than I need to. Tell me something useful. Were they even robbed? Or was that more media speculation?'

A long enough pause allows a little hope to enter.

'We think cash and jewellery were missing,' says Elliott.

'That means someone stepped right over two bodies to steal from them? That'd take nerves of steel.'

'Exactly, ruthless. They might've only stepped over one body. Carrie's body was further down the back of the hall.'

'They had recently arrived home. Possibly dumped bags, maybe even cash or jewellery just inside. Kitchen's at the front?' I say, looking ahead at the attractive cottage that hides a terrible secret. 'Someone might have seen cash and jewellery through the window? But why would someone be here at all? Burglary was less motive, more cover?'

'You can speculate all you like, Keera.'

'Please can we get past this bit and agree you're not going to stop me. Please can we move on? What can I say that will make you help me? And before you answer, just give the impression that you are at least considering it.'

25

Keera

Eliza's outside her shop early, in a colourful strappy summer dress, her hair loose, like someone who shouldn't have a care in the world. But she's busy with broom.

A mess of broken glass glitters in the morning light, making the pavement look more like a shimmering stream of bright water.

'What's happened?' I call. 'Not another lorry sending a stone through your window?' I say, more in hope than expectation that this is purely an accident.

It's obvious there's been another incident. Already. And we thought it was a smart move, sending Verity in to tell Benj we're all looking out for Eliza, warn him off. Then I went in and… possibly upset him? Did more harm than good?

The plate glass front of her shop is intact and I recall Benj Beresford's parting words about having a lot of broken glass to deal with. Where's all this come from?

'Someone's had fun with the bins again,' Eliza says, her face grim. 'Smashing bottles right outside my shop.'

'I'll come and help.'

We sweep very carefully, I'm mindful that the soles of my shoes are very worn. We're dealing with huge, shockingly jagged pieces to tiny shards of ground glass.

'Verity went to talk to Benj,' Eliza says. 'I had hopes it might be over. Now this!'

We glance at the windows of Benj's Crossways Cafe.

'This time I'm taking photographs,' I tell her.

'I'm not going to the police,' says Eliza.

I want to ask why not, but Verity arrives for work with Jackson Brodie in tow and we need to get the cat to mind his paws.

'No police,' says Eliza determinedly, as I insist on taking photographs.

'Fair enough. But think about it,' I say.

It's difficult to keep Jackson away. He's too curious about what we're doing.

'Curiosity's going to get you glass in your paws,' I tell him, heading to fetch some food and placing the bowl further along the pavement. 'Lucky bookselling involves plenty of cardboard,' I say, 'so it's nice to find a use for that.' I dump broken glass into a box.

'His paws are dirty from digging again,' Verity says, trying to entice Jackson away as the shiny splintered bits are a nightmare to sweep up. 'I'll shut him in the shop.'

Verity likes digging too, albeit in a different way. I wonder if between us we've managed to do the opposite we intended and have antagonised Benj and I'm mindful of all super-cautious Elliott's warnings. Mitch went to talk to him too. Liv and I are asking questions. And I don't trust that Verity isn't seeking an outlet to an otherwise dull summer.

This nastiness is targeted at Eliza, but proves there's someone more than unpleasant here, someone ruthless is living in Crossways. Benj? I wonder what Benj is capable of. How do we get any proof. Of anything.

There might be a danger in trying to bring justice for that poor Winter couple. But I can't just turn it off. I burn inside whenever I see injustice. And the attacks on Eliza started before Mitch started going around telling everyone about what's in his book.

'You must think this is a nice place you've moved into,' I say. 'Not thinking of giving up, moving on?'

'Give into intimidation? Not bloody likely.'

Last time Eliza was ranting and angry. Now she looks grim-faced, shocked and unsettled. Verity and I try to tell Eliza that we'll deal with it. Eliza covers up her injuries well, but she still has difficulty bending. She won't leave us to it. I wonder about her injuries. There's that rumour about a vengeful ex-lover. She's secretive about her background, what brought her here. Eliza is so reticent about herself.

And Benj hinted something about her. I know he was trying to deflect scrutiny of him. He accused her of lying, insisted he had no reason to wage any vendetta against her as she was on a short lease and never had any plans to stay.

I pick up another jagged bottle, a local brand of beer Benj serves in his cafe, suddenly tired of all the mystery.

'I don't suppose you can think of anyone else who'd want to do this? Anyone you've upset? Anything you want to tell me? We've told Benj we're watching him. If he's smashed glass just on your bit of pavement from his own bins, well. He's not exactly been a criminal mastermind about it.'

'Who else might it be?' asks Verity.

We both look at Eliza, who doesn't reply. I thought she'd be quick to deny she'd upset anyone.

Jackson Brodie miaows loudly, shut in Between the Lines.

'Liv's son is in the police and I do grudgingly admit it can be useful to have a police insider. Elliott would handle this sensitively, if you want me to have a quiet word. In order to get this to stop we need evidence,' I say.

'They'll just ask awkward questions,' says Eliza.

'What questions might you want to avoid answering?'

'No police,' says Eliza.

With a sudden flash of purple Benj disappears off on his bike, not stopping to help. He must have seen the three of us, plus cat, clearing up.

'Earlier than usual,' says Eliza. 'I need to talk to him myself.'

Eliza balls the last of the broken glass into newspaper and drops it into my surplus boxes. We dump the boxes full of broken glass back into the Crossways Cafe bins.

I want to ask if Benj told the truth about Eliza's short lease. But she closes down conversations about herself. I need to get her to trust me.

Eliza strides off into her shop. Jackson miaows accusingly when I open my door. He shoots off, his broken tail in the air. At least his paws are safe.

If Liv were here, she'd offer me the sound advice that the most obvious answer is usually the right one.

The obvious answer is Benj Beresford.

It's just that I feel Eliza's covering up for a whole lot going on that I need to know about.

'Try to get her to take some rest,' I say to Verity before she goes too. 'Eliza's going to have difficulty finding chatty small talk as she serves her customers today and I could tell her ribs were hurting. Lucky how quickly Ashley sensed Eliza needed help this summer. You're in the best place to keep an eye on her.'

Maybe I need to work on getting Verity to trust me too.

For now, all I can do is spend a distracted morning thinking of the mystery of Eliza, just the other side of the wall, yet she feels a much further distance away. And answers are even further away. There are too many people in Crossways getting away with their crimes. And I don't like that one bit.

It was imperative she saw the footage first.

Of course, if she'd done a good job and fixed the camera correctly and the camera had done its job, it would show Benj, who had every reason to feel bitter about Eliza and wage a war to drive her out.

But just in case… Until Verity saw it for herself and she knew there were no nasty surprises… Because Crossways hid its secrets too well. Since deciding she needed to find a sliver of a secret about everyone, it was disturbing that at every turn she was faced with the fact that Grandma was definitely keeping secrets. And to learn Grandma was such a terrifically good liar.

How was it possible that of all the people in Crossways, it was Grandma who was behaving suspiciously and had a secret life?

All those jaunty lies on the mini-chalkboard about what a busy, fun, but respectable time Grandma was having had rattled Verity. What was Grandma really doing? Where was she really? And there was more. Like why had she lied about not moving here until after the Crossways Killings? Bookgroup Investigates said Grandma was most definitely living here at the time.

But Verity could trust Grandma. Couldn't she?

26

Verity

Verity had started having very real nightmares about what exactly Grandma was really up to. Not outside Eliza's smashing bottles in the middle of the night, that was for sure. That was ridiculous.

Even so, Verity needed to see that footage first.

She could allow the smallest chance it was Grandma who'd appear on that tiny screen, and certainly not with Bookgroup Investigates watching. Why was Grandma telling so many lies?

The shop was busy and Verity kept a look-out for any members of Bookgroup Investigates on the prowl who might poke their collective noses in and scupper her chances to be sure it showed Benj. Of course it was Benj.

Even though Grandma had not come home last night.

On the mini-chalkboard on the fridge, Grandma claimed she was out *working late, wining and dining a visiting dignitary.* Nothing about being out all night. So far that chalkboard had been a hotbed of nothing but lies.

And Bookgroup Investigates described Grandma getting Verity working in the deli as *being undercover.*

Keeping an eye on Eliza was just a kind and friendly thing to do. Just like Grandma. Grandma hadn't got Verity in here for quite some other reason, nothing along the lines of keeping your enemies close. No secret agenda.

Grandma was not in some secret war against Eliza.

It was all just Verity's imagination.

But when and how had Grandma become this woman with a secret life? That was not just Verity's imagination.

But it was still ridiculous to even imagine the covert surveillance she'd set up was going to end up being a means to an end for proving it was Grandma who was the mysterious person waging some vindictive war on Eliza. Absolutely not going to happen.

But Verity had to see it first. Because Verity wished she could be more sure. She was so shaken by Grandma's lies. But the shop was too busy. She was running out of time to see that footage first.

'What happened this morning was really upsetting. Do you need to take a break?' Eliza asked, after Verity had twice given customers the wrong olives.

'It's you who needs a break!' Verity shook her head. 'I am fine. This is tough on you and you're still recovering and I am very much down to help you. So you should go and rest up.'

'I'm better off keeping busy,' said Eliza.

'You say that, but you're probably not,' said Verity. 'I'd grab a rest while you can. Honestly. Make the most of the fact you only live upstairs.'

Verity needed to get Eliza out of the way. Otherwise what possible excuse could she have for a sudden need to retrieve a handily placed set of steps outside?

She needed to see that footage. And she'd see Benj. Because what possible reason could Grandma have for waging some kind of war against Eliza? Although why would anyone? Apart from Benj.

There was a sudden lull in the rush for olives and posh sausages and fresh salads. So far Belinda, Isha and Margot had remained remarkably absent. Now or never.

'Honestly, you spent all morning doing way more than you should if you want your ribs to recover. Go! Please!' Verity held her breath until Eliza gave a short nod.

'Thanks Verity, Ashley suggesting you come and help me has been brilliant. I hope it's not too dull for you, because I'm beginning to wonder how I'd cope without you.'

'Well, you probably wouldn't have to keep giving refunds when I serve the wrong olives!'

Eliza gave Verity a grateful glance and disappeared through the discreet white door that led to her flat above the shop.

The second she disappeared, Verity raced to turn the shop sign to Closed before any unwanted customers could come in.

Verity probably had seconds to do everything in her power to make sure any secret Grandma had about her night-time activity did not get out.

She needed to retrieve those steps and see that footage before anyone else saw it. And if necessary, destroy it.

27

Verity

Verity dashed outside, but too late. Belinda, Isha and Margot bounded up to her, making Verity wonder when someone as poised and sophisticated as Belinda had last bounded anywhere.

'Were you three hiding around the corner or something?' Verity said irritably.

'What's on the camera?' asked Isha excitedly.

'I haven't had chance to look yet,' Verity pointed out. 'Not without Eliza noticing I was up a step ladder and that might, you know, make her suspicious. We agreed, this is our secret.'

'Until we know what we're dealing with,' said Belinda.

Desperate as she was to see that footage, Verity would love to ditch the help of Bookgroup Investigates even more. Bookgroup Investigates were not being helpful, they were being a terrible distraction.

'But you're about to look? Come on then,' said Margot briskly. 'Let's hope we caught something!'

'We're not fishing,' said Isha snappily. 'We are helping Eliza and this is serious.'

Verity retrieved the steps she'd placed just inside the garden gate. There was no way Grandma was going to appear in that footage, just because she'd been absent from home last night. There were other people with secrets. Verity hadn't even yet talked to the main witness, Grant Michaels.

Twice yesterday she'd tried to talk to the estate agent. Once Keera had been in there, but also annoyingly, Isha had beaten her to it. Why was Isha talking to the estate agent? That was another secret. Isha had definitely been evasive about paying for that holiday. And Eliza was a whole mystery that needed solving. This was about far more than Grandma.

Even so, Verity held the camera in her hand and tried to feel one hundred percent confident. Could she come up with a reason to watch the footage first? And if necessary, it might suffer a terrible accident.

Then Mitch Ravenscroft appeared and stopped, looking curious why the four of them were stood around the front of Eliza's Deli with a step ladder.

Then Isha said, 'Oh you're involving Mitch, what a very sensible idea. Let's show him what the camera's recorded.'

Verity threw daggers at Isha. 'No, I wasn't involving Mitch.'

'Involving Mitch in what?' said Mitch.

'Nothing that involves you,' said Verity.

Did Poirot find it this annoying having a sidekick? Was that why he was always sending Hastings away on errands that appeared to have nothing to do with the case?

'What camera? What recording?' said Mitch.

'It's just capturing the street outside the front door, all right. It not illegal,' Verity said defensively.

'Smart move,' said Mitch. 'Particularly if it captured whoever smashed all that glass last night. Let's have a look.'

Verity had no choice but to replay the footage. *It'll be Benj. It has to show Benj*, Verity said to herself as she lifted the tiny camera very close to her face, trying not to let the others see.

Verity did not miss the irony that the whole reason she ended up in Crossways to mend her ways was to do with this very camera and an illegal recording. Only months ago she had set up this exact recording device without dreaming of the consequences. Grandma had brought her here to try to teach Verity a lesson that if you go delving obsessively into other people's business, sometimes the person who you harm most is yourself.

Verity's own path to the wrong side might be rather eclipsed if Grandma was caught on camera having a smashing frenzy outside the deli.

But that was not going to happen. History was not repeating itself.

The images were small, flickering black and white, the others crowded in trying to see, elbowing each other for a better view.

'This way none of us are going to see anything,' snapped Verity.

At first nothing was happening on Crossways' very bland, night-time high street. Jackson Brodie was the first creature to appear, his tail, fluffy, and bent like a broken finger.

'No one's getting a good look,' grumbled Belinda.

'I'm leaving soon for a weekend away,' Margot said airily. 'So I should be first to see. This is far more exciting than David droning on about some plant or other.'

'It's not a bad capture for a cheap camera,' Mitch said as they were all sandwiched together and glued to the screen of the tiny camera, awaiting something extraordinary to be revealed on the night of the broken bottles.

'You can get some very fancy ones that load up on your phone and livestream,' said Margot. 'A friend has one of those doorbells and she can speak to the person who's been caught on camera.'

Verity's heart was hammering so hard she thought the others might hear as she raced through the grainy footage.

If she suddenly saw Grandma, she'd have an *oops butterfingers* moment, drop the camera, step on it and smash it. In the dim of the street lights, she hoped the images would be too grainy for anything to be clear.

Then all of a sudden, something did appear and Verity's heart nearly left her chest. The camera had done its work and caught a figure that set about smashing broken bottles right outside Eliza's Deli.

'Wow this camera's done a great job, actually,' said Belinda. 'But who is it?'

'Well done Verity,' said Isha.

'They've got their hood up,' said Margot disappointedly.

'Does it look like Benj?' Belinda said.

'Ah, Benj Beresford,' said Mitch. 'There's a name that crops up a lot lately. You think he smashed the bottles?'

'We know you went to talk to him,' said Belinda.

'Did he admit anything?' said Isha. 'From the angle it's impossible to get any perspective, to tell the height of the person even,' she grumbled, nudging everyone else out of the way and trying to take the camera from Verity to get a closer look.

They all bumped heads in their eagerness to see.

'The grey figure's never still enough,' complained Belinda. 'And the smashing frenzy didn't last long. Notice how they never look up. We never once get a glimpse of their face.'

'It's really disappointing isn't it,' said Margot.

'It must have been noisy, but over in minutes,' frowned Belinda. 'It was so slick and anonymous.'

The grey, hooded figure disappeared from the screen and Verity breathed. She finally allowed them all to pass the camera around, safe in the knowledge that no one could prove that was Grandma. But who was it?

Because it was also impossible to say that footage ruled out Grandma.

'I thought we'd been so clever,' complained Isha. 'But this proves nothing. You can't even tell the basics like age or gender. It's just a shapeless figure in a hoodie.'

'Apart from the fact that it's not someone built like a fridge or beanpole tall, it really could be almost anyone,' grumbled Margot. 'But it could be Benj.'

'What were you expecting? Someone turns up to smash a load of bottles at three in the morning wearing purple cycling Lycra?' said Belinda, squinting at the screen. 'Do you think they suspected there was a camera there?'

'It's possible,' said Mitch. 'Why do you think Benj smashed those bottles?'

Verity shared the story that Benj had lost out on Eliza's property. No one mentioned Grandma's lies at all. Verity had been driving herself slowly mad, obsessed for no reason other than she'd caught out Grandma in a few lies (well, quite a few).

'I should get back to work,' Verity said, hugely relieved and giving her cue that the others should be gone.

'Let me look one more time,' said Isha. She put the tiny screen really close to her face.

'There's nothing more we can do,' sighed Margot.

'Actually, there is,' said Belinda. 'What about other cameras locally? The pubs both have cameras.'

'They'll be trained on the car parks or entrance,' said Margot. 'They won't have caught the smasher.'

'He won't have passed those anyway, he's only next door,' said Isha.

'Several cases have been cracked by collecting street footage,' insisted Belinda. 'We might see our grey hoodie pass, see where they came from. And if no one passes, doesn't that mean it has to be Benj?'

'You are so smart!' said Isha.

Verity had forgotten Belinda was a true-crime enthusiast. Sadly, this meant Grandma wasn't safely out of the woods yet.

'Mitch, I know you're retired, but I'm sure the pubs would show you their footage if you asked.' Belinda went on. 'Maybe check any doorcams too.'

'Actually, that's brilliant,' says Mitch. 'I could also enhance this image. Actually, I couldn't, but I know someone who could.'

'Ooh so you'll get one of your tech wizards to clean it up?' said Isha, who had the tiny screen very close to her face and had been replaying it over and over. 'We might see more detail. Like this bit.' She pointed. 'This fuzzy bit, just there.'

Now they all wanted to see what Isha had spotted.

'You're right. Is it some sort of logo?' hazarded Belinda.

'It's too difficult to see properly,' said Margot.

‘I’d better take the footage,’ said Mitch, holding out his hand.

‘I’m going to put the camera back up,’ said Verity quickly. ‘I’ll send you a copy.’

Because Verity recognised that logo instantly. She’d seen it enough times. It was very familiar. Crossways golf club.

Grandma had a grey golf club hoodie with that logo hanging on the hatstand in the hall.

28

Keera

Questions get fired at Mitch before he's even taken a sip of chilled elderflower presse (he said he'll have a wine after, but he's looking like he might be regretting that decision).

Before he can even begin his How To Write Crime Fiction talk (he has everything on little organised cards) he's bombarded.

How did he find a publisher? (from Isha). Is it true that crime-scene DNA gets washed away by rain? (David). How many people are reported missing each year, but never found? (Cal Kinsky – lovely to see young people here).

But is everybody writing a crime novel? Does everyone sit around wondering how quickly does a body decompose? What would a body look like and what state would it be in after it was buried for, say, four or five years? Nothing like that ever appeared in Isha's poetry. I lose track, but some of the goriest questions come from the unlikeliest of sources. Who'd have thought Margot would be straight in with the squelchy body questions?

Mitch shuffles his prepared talk cards with the air of someone rapidly rethinking. But he gives considered replies. The one about the rate of decomposition and what forensics can be extracted from a long-buried body is so astonishingly detailed I'm surprised no one needs to rush out for fresh air, apart from Mitch, who I slide a glass of chilled white wine which he receives with a grateful look. He has a sheen of sweat on his brow.

The room is packed. More eager questions flood in. I'm thrilled and hope everyone's going to sign up for the full six weeks. Maybe we should go with Mitch's first suggestion and have a twelve-week workshop, why not. There are people here I wouldn't have expected. More than just the usual suspects with their notepads ready, pens poised.

And everyone has paid far more than I'd have asked in my wildest dreams. Liv Trent's dreams are wilder.

There's the ringing sound of a spoon against a wineglass. 'Can I make a suggestion,' Ashley says, as chatter dies down. 'Can we leave questions until after Mitch has delivered his talk otherwise we'll never hear all Mitch's wisdom about writing crime fiction.'

Ashley receives a grateful look from Mitch, who takes a big gulp of wine and raises his glass to her. Ashley smiles back, more a simper; could be described as flirting. Mitch is a celebrity and Ashley's looking positively slinky in tight black trousers and a top with just the right amount of sparkle for a summer evening. All very glamorous for a crime-writing workshop. Even though I had Ashley down as writing popular science, not crime.

It probably should have been me that stepped in to calm the bristling hands, but Mitch looks right at home in his role as an author tonight. Who's next to get published? How exciting to think maybe I'll have their books on my shelves one day.

Grant Michaels has his umbrella tucked under his chair (didn't Grant say he had a brilliant idea for a novel but no motivation to write it?). Verity's here, notebook in hand. Mrs Kinsky – certainly didn't have her as a closet crime writer. Belinda Messenger is not here, adding fuel to the Crossways rumour that the two women avoid each other, because of friction between Cal and Taylor, practically the only teenagers in Crossways. Cal Kinsky's scribbling away diligently. Taylor Messenger cannot be writing a crime novel too? But she's sitting cosily with Cal, heads close and giggling. Are rumours about them true?

And there are people I've never seen before.

Writing a book must appeal more to Crossways folk than reading them. Or perhaps, strictly, as an author once pointed out, it's not so much the joy of doing the actual writing that motivates so many to make a start. More the attractiveness of being able to say you've written a book.

Or the lottery-win allure that it may be a bestseller.

Mitch gets down to his talk, saying he's not an expert in everything, he's sound on the procedural stuff. But will do his best, even about specific things even an expert would struggle to answer, like the question on money laundering. (From Cal?).

Mitch clears his throat with the relief at the well-behaved silence and takes a fortifying gulp of wine and is on firmer footing delivering a funny story.

Mitch takes everyone through the basics, delivering notes on plotting and reveals. He goes around asking us all whether we have ever done any writing (answer – all complete novices, goodness knows where anyone gets the idea that we can write).

Next door it's a wild Crossways Friday night. Mitch has to compete with the sound filtering through from the main bar, the clink of fishbowl glasses serving the local gin, probably having heated conversations about traffic and gardening. But in here it's all about the crime.

His talk is well put together and interesting. A dry run for the talks he hopes will publicise his memoir?

The moment Mitch takes another pause and a sip of wine, hands go up with more questions. There is rapid fire from all directions and looking at the eager hands, I wonder why I ever hesitated thinking Crossways was too genteel for true crime?

'How easy is it to get hold of a new identity? This from Cal Kinsky. 'Could you get a new identity by picking someone who died young from a cemetery gravestone? Or does that just happen in books?' Even Cal isn't just here because there's not much else to do as he asked several intelligent questions (How do you balance pace with character? Answer: only with a lot of practice.)

I'd love to know what Verity's writing in her Doodles of an Evil Genius notebook.

Eliza suggests if Mitch is going to encourage us with our writing, maybe we need a regular group. 'We can swap our writing and learn how to give feedback.'

And then it's time for a break.

Jaxx is suddenly very busy at the bar, not least because Taylor Messenger is attending the crime writing workshop. Jaxx's partner, Maya, tends to stay in the kitchen, delivering the food orders.

I introduce myself to the people here I don't recognise, being a dutiful and welcoming host and hoping Liv is watching and will be proud of me as I tell them I'd love to help them with any of their bookish needs (everyone has those, don't they?).

Then everyone is back for round two. Ashley seats Mitch back down in the chair to await more torture, but hands him another glass of wine.

Or is it torture? Although there's another effort to sidetrack Mitch from his talk with more questions, this one from Isha about the trend for unlikeable narrators.

'They infuriate me, I can't see why people read them.'

'There's something for everyone,' chuckles Mitch. 'The secret of good crime fiction isn't even understanding how the police really work. Focus on the storytelling first. I tell that to all the bestselling authors I've advised.'

'Who have you worked with? Anyone famous?' asks Grant.

'My lips are sealed. But my tip is always the same. The most important thing is to write an entertaining story. Have fun with it, because writing takes a lot of time.'

'Trying to work out what's going to sell to a publisher's a tricky business,' says Eliza. 'I remember my mum saying many readers think they could write a bestseller because they've read a bestseller they didn't think was very good. She taught English, so her standards were very high.'

'Just because you don't like something, doesn't mean it's not any good,' Mitch chuckles. 'You can't please everyone, so you shouldn't even try.'

I'm waiting to see if he'll steer the conversation around to the Crossways Killings. He may want to stir things up, remind people it's not over. But Liv's right (again). Mitch's main interest is promoting his book.

'You have to spice up even true crime as so much police work is very dull,' admits Mitch. 'No one wants to read about knocking on a hundred doors trying vainly to get someone, anyone, to talk or be a reliable witness. Difficult to turn that into an interesting chapter,' he chuckles and takes another sip of wine. 'You have to skip all that.'

'But you must have exciting cases if you've written a book about them?' asks Taylor Messenger, picking at her black nail varnish.

'The rumour is you've written about the Crossways Killings?' says Verity, repeating behaviour from bookgroup; sitting demurely, then bringing up a brutal local murder. 'Two people gunned down in a place where everyone noses into everyone else's business—how is it possible the Crossways Killer's never been found?'

'Because it wasn't a Crossways Killer,' says Isha. 'Because they were outsiders. The killer came from outside. It was terrible. It sounded like they were a lovely couple. But no one knew them or anything about it. I only know what I read about it. Seem to remember he was a scientist, wasn't he?'

'There are a lot of scientists about here,' David Purkiss says, more than a little defensive.

It's not only David who looks uncomfortable. I can count three scientists in this room. Mrs Kinsky, David Purkiss and Ashley Smollett.

'You could say the same of teachers. She was a teacher, wasn't she?' David bats back to Isha. 'Bet in a room at any time in Crossways there are teachers. Doesn't mean any teachers here knew her.'

'Did the police ever find a motive?' says Eliza.

'It was a burglary that went wrong,' says Ashley.

'They were followed from the airport,' says Mrs Kinsky.

'Just a random tragedy,' agrees Isha. 'Mitch, it's not true you're raking all that up again?'

'Going over it all again won't be any more fruitful, it'll only upset people all over again,' says Mrs Kinsky.

'Well Mitch,' says Grant with his usual dry chuckle. 'That's put you on the spot.'

If Mitch thought this evening was going to get secrets tumbling out, he'll be disappointed. Everyone is looking at everyone else. But no one speaks. Liv's right. Everyone's traumatised at the thought the gossip might shift from gardens and holidays.

And afraid of what might come out? Afraid the answer is local. That there is a Crossways Killer?

'People should be brave enough to speak about it,' Verity says. 'Historic cases rely on people speaking up to get solved. Otherwise you just become part of the cover up.'

'Sure,' says Grant. 'If anyone can answer how two strangers were murdered in Crossways and no one saw a blasted thing—do talk to Mitch. Don't be a silent conspirator. Maybe we should all start talking about it.'

Ashley gets to her feet. 'But not tonight. Mitch has worked really hard this evening. Thank you Mitch, I think I speak for everyone when I say that was brilliant. Let's show our thanks and good luck with your writing everyone!'

Ashley leads a round of applause that definitely signals a sudden end of the evening.

'Have to admit it has taken it out of me more than I realised,' says Mitch. 'Such very good questions. All of them. See you all very soon and next time I'll be even better prepared. And don't forget to buy my book when it's published.'

29

Verity

One minute Grandma was there, learning how to write crime fiction, the next she'd disappeared. But she'd been home. When? Because there was a new message on the mini-chalkboard on the fridge.

Had to do farewells with visiting dignitary who leaves early tomorrow. Pop and ping curry in the freezer x

Incredibly smart that her lies were scribbled in chalk, because the evidence was always wiped away.

No chance to talk to Grandma. Again.

The workshop hadn't finished late. Verity was restless and failed to settle, even though she tried to distract herself with television and a very large glass of Grandma's most expensive wine.

Grandma's grey golf-club hoodie was there, hanging on the hatstand in the hall. Verity couldn't stop herself checking if it contained any evidence of illicit night-time activity. But there wasn't so much as a tiny shard of glass. But absence of evidence never proved anything.

Verity bit her nails and went over her case-notes. What linked someone here in Crossways to a quiet retired couple?

What was the motive? Why was Grandma lying about so much? Verity read Mitch's chapter again, thinking she needed to go back to the beginning.

Grant stood out as the only witness. The trouble with only one testimony was that who could corroborate anything he said? The whole story of the Winters chancing to be in Crossways – all that evidence rested solely on Grant. But why would Grant lie about it?

Verity topped up her wine. She wanted Grandma to still be the person she'd known all her life. But she had to face it, Grandma had changed since moving to Crossways.

Verity watched the glass-smashing footage again, willing to be convinced there was no way it could be Grandma. How long before Mitch pestered her to hand it over so he could enhance the detail? How quickly would he track down any other CCTV footage that would prove where that figure in the grey hoodie came from? And it was a golf-club hoodie. If Verity and Bookgroup Investigates knew Grandma had secrets, how long before Mitch Ravenscroft took an interest?

Was Grandma targeting Eliza? Why? Why had Grandma arranged for Verity to work with her all summer?

One thing Verity had learned from almost three years of university was that one secret almost always led on to others. People behaving suspiciously always had something to hide. Bad enough to think Grandma was the one waging some war against the arrival of Eliza Somers. But was Grandma hiding the fact that she had shot and killed two people?

What Verity wanted really badly was to eliminate Grandma from her enquiries.

A noise outside made Verity leap up. Someone was outside. Grandma? She opened the door. No one.

Did she imagine the scuffling sound of someone moving quickly, as if someone took off at speed past the house where the old couple lived that the whole street relied on to know which bins to put out?

Verity's skin prickled with the thought that someone was out there, wondering what her next move would be.

What was her next move?

Lack of evidence wasn't proof of anything. So there was nothing for it but to take the sensible girl's approach; she needed to search the house. If something connected Grandma to Eliza, or the Winters, or there was some reason she had become a different person, Verity wanted to find it.

Grandma's room was first. It was tidy and didn't take long. Grandma had a big clear-out when she downsized after Grandpa Smollett's death. Grandma's clothes were organised in the wardrobe by colours and seasons and paired things that went well together. Verity found evidence of upmarket tastes, down to underwear and very on-brand yoga gear, which wasn't even being used. What could she read into a drawer of sheer tights, apart from the fact that none of them were old and bobbly?

Grandma had updated her home and refreshed her wardrobe. She had new, expensive brands of make-up. And she'd gone to some up-market perfumier and had a scent mixed just for her. Now that felt like something old Grandma would do. Verity could imagine her being a pain of a client, wanting to know all the chemistry behind it.

Grandma's to-be-read pile of books was organised by author on a bookcase by her bed rather than an untidy pile on the floor. A surprising number of spicy romantasy books, but then everyone was reading those.

Verity knew the nooks and crannies of the kitchen, so didn't bother with that. Grandma didn't have anything so fancy as an office, just a desk. Verity searched it, scouring the little paperwork she found. But everything would be on the slimline laptop that went everywhere with Grandma.

After a thorough search Verity wished it made her feel better. There was no evidence to connect Grandma to the poor, dead Winter couple, or even to a reason she'd want to wage a vendetta to get Eliza out.

Trouble was, there already was a connection. Grandma had downsized and made the sudden decision to move here just about the same time as the Winters had moved here. And Grandma had lied about that.

And this evening, another connection had been thrown in front of her.

Chris Winter was a scientist, same as Grandma. That had got Verity thinking. She went right to the back of every cupboard, the bottom of every drawer, under the bed. Verity knew what she was really dreading finding, even though it was ridiculous even to imagine… Grandma had a tiny suburban garden. She had a bird feeder, a nesting box for blue tits, she didn't even have rabbits. Not even vegetables. Why would Grandma ever need, or want, or know how to get hold of a gun? Ridiculous to imagine Grandma with a gun. Of course Verity wouldn't find one. And she hadn't. But if Grandma had ever had a gun… Grandma would have got rid of it surely. Especially if she'd used it.

Grandma was spending so little time in Crossways she might not realise it was all being raked up again. Was Grandma in danger?

Verity had started out looking for someone with a new secret, something to share with Mitch Ravenscroft to persuade him they needed to work together. And so far, she'd found nothing, except Grandma.

She had to be careful. Could Verity get on the inside track and find out which way Mitch's mind was working? Just in case… But what did she have to offer?

Verity believed she had the skills to uncover truths and now she had to prove it to herself. She had never needed those skills more. So who was her best suspect?

It was impossible to sleep. Was it really just twigs scratching the window? Verity threw back the curtains dramatically, just in case that figure she imagined was outside was still out there watching.

That's when she realised she was staring at the shed.

The one place she hadn't searched. Would Grandma keep a gun in that shed? Well, there was no way she was going to search that, not in the middle of the night.

30

Verity

'I have a secret I need to share,' said Verity.

'That sounds worrying. I hope I'm ready for it,' Eliza smoothed today's dress, a bright shade of grass green.

'You could win any award for the best-dressed deli-owner ever,' said Verity.

'That's it? I'm going to be presented with an award because I have a large collection of pretty dresses?' Eliza smiled.

There was a lull in the rush of the day's customers. Eliza was busy preparing more salad ingredients.

Verity shook her head. 'It's this. I'm supposed to find a ruse to get you out of the way.'

'Actually, now you are worrying me. Something bad is happening?'

'Don't you feel lots of bad has already happened?' Verity said.

Eliza looked at her keenly, her sharp knife hovering over perfectly ripe tomatoes as she chopped things ready for the next rush on the day's salads. Eliza's tumble of dark hair was up in a high ponytail, a smear of dark lipstick still in place. Was there any way Verity could get her talking about her secrets?

'I know you use heavy make-up to cover fading bruises. Do you ever think your crashing down the concrete steps out back could have been worse? I'm actually amazed you only cracked a few ribs. You could have easily broken a leg, or worse. Everyone's worried about you. What's really going on?'

Eliza and Verity looked at each other.

'You haven't explained why you need to get me out of the way,' said Eliza. She handed Verity a stack of containers from the fridge. 'Could you take these through?'

But Verity didn't move, just looked at Eliza and waited.

'Is it only Benj you've upset?' asked Verity. 'Or has someone else got it in for you?'

Eliza sighed. 'Ignore things or upset people? Your path through life involves a lot of choices. I feel you might be like me, Verity, and not want to simply ignore things.' Eliza sliced another tomato easily. The knife must be very sharp. 'Do the thing that scares you most. Isn't that the advice for stopping overthinking and stopping your anxiety and being scared of the consequences?'

'And what are you most scared of?' Verity asked, for the first time thinking she might be on the verge of mysterious Eliza finally sharing something about herself.

But Eliza gave herself a little shake. 'Right now it's not getting these salads ready in time.' She gave a half smile.

But Verity couldn't let it stop there.

'You've put a bolt on the back gate. Those locks on the front door are new. Even the door from the shop that leads to your flat above has serious security. Everyone thinks someone's out to get you. What do you think?'

'I think you are very observant,' said Eliza. 'But weren't you in the middle of telling me a secret? Speak now, because you might not get a chance once more customers arrive.'

'Yes, sorry. So everyone knows about the bins and all the other crap you've been dealing with. So Liv, you know Liv who helps Keera next door, hatched this plan to show we're all rallying round and supporting you.'

'Yes I know Liv,' said Eliza quietly.

'Everyone says she's the one who keeps Between the Lines from going under and that Keera's just the bookseller.'

'Yes, people do say that, but no one's *just* anything are they? Everyone has their hopes and dreams and their secret inner lives, don't they?'

'I guess. Do you? Have secrets?'

'We're not talking about me. We're talking about Liv's secret plan.'

'Yes. Well, Liv knows you got injured falling down those concrete steps out back.'

Grant Michael raps on the door at that moment. He pops his head in most days, just asking how we are.

'Three brain eating aliens want a secluded place to start their invasion of Earth,' he says, 'and I think I've found the perfect pad so I can lure them in and kill them.'

He didn't. Verity never paid much attention to what he did say, but it was enough to break any moment where Eliza might finally have shared something.

'So what's Liv up to?' said Eliza when Grant had gone.

'Liv says the whole of your garden is a bio-hazard. So your neighbours and customers want to show you that you are very welcome here. Basically, they want to tidy the garden and make it all lovely and safe for you,' said Verity.

'How many of my neighbours and customers?'

'Quite a lot. But it is a surprise. It's my job to think of a ruse to get you to leave for the evening, because you live above the shop.'

Verity twiddled with the short end of fishing line she'd removed from being wrapped around the bottom of the jasmine just outside the back door. She kept it in her pocket. It was just the end of a piece of new-looking fishing line. Would anyone else be convinced it proved someone meant Eliza serious harm?

'You thought you'd just tell me.' Eliza paused. 'I'm grateful because I hate surprises. I think you guessed that because I think we have more in common than we realise.'

'If you could just go out, then come back and act surprised and not tell anyone I spoiled the plan. Some people are bringing plants and even flapjacks and the whole thing has pretty much spiralled and it's all up to me to make sure it doesn't go wrong. Just go out, come back, act surprised, and you'll make everyone happy.'

Eliza nodded. Verity didn't miss that she wiped a tear from the corner of her eye. '

I can do that,' she said in a choked voice. 'And thank you, Verity, you really are kind and I don't know what I'd have done without you.'

Verity felt she hardly deserved thanks. She wasn't even kind. She only grudgingly helped Eliza. She mostly focused on proving Grandma wrong about her obsessive nature by finding small cases to get interested in to defy Grandma.

She had not even managed to solve Who Shot Jackson Brodie, but hadn't forgotten Operation Workshop would be solved tonight. One success.

It wasn't the size of the mystery, there was the thrill from knowing the truth of secrets everyone only gossiped about.

'I don't deserve it,' said Eliza, with a small sniffle as she topped up the big colourful olive display bowls from a giant plastic pot. 'Thanks to your help and sending me off for frequent rests and managing the shop by yourself, I'm recovering pretty quickly. I haven't driven since my accident. I shall risk a drive this evening. Head out into the countryside.'

'If you can get your car out from between Grant's monster and that black four-by-four that always parks too close to you.'

If Eliza was ready for driving, maybe Verity needed to accelerate the question of what she should do after Crossways. She couldn't carry on living with Grandma. Eliza may remain another mystery that Verity failed to solve, but she'd been pretty tolerant of Verity.

The truth was that it could not have been easy for Eliza to have a disgruntled granddaughter thrust upon her. Verity, with her low people skills and zero retail experience and acting like she was the one doing everyone a huge favour.

'So pleased you feel recovered enough to drive, even if it means you won't even need me soon!' Verity said. 'I shall have to find someone else to annoy.'

'I could not have managed without you Verity.'

'You say that, but everyone would have just stepped in to help out, wouldn't they. Crossways is like that. If it takes to you.'

'When do I have to go out, come back and act surprised?'

'Soon actually.'

Verity would like to stop this awful vendetta against Eliza. Was it true Benj was the only suspect? Who was really targeting Eliza and why. Unless of course, it really was Grandma. Or perhaps, particularly if it was Grandma. Verity needed to know. She couldn't leave Crossways before she did know.

Eliza was silent a moment. She seemed on the verge of saying something. Eliza herself was a little piece of mystery that definitely needed solving.

'Ok, guess I should go,' said Eliza.

'Oh. As it's hot and lots of people are coming over, I thought I might use your flat upstairs,' said Verity, trying to sound very normal and not give away how important this was. 'I could put a few things in your fridge. If you've got a spare set of keys.'

The deal was done and Verity got a thrill from a little successful subterfuge. So far she'd managed to go into Eliza's flat once and had been intrigued by some project spread out across a dining sized table.

Tonight she also planned to solve the mystery of Eliza Somers.

31

Keera

'What was the one interesting thing Benj told you?' Liv asks as we wait for the signal that Verity has succeeded in getting Eliza out early and Project Biohazard is go.

'Benj says he doesn't need to do anything to get Eliza out. She only wanted a short lease. She'll be gone in a year. I meant to check with Grant as he'll know if it's true or not.'

'That doesn't sound right,' says Liv. 'Why would you bother to go to the effort of starting a business if you don't mean to put down roots? Sounds like Benj grasping for a reason not to be behind the vendetta against Eliza. But it's a silly thing to say as it's so easy to check.'

'Let's hope this idea of everyone pitching in to make Eliza's garden usable in a show of support will work. It's a brilliant idea Liv. You are always full of them.'

'We tried to warn Benj off and another incident happened right away. We had to do something else. I don't like to think of Eliza being in that shop alone. And this way is better than you going around again and risk causing more chaos and Eliza gets a usable garden. Also, a gathering of Crossways people means chatter and gossip and we can listen in. Because the other way to stop nasty things happening is prove who's behind them.'

'Do you mean you don't think it's Benj? Or are you talking about the Crossways Killings?'

'I think I'm talking about both,' says Liv.

'It sounds like you're starting to think the two are connected?'

'Oh there she goes! Eliza's going for a drive. Good sign. She must be feeling better. Although probably means Verity's days are numbered. Maybe she could help you? And before you say you don't need any help, can I just remind you that I have no plans for my volunteering to become permanent.'

'You say that, but you have way too much fun, not just selling books, but organising my events. And organising me. And where better than a bookshop for the gossip?'

'Talking of gossip, let's go and get started. Eliza's still recovering. She might not be gone for long.'

The garden project starts with a little fracas as both Ashley and Mrs Kinsky try to take charge, before they're interrupted by a roar and poet Isha Cheema appears through the hedge with a chainsaw, carrying a not insubstantial axe in her belt. Everyone stares at her with renewed respect.

'One way of dealing with an overgrown hedge and an argument at the same time,' says Liv.

'Slicing through like some terminator robot, I like it,' I say.

'The garden's so long we won't chop back everything in one go,' says Isha. Her long hair threaded with grey, is tied back as well as being topped with her green beanie, along with ear-defenders. 'Let's focus on nearest the shop and worry about the far end when we can see progress.'

Ashley and Mrs Kinsky agree and hand out forks and trowels. Taylor dons ear protectors and tears through to rediscover the overgrown lawn with a huge mower.

'I'm nervous of weeding in case I take out the wrong thing,' Cal says.

'Don't worry, it's all weeds,' says Mrs Kinsky.

Every time the explosion of the chainsaw or lawnmower dies down seems to coincide with the firing of a distant crow scarer.

'Whoever said the countryside was peaceful never came to Crossways,' I say to Verity.

'I've never seen so many sharp blades in one place,' says Verity. 'It feels like half of Crossways is giving up a Saturday evening. Is it just to have an excuse to wield a lethal weapon?'

'Although it might be because Isha's throwing a garden after-party,' says Grant. 'People are wary of her homemade samosas, but what's really lethal is her gooseberry wine.'

'Steer clear if you don't want a headache tomorrow,' says Liv. 'Are you coming to the after-party? Not much to do in Crossways for young people.'

'Oh I've been finding ways of having fun,' says Verity. 'Is Isha a secret prepper? She does have a lot of well-organised vegetables and fruit. And I had heard she has a gun. Her father's. What happened to that?'

'I doubt Isha's ever had a gun,' says Grant.

'Crossways gossip is that the way her dad kept himself busy was shooting at rabbits and crows,' says Verity.

'It's the country,' Taylor says, taking a break from mowing to grab a drink. 'Lots of people have guns.'

'And shoot things?' says Verity. 'Someone must have had a gun to shoot those two newcomers.'

Taylor flashes Verity a look. 'That was outsiders. People just shoot vermin. It is allowed.'

'What classes as vermin?'

Taylor grins. 'More than you think. Squirrels.'

'People around here are ok with shooting to kill nut-munching fluffy tailed squirrels that scamper around the park?' says Verity.

'Only the greys. And Isha's dad was always shooting at rabbits after his vegetables. That's allowed too.'

'What did Isha's dad do with them all?'

'Ate them I think.'

'I meant the vegetables.'

'Yeah, I meant both,' says Taylor. 'Probably sold what he couldn't eat to the pub—same as the rabbits. Not the squirrels. Waggon and Horses say people don't buy it on the menu. Even in a pie.'

'What another new and unpleasant side to Crossways,' says Verity. 'I hope you're joking.'

'You can shoot feral cats and crows and rooks I think too—but don't try selling them to the pub for putting in their burgers either,' Taylor goes on. 'Her dad tried to teach her, but Isha never really got the hang of shooting. Never hit much. 'Spect she thought that stray cat Eliza's adopted was a rabbit. Is it me or is this huge pile of clippings giving vibes like the party later is going to involve some ritual sacrifice?'

'Isha shot Jackson Brodie?' says Verity. 'She thought he was a rabbit? How do you know that?'

Taylor shrugs.

'One of my caseloads solved,' mutters Verity. 'And she does still have the gun.'

Or at least that's what I think she said.

Part of Liv's show of support for Eliza was to gather together people who really know Crossways and listen to the chatter. A fine plan, but not easy, not with the power tools. The conversation only stutters when the chainsaw and the mower die down.

Taylor's asking Isha if she can take a turn with the chainsaw. Grant Michaels is tackling the lethal concrete steps, replacing it with a brick-edged gentle cement slope, complete with handrail. We all told him that sounds brilliant and left him to it. Verity sidles up to him and I don't think it's because she's good with bricks and cement or wants to learn. I sidle closer to listen to what she's saying to Grant.

'You know everything that happens in Crossways.' Verity smiles.

'So everyone says, but I have no clue about one important thing,' Grant replies as Jackson Brodie also sidles up and makes a contribution by digging and covering everyone in dirt. Verity tries to manoeuvre Jackson away. 'I mean the question of what we are going to do about the far end of the garden? Someone suggested we leave it and call it a wildlife space. But whoever called this garden a biohazard is right. These gardens are far too long and most of them could be hiding something that could be a threat to life.'

'We could do what I noticed Isha's done,' says Liv. 'Isha's blocked off the end of her garden with some serious boarding. I'm surprised. I thought she used every inch for growing vegetables.'

'I said she looks like a prepper,' says Verity.

'Where is the horrible neighbour?' I hear Ashley say to Mitch Ravenscroft. 'Pretty much everyone's here except Benj. Significant after what happened with his bins?'

Liv was right that once people knew how many were turning up and helping, more would join in. Having an after-party also helped I'm sure.

'Benj never turns up for any community events,' says Mrs Kinsky. 'Not even that karaoke we had for the village hall roof fundraiser.'

'Although most of the crowd wished they hadn't turned out for that,' says Grant.

There's plenty of general chit-chat to eavesdrop. But I have an urge to say something to get people talking about the Crossways Killings. It never seems to get brought up. And if it does, someone always shuts it down. But why? Everything's a subject for chit-chat, even that Isha's tackled the brambly, boggy, unloved end of her very long garden by boarding it up. Is Liv's non-confrontational, do a lot of eavesdropping plan getting us very far?. But then I overhear Verity asking Ashley quietly where she was last night and the night before. News to me that Ashley's movements are a subject of Verity's suspicions. And the last couple of times we've almost ended up discussing the Crossways Killings, hasn't it been Ashley who's been quickest to shut it down?

I risk sidling closer. News that Ashley is going walkabout. And interesting that Ashley refuses to answer.

'Not now Verity,' Ashley says briskly and firmly.

But definitely evasively.

I dig in my spade viciously to find the roots of a giant prickly thistle to pretend I'm not eavesdropping. But Ashley moves off in such a way I can only describe as stalking off. She definitely didn't want to be questioned about what she's up to. Interesting.

I look up and unexpectedly catch sight of Benj Beresford.

So he's around. But instead of helping, he's spying on all the community positive action for Eliza from an upstairs window. A definite decision from him not to help.

'Hey Mitch—any luck with camera footage?' I hear Isha ask.

Camera footage? Something else going on in Crossways that I feel I should know about.

'Already talked to a few with cameras. Positive reaction. They're happy to show me,' Mitch tells her in a low voice I have to strain to hear. 'It'll take me a while to view it all.'

'Can we help?' Isha asks.

So they are gathering data from cameras in Crossways. My guess is they're going to see if there's any capture of anyone making their way to smash the bottles last night. Smart move and I wish I'd thought of it. Maybe Mitch isn't quite so useless and is doing more than just stirring up trouble for publicity for his book.

Would be great if they get the evidence we need to confront Benj Beresford properly.

'No chance yet to get anyone to enhance that film,' Mitch goes on. 'Still waiting for Verity to send that through to me. I should ask her.' He looks about.

But I already know Verity's disappeared. Because only a moment ago I saw something that definitely got my suspicion antennae firing.

I watched Verity taking a quick glance around, as if checking no one was watching, then slipping out the gate.

I wait a few seconds and then follow her. Where's she going? I'm just in time to see Verity use a key to let herself into the silent and empty deli in a way I can only describe as furtive. But she works there, she's in there every day. What can she be up to now?

32

Verity

With a last glance over her shoulder to check she was unobserved, Verity let herself into the empty shop and went straight to the white door to Eliza's flat, unlocked it and climbed the steep stairs.

All was quiet and she could not help but think of Grant Michaels, walking into what he thought was an empty house and finding two dead bodies. It made her more on edge than worrying Eliza might return early. Or might even be up there now, secretly drinking in the sappy smell of newly mown grass and quietly watching all the activity below.

Everything was as she pictured from her first visit; a tiny flat with furniture too large for the space, as if it had been brought from somewhere bigger. Bookshelves were the quality, solid old-fashioned kind that pre-dated flat-packs and Ikea. The kitchen area was tidy, part of the one-room living space. Two doors led off that Verity could guess were bedroom and bathroom.

She went straight to the dining table, unfortunately placed right under the window overlooking the garden. She needed to be careful. But her one trip up here had left her fascinated by why Eliza should be doing a research project. Her luck was in. It was all still there.

She stepped closer to the thick pile of notes, avoiding getting too close to the window and risk someone seeing she was up here. She had a good view, not only of everyone working below, but along the back gardens that stretched to the right.

First was Isha's, with its boarded-up end of the improbably long garden. Crossways was beginning to buzz with a rumour that Jaxx and Maya at Halfway wanted to buy up the unused ends of people's gardens to extend their accommodation offering.

Further along would be Margot and David's, where later, Verity and Cal were going to find out what David really used his shed for.

Verity felt a thrill just thinking of that, but right now she couldn't waste this opportunity.

Things already looked better in the garden. Everyone was too busy to wonder where she'd disappeared to. There was a mound of weeds and shrubby cuttings, actually more of a mountain and no one knew what to do with any of it.

'But let's just focus on the enthusiasm for now and not go looking for problems,' (Grandma had said to Verity when she'd asked).

Verity's attention went to the stack of notes. On the top was a print-out of a magazine piece covering some science awards at a swanky black tie evening banquet.

Verity's university had invited her to something similar. A chance to chat with old friends, make new acquaintances and potential future business colleagues. Networking. That was what her uni gig had been about. Verity understood it. Wasn't any good at it. Why was Eliza interested in this?

The article featured two photos. Photos were always useful. Verity was drawn to look at these first, took out her phone and snapped the piece to look at properly later.

One photo was of a small group. Two guys in bow ties, three gals in dark frocks, seated at a white-covered table with folded napkins and three different types of glassware that nobody knows what to do with. She could imagine the hubbub of anticipation and chatter.

Verity turned to the rest of the stack of paperwork. The first was a print-out of correspondence offering condolences on the death of parents, and apologies for having no information to add. A quick sift told her there were print outs of lots of similar correspondence, emails mostly. What was all this?

Verity couldn't read all of it, couldn't even photograph all of it. Whatever this was, Eliza had clearly been at this a long time. It was evidence of serious digging. Seriously impressive digging. What was important? Just glancing through wasn't telling her much.

Something else caught her attention, an A4 brown reinforced envelope stamped with the word *photographs*. It hadn't been opened. It had arrived in the post that day. Research that Eliza hadn't even looked at yet.

If she was careful she could open it, look at it before Eliza even saw it. Even if Eliza noticed it was open, she'd probably blame damage in the post. Hopefully she'd never dream Verity had been up here snooping. She took a risk, opened it and carefully slid out what was inside to avoid leaving finger marks on the photograph. An accompanying brief letter apologised for the delay, making excuses about being difficult to track down exactly what Eliza had asked for. It acknowledged a payment and said this was the best photograph taken on the night in question.

Astonishingly, Verity was staring at glossy prints of the same photos as in the magazine article. Eliza had been interested enough in this awards dinner to trace the professional photographer whose shots were used in the science mag piece. Eliza had ordered a high-res image.

This was taking obsession to a whole new level.

Verity put aside her plan to photograph everything quickly and turned to look closely at the pictures Eliza had gone to so much trouble over. An assortment of snaps of a few key addresses from an awards podium where winners collected their accolades. A blown-up image of the group shot that appeared in the magazine that was much clearer than the one in the article. Why was Eliza interested in this?

The idea of taking pictures and getting out quickly went out of the window the moment Verity recognised a couple in the photo. She was looking at Chris and Carrie Winter, right there smiling up from the middle of Eliza's dining room table.

Eliza's research was into the Winters.

Somehow, Verity found this was not the surprise it might have been.

Things were falling into place and she couldn't leave now as Chris Winter stared up at her, instantly recognisable with that high domed head and a hint of remaining black hair tufting around the sides. He was in his sixties, recently retired when he was shot dead. This awards dinner wasn't long before that. Chris was sitting in the front row of the big group alongside a smaller, pretty woman with a cloud of brown curly hair. His wife, Carrie.

Verity scanned the research again. This time things made more sense. No wonder Eliza was always shady about her past and what brought her to Crossways. Eliza was fascinated by Crossways' darkest secret.

From below came chatter every time Isha's chainsaw took a break and Verity risked staying a little longer.

She re-read some of the email print outs. Eliza had followed up an awful lot of leads. She must have devoted hours to this. Correspondence with what sounded like friends of the dead couple, mostly apologising about nothing to add, having heard nothing from the couple while away on their long holiday, that they had never explained if there was any particular reason behind their surprise move to Crossways. Most offered condolences on the death of her parents. The emails were to Eliza Winter, a detail Verity had missed on her first scan through.

Eliza had been keeping her own secrets.

Easy to understand why Eliza might not want to arrive in Crossways with a giveaway surname like Winter.

Verity had read Mitch's chapters enough times to remember Carrie had a daughter from her first marriage.

Now things were making even more sense. This was why Eliza had burrowed herself into Crossways, making herself a chatty, friendly part of the community, while hiding a secret agenda of trying to find out the truth of what had happened to her parents.

So had Eliza succeeded where the police had failed and found out anything that pointed to why the Winters were killed? Had all of this research led to a new lead, someone not talked to by the police? A detail overlooked? Did Eliza have a main suspect? Finally, Verity might be able to stop worrying about the reason for Grandma's secrets.

One thing Verity knew was that high-res photo was Eliza's most recent step in her research. Verity re-examined the original of the group shot that Eliza had taken so much trouble to track down. Exactly why had Eliza sourced this photo? Verity scrutinised it, making sure the photo on her phone was clear enough to look again later.

What had Eliza been looking for in this photo?

It was hard to make out faces clearly. It was likely done in the hope that everyone in the photo might be motivated to buy a copy of the magazine. The magazine name-checked everyone. Along with a high-res image of the photo, the photographer had sent Eliza a print-out of the same list of elite scientists in the photograph.

Then Verity was staring at a small image of another face she recognised, a tiny face, but unmistakeable, in a line of other faces. Even with the previous bad hairstyle that she looked much better without, there, without any doubt, right behind the Winters, was Grandma.

33

Verity

Verity stared at the photo of Grandma with the Winters.

Leaving no room for doubt, Ashley Smollett was name-checked in the line-up.

So what if Eliza had been doing in-depth research into the Crossways Killings and had found a connection? An elusive new connection that no one else had found.

So what if Grandma had known the dead couple? And never mentioned it. And lied about even being in Crossways when it happened. And kept a lot of secrets.

So what if it had been called an impossible crime, the police left with no option but to land on that unlikely theory that the couple were followed from the airport? So what if someone was waging some vendetta to get Eliza out and make it clear she was very much not welcome in Crossways.

This was simply a coincidence. All of it.

There would be a very good explanation for Grandma knowing the Winters. And never mentioning it. If Verity asked Eliza, she'd laugh and say how hilarious that her research had come up with a connection to Grandma. Of all people. Of course it was Benj who was waging war on

Eliza to get her out of Crossways. Benj wanted her garden. The simple answers were always right.

If Verity asked Grandma, Grandma would also just laugh and have perfectly good explanations for never being at home, but never being at YogaGals either, or golf. Or having that incriminating grey golf hoodie in her hall. Of lying to her friends and Verity. Of keeping so many secrets.

Life felt like it was twisting away from her and going in bad directions. Messy. Verity liked things to be ordered, understandable. She thought she'd been the clever one, injecting a little investigative fun into her summer of shame and doing it right under Grandma's nose.

And this photo was the result. Proof that Grandma was someone in Crossways who knew the Winters and had kept it a secret.

What was Eliza going to do about it? What should Verity do?

Verity went down the stairs, using the keys to secure the new locks Eliza had put in, noticing her hand trembling. Eliza had known full well what she was doing might be dangerous. Digging into a double murder. Because she was convinced the killer was still here in Crossways.

Verity gave a little shiver as she left the deli. She felt light-headed as she twiddled with the end of fishing line in her pocket. Someone had placed a tripwire across Eliza's hard concrete steps. Someone caused Eliza to have a terrible accident.

It very much looked like she wasn't the only person who'd worked out the real reason Eliza was here.

Was that Grandma?

Grandma wanted Verity to mend her ways. Because when you started trying to find the truth, you never knew where or what or even who you were digging towards.

What was she going to do?

Warn Grandma, obviously. Funnily enough, this might finally be the thing Verity could do that would impress Grandma, let her know how close Eliza was getting. But then Verity was pretty sure Grandma had manoeuvred Verity right into position, working for Eliza, keeping her enemy close, for that exact reason.

Verity reached the side gate and opened it. And there was Grandma hacking at an overgrown shrub with a lethal looking blade.

'Ah Verity!' Grandma turned. 'I've been looking all over for you. I think we're nearly done, well for today,' Grandma said, in her familiar brisk no-nonsense tone, dusting crumbs of earth from her gardening gloves and putting down some lopping tool that could do serious damage to fingers.

'Well I guess that's what happens when a poet with a chainsaw takes charge,' Verity said, her voice sounding forced and choked.

She had to tell Grandma. But not here. But then she hardly saw Grandma. When? Soon.

'Isha's invited us all over to hers. Apparently she does a mean peach liqueur,' said Grandma. 'Or was it gooseberry wine?'

'Either way, I'd steer clear if it's home-brewed,' said Verity.

What was going on inside Grandma's head? How could they be having such a normal conversation? Verity simply did not know Grandma any more.

It was one thing to discover that Grandma was an expert liar, another to find photographic evidence of her secret keeping. Verity twiddled with the end of fishing line in her pocket. Easy to put a lethal tripwire across some concrete steps. Getting up close and personal and shooting two people was a completely different matter.

Verity scoured her face for the old Grandma she remembered growing up. Was she still there? Grandma had changed since moving to Crossways.

Killing two people, that would change a person.

'Cal's looking for you,' Grandma said to Verity, with a knowing smile. 'Off to see some band at the pub.'

There was nothing like contemplating whether your grandmother was capable of executing a double murder and realising she absolutely could have done it.

If Grandma had planned a double murder and pulled the trigger, yes, Verity would fully expect the crime to remain unsolved. Grandma would have got away with it. For four years. In fact, if you wanted someone to organise a really well-planned murder and leave no trace and completely get away with it and even have it declared an impossible crime… Yes. There was one person in Crossways who would be your obvious choice. Grandma had a forensic attention to detail, she was a chemist. She was a planner. She was smart. She knew the dead couple and had kept quiet about it.

But did Verity really think Grandma was capable?

What was the reason?

What had driven Grandma to do it. That's what Verity was missing.

Verity pressed a hand to her forehead. Should she break the news Eliza was closing in right here, right now?

Instead she said, 'Isha does seem very good at gardening. Why does she want to board up so much of her garden? She'd have enough room to grow vegetables and potatoes to survive a major apocalypse.'

'Just grateful for the money I think,' said Grandma.

'Hmm?'

'Halfway are buying up back gardens to expand again. Bet Isha couldn't believe her luck when someone offered cash for a bit of her garden. She was pretty broke.'

'She sold it?'

Grandma gave a small but complicit smile. 'That's my guess, but a Crossways secret, don't tell anyone.'

'That's how Isha afforded her long winter holiday,' Verity muttered. Another of her caseload suddenly solved.

Above the general chatter, Verity could hear Keera and Elliott Trent arguing.

'This is not a sensible way to do things,' said Elliott.

'You are not my boss,' said Keera. 'Do I have to make a vow to be sensible all the time? No one ever achieved much by sticking to the rules. No one else is doing anything.'

'How do you know what anyone's doing? And sticking to rules is the only way things get done properly. Who knows what harm you might have done—without my even going into the danger you might be putting yourself in.'

'Oh danger, danger, danger. Anyway, it wasn't me that started stirring up everything. Mitch said he wants to look into it, but to be honest, he's way too distracted.'

'Why can't you leave things alone?' Elliott said.

'I don't know. I can't help it. I see injustice and I can't walk away. What if it was me who got shot four years ago and no one was doing anything about it?'

'Don't feel you have to hang around and come to Isha's after party,' said Grandma. 'Go and have some fun.'

Fun? What they urgently needed was to hatch some clever plan together, something to explain away all that damning evidence that Grandma knew the dead couple and had not breathed a word about it. The connection between the dead couple and someone in Crossways. The connection everyone had missed. Until now. She had to warn Grandma. Should she just come out with it?

But Cal appeared and Verity had never needed his soft smile more.

He leaned in to whisper in her ear. 'You asked me what people around here did for fun. Well, this evening is it.'

They were breaking into David and Margot's garden. Verity felt a rush of adrenaline just thinking about it. Grandma would go to the after-party. Verity could join the breaking and entering party with Cal. They'd talk later. Properly. At home. If Grandma ever came home.

'The band we usually go see was called Primordial Soup,' chattered Cal. 'But no one could spell it and it wasn't ideal the way everyone shortened it to Soup. But they're quite good. Well, better than a band known locally as Soup you might think would be anyway. Up for this?'

Cal moved in close. 'For fun we also do a bit of spying on the neighbours and breaking into their sheds later.'

'I haven't forgotten. Now?'

'Oh yes,' said Cal. 'Operation Workshop is on.'

34

Verity

'But beer first?' said Cal.

'Of course.' Verity felt an unhinged smile crack across her face. 'I'm ready for anything.'

There was only one available outside table at the Waggon and Horses, rejected by everyone else for being so seriously wonky it nearly tipped over when they sat down. Then they were joined by Taylor Messenger.

'You here to see the second rate band?' Verity asked.

What she really wanted to know was if Taylor was in on the Operation Workshop part of the evening? And were Taylor and Cal an item? Verity couldn't quite work it out.

'Second rate bands are Fridays,' said Taylor. 'Cal got it wrong. When's the breaking and entering party?'

That answered that question.

'When it's dark,' said Cal.

'Great, then time for another beer,' said Taylor.

'People go on about lovely light summer evenings,' said Verity, as Taylor sank another drink, drawing attention to the tattoo of a bad fairy on her wrist. 'Never about how long you wait to break into someone's shed after dark.'

She didn't fancy doing this with Taylor, a drunk Taylor even less. Verity was feeling light-headed, maybe from the beer, but also from the revelations about Grandma. She felt wired. She wanted to get going.

'If we go sooner Isha's garden party's good cover,' said Verity. 'Margot and David live on the high street, right?'

'You're new to this and already you got a better plan?' grinned Taylor.

'You mean you're *not* new to breaking and entering?' Verity said it as a joke, but the look that passed between Cal and Taylor might be telling a story she should know about.

'Just saying,' said Taylor, 'I had you down as serious, a studier. Didn't have you down as the most likely to want to join the breaking and entering club.'

'There's a club?'

'There's a club for everything around here,' said Cal quickly. 'Even gardening. We should start one.'

'Cal says you've caseloads to solve about Crossways,' said Taylor. 'That must take serious imagination cos I'd've thought you were a bit light on material around here.'

'I am light on material. Why else do you think I'm solving the mystery of David Purkiss's shed? I am open to clues on bigger mysteries. Like about breaking and entering.'

'Verity wants to know who shot the cat,' said Cal.

'Told you, Isha is a terrible shot and has bad eyesight. Probably thought he was a rabbit in her rotten cabbages.'

Isha shot Jackson Brodie. And Isha sold the end of her garden to Halfway to pay for her winter holiday. Two caseloads solved. Perhaps more importantly, was Isha looking a likely person to muddy the waters from all the secrets being about Grandma?

'If I were you I wouldn't bother with all that small stuff,' said Taylor. 'I'd go for the big one. The Crossways Killings. Tell me you're not interested.'

'I'm interested.' Verity sipped her drink carefully. 'Has everyone around here got a secret theory who did it?'

'Some said it was the done by the same people as those burglars who went into empty houses,' said Taylor, starting to pick at her black nail varnish. 'But it wasn't.'

'You sound very sure. But someone local knew the house was supposed to be empty. If you reckon everyone knows Isha shot Jackson Brodie and got him in the tail, but everyone's covering up, it sounds the same happened with those burglaries.'

Taylor started chewing her lip. 'Let's get another beer.'

'For someone who's in a breaking and entering club I'd have thought the sensible girl's suggestion would be we all switch to lemonade,' said Verity quickly.

'Sounds like you want out,' said Taylor, pausing on her way to the bar. 'You're in the wrong club if you're worried about being sensible.' The rosy glow of low evening sun glinting off her lip piercing as she grinned. 'Now's the time to play.'

'Dare you to see it through,' Cal said, raising his eyebrows at Verity.

'Dare me? Seriously? This is like doing breaking and entering at school.' But Verity had to admit she felt a thrill.

'That mean you're not accepting the dare to break into David's shed?' said Taylor.

'It's walking into someone's garden while they are away and checking an outside building. I'm not sure you could even call it breaking and entering,' says Cal. 'Technically.'

'Very knowledgeable,' said Verity. 'I thought you were studying medicine, not the law.'

'Chill. It'll be super easy,' Taylor said. 'David won't have security, not for a garden. Most bolts on garden gates would not fool a toddler as long as they were tall enough to reach over. Or could climb a set of steps without falling off. Which I think is most toddlers isn't it?' Taylor sat down again. 'Do you mind living with your gran? Or getting kicked out of uni?'

'I left because it was better than the alternative offered,' Verity said.

'Which was to be kicked out? Bad luck. Uni sounds terrible. But better than staying here forever. But then you went to uni and you still ended up here. Rotten.'

Verity swallowed the urge to tell Taylor she should get out of slitheringly dark and properly poisonous Crossways as soon as she could. And once she'd kicked its dust from her heels she shouldn't look back. Unlike Isha who left, but came back. Or David and Margot who sounded like they were trying to leave but never managed more than yet another minibreak. Or Grandma, who had become quite a different person since moving here. Crossways changed people.

'Sounds like you made uni more interesting than most people,' said Taylor.

'More interesting, but less successful. My grandma does not approve of the ways I make my own entertainment.'

'Don't they say smart people learn from other people's mistakes?' said Taylor.

'I have heard that.'

'Your gran brought you in as a smart person to investigate what's really going on with Eliza?' Taylor scratched at the back of her neck. 'Because you were smart enough to get the dirt before on someone at uni?'

'Did you overhear our entire conversation in Halfway when you were clearing tables that didn't need clearing?'

'Nah, I couldn't get most of it. But did she?'

'Maybe we swap. You tell me about the burglaries.'

'So are we doing this?' asked Cal, springing to his feet.

'I thought we were waiting until dark?' said Verity. 'And how do we get into the shed?'

'Couldn't we just look in a window?' said Cal.

'Not all sheds have windows,' Taylor pointed out.

'If we wait until it's dark, will we see anything?' Verity pointed out. 'Inside a shed?'

'You're right,' said Cal. 'Forget waiting until dark. Let's do it now.'

35

Verity

'If we weren't going to wait until dark, couldn't we have done this before reaching the stage where Taylor staggered when she stood up?' said Verity.

She was expecting a sharp remark from Taylor, walking slightly in front, but the girl stopped and listened, swaying gently, a finger to her lips as the distant, but still throaty roar of the chainsaw subsided.

'What are you listening for?' Verity asked. 'You think it sounds like the garden party is ready to become the after-party?' She ducked as something swooped right by her.

'It's just a bat,' said Taylor casually.

'I hate the countryside,' said Verity, having to catch Taylor as she stumbled on an uneven paving slab. 'Don't worry, someone in Crossways will have reported it.'

Progress was slow with Taylor's stumbling walk from the Waggon and Horses at one end of the high street.

'Don't you love this time of day?' whispered Taylor.

The high street did look different with long evening shadows and minus the constant background buzz of cars. Now the chainsaw had stopped, the soft music of late-evening bird song was allowed in.

'It's as if the birds are all singing their own tunes on their way back from the pub, but only remember the chorus and just sing the same bits over and over again,' said Taylor.

'Very poetic,' said Verity. 'All I can hear are noisy crows. All those clicks and chirrups are more like a human conversation. Hardly bird song.'

'That's it exactly!' said Taylor. 'They communicate about where the next meal is coming from, who's forming which hunting party to go get it in the morning. It's all been researched you know. If one of them sees a dead crow they're on it, making sure it doesn't happen to everyone else. You've heard of a murder of crows? Should be a murder investigation of crows.'

'Is that even true?' asked Cal.

Something spooked the crows and they all launched into the air as one.

'Vampires,' said Taylor unexpectedly. 'Don't you think crows look like a storm of vampires. Or witches.'

'A storm of vampires?' said Cal. 'Making that up too.'

'Crossways is a very weird place. Wouldn't surprise me if you were all secretly vampires. And everyone has such a conspiracy of silence over the Crossways Killings I instantly thought cult,' said Verity. 'Makes me wonder if joining a breaking and entering club is a great idea in a village full of cults, or even people with guns and poor eyesight?'

'Not everyone has poor eyesight,' said Cal.

'Don't feel that's as reassuring as I think you meant it to be. You have noticed bad things do happen in Crossways?' said Verity.

'Nah, not that much ever happens in Crossways, it's just dull really,' said Taylor.

Verity couldn't believe how strung out she felt. She wasn't swaying unsteadily like Taylor, but two pints and no dinner had hit her bloodstream. Even birdsong seemed unnaturally loud. She was glad of the slow pace giving her time to ask herself if she definitely wanted to do this. It was just a garden. Just a shed. But what happened to the Winters cast a long shadow.

'Do we really want to do this? How sensible is it to join a breaking and entering club when two people ended up dead after a burglary that went wrong?' Verity said.

'Yeah, we do. Come on, we're in this together,' said Cal, his fingers reaching and touching Verity's and sending a thrill through her even bigger than his smile.

'You do know this is going to be so disappointing because we are very likely going to find a miniature railway tonight,' Taylor said.

Eliza had said earlier that the way to deal with anxiety was to do the thing you were most afraid of. What was Verity most afraid of? All those evenings home alone with Grandma's lies on the mini-chalkboard and only an annoying owl for company?

'Although what would a chemistry lab even look like?' said Taylor. 'Bunsen burners and all that glass is just in films, right? Guess we'll cross that bridge when we burn it. Did you really get kicked out of university for spying on one of your lecturers?'

'My Grandma is trying to teach me it's rude to be intrusively interested in other people,' said Verity.

'But what did you do at uni exactly?'

'I studied English.'

'No I mean what did you do that got you kicked out?'

'I left. I did not get kicked out.' Everyone had their little secrets. Verity was still trying to keep hers.

'I heard you spied and you got caught. That true? You can tell us. Now you're in the breaking and entering club.'

Was she properly part of a breaking and entering club?

Maybe it was time Verity faced some of the things she was afraid of. Instead of being obsessively interested in people, maybe she should do something else not strong in her skillset – make friends.

'I do like digging. But here I'm digging in the dark. You know Crossways better than me,' Verity said, grabbing Taylor's elbow to help her walk. 'From the outside, what looks like small potatoes looks life or death to people in Crossways. We're breaking into someone's place to answer an entirely irrelevant mini-mystery, except to people in Crossways. You could help me understand.'

'Is that like a weird way of saying you really do think someone's got it in seriously for Eliza?' asked Taylor.

'Partly. But you could tell me about the burglaries.'

'But those burglaries aren't connected to Eliza being injured,' said Cal.

'Again, you sound so sure. I'll tell what happened to me at uni if you tell about the burglaries.'

They were nearing the Crossways Cafe.

'We don't know anything,' said Cal. 'Chainsaw sounds have definitely stopped. After-party's starting.'

Maybe Grandma was a little bit right that being obsessively interested in people was not the best way to move forward in life. This time she felt she was on the inside track, properly part of something, part of Crossways. She hadn't realised how much she needed this. Even though Verity could easily imagine they weren't on their way to investigate a shed so much as she was being lured to her initiation.

Even that wouldn't stop her.

Should breaking into a back garden with a drunk girl scare her? Maybe knowing people had guns did. But leaving without knowing the truth, never knowing just how much Grandma had changed and why? That was what properly scared her. She had to keep digging.

Last time she'd carried out a little investigation, the tables had been turned and she'd ended up being the one most damaged by it all. She should learn that these were the consequences. But once she started, she needed the truth. Whatever the cost.

Eliza had given up so much to come to Crossways and find out the truth. Verity wanted her to have an answer, but not one that meant she had to betray Grandma.

How was this going to end?

'If people don't talk, secrets go deep,' she said. 'I'm beginning to think everyone knows what happened to the Winter couple and it's a huge Crossways secret and that's why no one talks about it. Crossways reminds me of those fungal cordyceps. Pull on one and you never know what it'll be connected to and how far the connections go. So talk about those burglaries.'

'And you'll fess up why you got kicked out?' said Taylor. 'You first.'

'All right. I got curious about why someone in my year was getting such good grades when she didn't work hard or was particularly smart,' Verity shrugged. 'I thought it was the usual, her paying someone to write her essays. Then I noticed she spent a lot of time with one of my lecturers.'

'You suspected he was giving her something other than extra tuition?' said Taylor.

'He was old enough to be her father. Supposedly happily married.'

'You caught them together? And got kicked out for revealing the truth?' asked Cal.

'Sort of. The university wasn't keen I'd used an illegal recording device in his office. Nobody liked the truth. Turned out he was her father—by their cleaner at the family home. Hardly my fault he'd kept it a secret from his wife, including the fact that he'd been paying her mother for years. Sometimes you get an answer you weren't prepared for.'

Taylor nodded. 'What you imagine can sometimes be worse can't it.'

Cal paused outside a narrow, semi-detached home. Party laughter from Isha's filled the evening air.

'Now you expect us to tell you how we know so much about the burglaries?' said Taylor.

'It's important. It might be getting in the way of finding out what really happened to the Winters,' said Verity. 'And I think I might have guessed part of it anyway. Don't be afraid of the truth.'

Cal reached up with one hand over a wooden gate between this cottage and one of the many hairdressing salons in Crossways. He fumbled a little, then came the sound of the bolt being thrown back. He lifted the latch, opened the gate and turned to give a triumphant grin. 'Easy as that! The simplest plans are the best. All clear for Operation Workshop.'

'I've heard the Winters' place was supposed to be empty, but they came back a day early and we all know what happened,' said Verity, as she followed Cal, padding up a short dim paved passage along the side of the house. 'Perhaps it was a terrible accident.'

Taylor stumbled in the sudden dark of the alley. At the end, Cal hesitated.

'Bit late to go all cautious now,' Verity said. 'If you were worried maybe the sensible thing would have been to knock on the front door, make sure they're not in.'

'Actually.' He nodded. 'Great plan. Would you…?'

'How come I am the one with the plans when I am new to the breaking and entering club,' said Verity, rolling her eyes.

She retraced her steps to knock on the red-painted front door, avoiding being clunked in the head with a very colourful but terribly positioned hanging basket.

No answer. Crossways intel was right for once. Margot and David would never know Operation Workshop had ever happened.

As long as they didn't screw up.

Cal was waiting at the end of the alley. Verity sounded the all clear, but Taylor had vanished.

'Where's she staggered off to?' Verity whispered.

Cal wasted no further time stepping into the garden, which was very long. Verity couldn't even see the end as they emerged from the side alley.

'Where even is the shed?'

Near the house was a patio and a narrow regimented bed with geometric edging, sharp corners, a lot of very white gravel and some waxy plants that Verity wasn't even sure were real. Geometric decking was arranged on the diagonal.

'Margot must get through heaps of bleach to keep the gravel white,' said Cal. 'Hey look, I think I've discovered something growing. Imagine having all this space to be a haven for getting things growing, wriggling, buzzing or flowering. Instead, I think these plants are all plastic.'

'The whole effect looks like it was arranged by someone who loves geometry and rules more than flowers. David's science-y influence?' said Verity.

Cal nodded.

All was quiet.

'We can be in and out in a matter of minutes,' said Cal. 'No one's going to know we were here. And even if Margot and David come back early and catch us, we're not doing anything wrong. It's looking inside a shed. Investigating a suspected model railway.'

'As long as we can finally reach the famous shed. My nerves are still jangling,' said Verity.

Cal gave his familiar warm smile and took Verity's hand and gave it a reassuring squeeze. 'Let's do this.'

The only curve in the place was one of those dangling egg chairs by a switched-off grey water feature.

They had hardly taken a dozen steps together out of the shadows when the egg chair started to turn.

They were not alone. There was someone waiting for them in the garden.

The grey hanging chair twirled very slowly towards them and a voice came out of the gathering gloom.

'Come on in. We've been expecting you.'

36

Verity

The egg-chair carried on twirling slowly.

All those rumours that the house was going to be empty were false. Verity could feel her heart pounding and the blood rushing in her ears.

The chair finally turned fully, revealing a smiling Taylor Messenger, stroking fluffy Jackson Brodie on her lap.

'We have been expecting you,' she repeated, 'Mr Bond.' She sprang out of the floating egg chair with a giggle and let Jackson slide to the floor. 'Well you are properly in the breaking and entering club now. Ready?'

'Ready for what exactly?' Verity's spine prickled.

'Do we feed you to the Crossways vampires. Or take your chances in the shark pool? For your initiation.'

Verity knew Taylor was messing with her, or at least, she hoped she was. She hated the way a shiver still involuntarily went down the full length of her spine.

'Taylor…' said Cal in a warning voice.

Taylor put a finger to her lips and talked in a loud whisper as she headed on down the garden, creeping through the shadows at the edge: 'If anyone spots us and asks what we're doing our cover is we say a ball went over the fence.'

'Sure. That might work if we were six,' Verity said. 'Are we checking this out or not?'

She tried to sound calm and in control and strode down the middle of the garden, Jackson Brodie tagging along.

'No one's going to catch us.,' she said. 'That hedge obscures any visibility from the neighbours. That side is a hair and nails salon with an empty back yard and no one there on Saturday night.'

Sounds of Isha's party getting into full swing could be heard. Crossways letting its collective hair down.

'Why live in the countryside and have a place with a huge garden if you hate anything that's actually real?' grumbled Cal treading on a bright green plastic lawn.

'I don't know why everyone doesn't do the same as Isha and sell a bit of their garden to Jaxx and Maya at Halfway.' said Verity. 'Although Margot wouldn't like it. Looks like the hairdressers have done it as they've got the end of their land boarded off the exact same as Isha.'

'Don't you think that's just another Crossways rumour?' said Cal.

'What, that Halfway are buying up gardens to expand? Grandma told me. She said it's a secret and not to tell anyone. So I assumed everyone knew.'

'I've got a proper secret,' said Cal. 'Want me to share?'

'Cal,' said Taylor warningly. 'Anyways, Margot's sandwiched between Isha and the hair salon. She won't sell cos they don't need the cash. So Halfway's got no chance.'

It was a moment of sharpness even after quite so much of the Gunners Gold local ale.

'Yeah, but you're missing the whole point,' said Cal.

'What d'you mean?' said Taylor. 'What whole point?'

'Let's take a look at this infamous workshop,' said Verity. 'And get to the bottom of one rumour tonight.'

A clipped hedge across the far end of the garden obscured a proper view of this shed and the fields beyond. Or potential science lab. Verity was still hoping for an exciting reveal and not a model railway.

'Oh good, someone's decided something actually growing might be nice,' said Cal. 'Nice hedge.'

'You think that's why Margot and David want to move?' suggested Taylor. 'Because they'll come under pressure if everyone else sells. Is that what you mean?'

Cal shook his head, making his hair bounce. 'Look at how far Halfway's up the high street. If Halfway were going to develop rooms all the way down to Isha's, that would be one heck of an expansion, right? Think about it.'

They reached the other side of the hedge and finally found something else ready to grow, presumably over the shed, as there were pots of climbing plants ready to go in where someone had prepared a bed, inexpertly digging down way further than was needed.

'If it's not a model railway, the shed can't be where he stores his lawn mower cos the lawn's plastic,' said Cal.

It was more than a shed. It was a proper garden room, sturdily built, with windows and even a veranda.

Unfortunately Taylor chose that moment to turn to say something and stumbled right into the hole and gave a yelp of pain. They all froze as Taylor rolled in the dirt clutching her ankle.

'I've twisted my ankle!' cried Taylor.

'Yeah I think we got that bit,' said Verity. She helped Taylor to her feet and out of the hole, but looked in dismay at the footprints in the freshly dug earth. 'You've also created enough of a mess it's going to be obvious someone's been here.'

Verity crouched to smooth it over.

Jackson Brodie thought this a great game and nudged at the soft dirt with his paws.

'You are more dog than cat, Jackson,' said Verity, ruffling his ears. 'But you keep on digging cos that's a useful cover, thank you. Good cat.'

Taylor sniggered at her for talking to the cat.

Cal was the first to peer through the windows.

'Why does he even have windows, there's not much of a view?' Taylor said.

'Maybe his secret is bird-watching?' Cal said. 'No one ever guessed bird watching.'

'Is that story actually true about David being minted cos of some science thing he did?' said Verity, squashing in right alongside Cal. His crinkly hair smelled of coffee. And of shortbread. The power of association, because he probably smelled of Waggon and Horses and local ale.

All three squashed together. There was enough light to see into the dim interior and they all peered in.

As Verity's eyes adjusted she could see a comfy chair, a desk and a bookcase.

'No science lab and not even a model railway,' said Cal. 'Typical Crossways. Think this shed is the definition of why it's more fun to speculate than to find out the truth. And now we think birdwatching?'

'It's so disappointing!' complained Taylor. She went to try the door handle and amazingly, it opened. She went in and started pulling books from the bookcase and fiddling with things. 'Maybe we can find out how much David Purkiss made from his science-y thing. I heard millions.'

Verity grudgingly had to admit Taylor was good at this, marching in, taking risks. One option if you're daughter of a headteacher at an elite school is you get a piercing in your eyebrow and your lower lip, a tattoo of a badass fairy on your left wrist and you start a breaking and entering club.

'Binoculars.' Taylor picked up some she found on a shelf and looked through them at Verity.

The smell was wood-resiny, the vibe comfy. Verity doubted they'd even find anything here to satisfy Grandma's curiosity about how much David made from that science spin-off. Jackson Brodie followed them, trailing specks of mud from his paws.

'Ok coming in wasn't such a smart move,' Verity said.

'We can leave the door open when we go so it looks like Jackson got in here by himself?' suggested Cal.

'Jackson is asking what are we all doing in this dull shed,' said Taylor, training the binoculars on the cat as Jackson started up his very loud purring. 'Which is a good question. Seen enough? Let's go.'

'Well maybe,' said Verity. 'Although now I am officially in the breaking-in club, wasn't there something about those burglaries four years ago you promised to tell me?'

37

Verity

Taylor perched half her bum on the desk and shared an intimate glance with Cal that spoke of closeness and secrets shared.

Verity rubbed Jackson under his chin. 'I told you the truth about why I got kicked out of uni and ended up with a summer of shame in Crossways. You promised to spill your secrets. So…'

'Should we tell her something?' Taylor looked at Cal.

'Yes, you definitely should,' said Verity. 'The case of Who Shot Jackson Brodie is solved: Isha mistook him for a rabbit. The Mystery of David Purkiss' Shed is solved: comfy birdwatching and reading hideout. Even though we still don't know how much he made from that science business spin-off. Taylor, you said I should go for the big one. It's only when people speak out that these things get solved. What do you two know about the Crossways Killings, let's say, starting with the burglaries?'

'I can let you in on one Crossways secret,' said Cal. 'If you like.'

'We like,' said Taylor.

Verity held her breath and tried to pick up the trail of mud crumbs left by Jackson with her fingers.

'I pointed it out earlier and neither of you worked it out. It's so obvious,' said Cal.

'I guess you don't mean you know who did the Crossways Killings?' said Verity.

'Stop being annoying and tell us,' said Taylor, punching Cal on the arm. 'What is it?'

'It's Verity's fault,' smiled Cal. 'She got me asking Benj questions. It was about his plans to expand and getting Eliza out. But that wasn't what he couldn't resist showing off about. He made me promise not to tell anyone.'

'That's all right, then,' said Taylor. 'We're not anyone.'

'No, but I mean, if you guess his secret, then it's not telling you is it?'

'Give us another clue,' said Verity.

'Ok. Think about it. Halfway's way up the street from Isha's. Why start with Isha's? They'd have to buy up loads of gardens to expand all the way down there.'

'Benj is buying up the gardens?' said Verity.

'You got it!'

'He's waiting for Eliza to finish her lease, then he'll have Eliza's shop, Isha's next door,' said Verity. 'And he's got the hairdresser next to Margot, and Margot and David want to leave. So he's got almost everyone.

'He showed off how easy it was to get the story put about that it's Halfway buying up the gardens. But you only have to think about it a second to realise it must be Benj. Halfway's too far away. And there's more. He got Isha to sell by lying he wants to expand the cafe and put in lodges or pods or something. His secret plan is a big one. He's going to build proper houses.'

'Well the pitchforks would be out if anyone knew that,' said Taylor. 'No wonder he kept that a secret.'

Taylor was still fiddling with everything. 'Oh!' She'd opened a drawer in the desk, now she took out a laptop and opened it. It flickered into life, not even password protected. She tapped at the keyboard, recovering the most recently used files.

'Well I wasn't expecting that! Do you want to know what David Purkiss's big secret really is?'

'Go for it,' said Verity. Hope it's something big.'

She and Cal edged in closer.

Taylor had opened up a document. They were looking at the title page. *The First Husband by Royston Millward.*

'David Purkiss is writing a novel?' said Cal. 'Is that his secret?'

'He's not just writing it. It's over a hundred thousand words. He's finished it. And he's chosen his pseudonym. Reckon this is the sneaky reason he and Margot disappear so often on all these mini-breaks? Secret publisher meetings.'

'Well they both say they hate visiting houses and gardens and blame the other for dragging them around,' said Verity.

'You are pretty good at spotting things, aren't you,' said Taylor.

'You two are very good too at finding things out. Do you always do it by breaking in?' said Verity. 'Now I've joined the club and I have as much to lose as you, I think it's time you tell me exactly what this club gets up to. Or got up to.'

Taylor started biting the skin around her nails, her face suddenly very anxious and very young. 'You know, don't you?'

'It wasn't exactly difficult to work it out,' replied Verity.

'We did those break-ins,' Taylor blurted out.

38

Verity

'They weren't break-ins, not really,' said Taylor. 'More… Dares.' She shared a glance with Cal.

'It did just sort of happen,' said Cal.

'We went to people's houses we knew were on holiday to look in their windows and make fun of stuff they had. We'd say what we'd bin,' explained Taylor. 'Not to break in. We dared each other to go into their back gardens and eat crisps there. We were bored.'

'Taylor dared me to try this back door—and it opened and we just looked at each other. And then she dared me and we were in, inside someone's house. It really was that easy,' says Cal.

'It wasn't breaking in,' said Taylor. 'Not even a little bit.'

'But thrilling,' said Verity. 'I bet it gave you a real rush. When did you start nicking things?'

Again that secretive look passed between them.

'It was just so ridiculously easy to get in,' said Taylor, chewing her nails even more. 'We got good at spotting when no one was in, not just on holiday. It was summer. People left windows open. I dared Cal to go in through a window.

I laughed at this hideous ornament of a pig. I dared him to pinch it.'

'We pinched just silly stuff. People didn't even seem to notice,' said Cal. 'Well, not at first.'

'Then the police got involved,' said Verity. She was definitely being initiated into a Crossways cult now.

Was this the real reason why Cal was known as the teenage tearaway? And why there was a frosty relationship between Belinda Messenger and Mrs Kinsky.

She'd worked out it was very likely the two bored teenagers. It wasn't much of a stretch to think others had reached the conclusion too. Was that why the burglary theory was always dismissed as 'just kids'.

Did that mean *everyone* knew the burglaries were Cal and Taylor? And did it explain a lot more?

Like why, in gossipy Crossways, everyone was so reluctant to share info that might track down what really happened that night when two people died and the police blamed it on burglars?

'We did it a few times and we thought someone would come after us,' said Taylor. 'But no one did.'

'Sometimes people had cash just sitting there,' said Cal. He looks guilty about it. 'I know we pushed it too far.'

'One finally got reported to the police,' said Taylor.

The really, really big question was if this confession was leading to them admitting to the shooting dead of two people. Had that also 'just happened'?

'And then one time,' Verity said carefully. 'The surprise was on you. They weren't supposed to be there… right? You got it wrong and the house wasn't empty.'

Cal and Taylor could not have looked more shocked.

'You think—' flapped Taylor, 'we broke into that house where those two people were killed? You think that was us?'

'Well did you?'

'No!' said Taylor.

'They were wealthy and the house was supposed to be empty? Must have been tempting,' said Verity.

'Empty? No chance. There were always people doing decorating and stuff.' said Cal. 'And Grant was always over, fussing, checking on things.'

Verity could understand that no one wanted to drop Taylor and Cal in it about the burglaries, not when the police were trying to connect the burglaries to a murder. So everyone had just kept quiet. No one had talked about what had really happened.

'You think we had a gun?' said Taylor. 'We never had a gun.'

'Stealing a gun would be the ultimate dare,' said Verity. 'If there was a break-in where you happened on a gun. Pretty likely in Crossways.'

'That's not what happened!' Taylor sounded outraged, but then she became tearful.

'That's not why we didn't say anything,' said Cal, putting an arm around her. 'We were scared that's all. When everyone said it was a burglary gone wrong we thought the police might start really looking for who did those stupid little burglaries. So we kept quiet.'

'It all went away. But it's all being brought up again, isn't it,' said Taylor, biting the skin around her fingernails.

'Guys I hate to be the one to break this to you,' said Verity. 'But there have literally never been any leads. It's been labelled an impossible crime. Crossways closed ranks, didn't really help the police. I think they were scared they'd say the wrong thing and drop you in it. With no one talking, people are more likely to have thought you were involved. Maybe it's not me you need to be coming clean to.'

'No,' said Taylor, 'You can't be serious—No one could've thought we killed that couple.'

'I've been here four weeks. If I worked out you two were the ones breaking into places when people were on holiday—everyone knows. What about your parents?'

'You mean, did we fess up to them?' asked Taylor.

'Well. Ever thought why even your mum, the supposed true-crime fan, never seemed at all interested in solving the biggest Crossways mystery?'

'I guess…' said Cal as he digested this idea. 'I guess… Taylor do you think—'

'No!' said Taylor.

'I can imagine you were terrified and why you never went to the police to own up,' said Verity. 'But there's always been a silence around the whole thing.'

'Us not coming clean is not the reason no one was ever caught for those murders.' Taylor bent to stroke the cat, not looking at anyone.

'But these things get solved because people talk. You get one small thing worth following up. Maybe it's time to say something,' said Verity. 'Maybe to Keera and Liv, because Elliott's in the police. Or Mitch.'

Getting them to talk to the police was the right thing to do, even though Taylor looked terrified.

And Verity was terrified too. This evening she might have solved another couple of mini-mysteries. But there was little satisfaction, not when it still left the big one.

It was just another avenue closed off. Another theory that had led to a dead end.

She was no nearer finding any answers that were not, inexorably, going to end up pointing a finger at Grandma.

39

Keera

The last person I want to see hanging about outside my shop before I've even opened up is Elliott Trent. What's he going to lecture me about this time?

'You are super keen to top up your TBR pile,' I say cheerily falling back on my go-to safe subject of books, while unlocking the door, all the while assuming he's here to tell me off about something.

'TBR?' repeats Elliott.

'To Be Read. You know, how sometimes there's a book we mean to read, but a more interesting one comes along and before you know it, you have a pile. That new-book smell is always strongest in the mornings. Do you sometimes feel it's because the books sleep and they wake up when you come in?' I say as Elliott follows me into my sleepy little shop. I've no idea why I always blather on when Elliott's around.

'If you asked Verity, she'd recite all the chemical compounds that create the smell. What's in the printing inks and paper. She said you can even tell the age of a book by the chemicals in it. Mitch said she knows more chemistry than David Purkiss and he won an award. But she knows all of this because she's the sort of girl who goes and looks it up.'

'I'm not here to buy a book,' says Elliott. 'I'm here bringing bad news.'

'Two bits of bad news then.'

'Sorry?'

'Well the fact that you're not here to buy a book is in itself bad news—when you are a bookseller, you know.' I tell myself to shut up, annoyed I'm so twittery with Elliott.

I put out my chalkboard onto the pavement and switch on lights. ' What's the other bad news?'

'Can I put the kettle on?' says Elliott.

I throw him a sharp look. 'You've never offered before. What sort of bad news?' Into my head pops the worst answer. Liv. But it can't be that anything's happened to Liv. He'd be in pieces.

He's already disappeared into my cramped back office. I hear him filling the kettle, starting a hunt for clean mugs.

'Check the milk's ok, because the fridge definitely isn't.'

Has something else happened with Eliza? I'd arrived at work glad to see everything was quiet. Apart from Elliott lurking. Eliza returned last night and was presented with the garden project and a celebratory glass of sour but strong gooseberry wine. Then I slipped away, tired.

There's only one time police officers offer to make tea and it's not because a lot of Crossways people might have sore heads this morning.

'Who died?'

Elliott's always adamant he cannot possibly discuss police business. But he's come here when something bad's happened. What's going on?

Elliott brings through tea and steers me towards the comfy reading chair.

'I'm not fragile or your ancient aunt. I have to get the shop ready. I have work to do. Just tell me. And then I think it might be time for you to talk to Benj. I believe there's be a final missing piece that connects someone in Crossways to the Winters. People are always careful what they say in official police statements and leave half of it out. You need to talk to him properly. He's the only other person, apart from Grant, who spoke to the dead couple. And Grant was interviewed properly, plus he's a terrible gossip and he was a suspect. So if he knew anything he wouldn't have kept it to himself. Benj is the opposite.'

'I can't talk to Benj.'

I sigh. 'I'm not asking for an official reopening, but honestly, Benj knows something. And I've been trying to get Eliza to make an official complaint against him because everyone thinks he's got it in for Eliza. If everyone thinks someone's responsible for something, they usually are.'

'He got knocked off his bike.'

'Oh no! That's terrible. He's hurt? That's why you can't talk to him? That's why you're here? How badly?'

Elliott's hesitating.

'How serious? Will he be all right?'

'Keera I'm really sorry to have to tell you Benj Beresford's dead.'

40

Keera

'How can Benj be dead? How can Benj get knocked off his bike and die? I can't take it in. I saw him yesterday evening.'

I sink into my cosy reading chair, blowing steam from my tea, holding the mug in both hands. 'What happened?'

'We don't know exactly. A tractor driver saw a mangled bike in a ditch in the early hours. Sadly Benj was dead at the scene. A hit and run,' says Elliott gently.

'Someone didn't stop after they hit him? That's awful. And Crossways is pretty much off-grid as far as CCTV goes, so how will you get who did it? Don't say this'll go the way of being another impossible Crossways crime.'

'We'll put out an appeal. Eyewitnesses may come forward.'

'Yeah well we both know the chances of that.'

'Let's not give up hope yet.'

'Someone knocked him off his bike and left him. You know what that is.'

'We haven't—'

'That's murder, Elliott. You can't let someone get away with this. What about tracing a damaged car?'

'We will do what we can. Honestly, Keera.'

'I'm not being rude or anything, but official channels never solved the Crossways Killings. Sometimes it really is more about listening to the community. Seeing as Benj is dead, it can't do any harm to tell me much scrutiny he came under. You can tell me everything he says in his police statement.'

'Not happening. You need to listen to me when I say you need to stop. This proves all my warnings are right. Stirring things up is dangerous.'

'You're not getting away with a lecture. It's not people talking about it again that's the problem. It's the fact it was never resolved in the first place. Leaving things festering.'

'Was he your number one for being the Crossways Killer?' Elliott asks.

I hesitate. Was he? I haven't even started to process what Benj's death means.

'He was my number one for being someone who never came under enough scrutiny. But all right, yes, probably. But now he's been killed, where does that leave us?'

Elliott draws a hand through his short, sandy hair. 'Someone sitting around in a car, following Benj Beresford until there was no one around and running him off the road. It seems an unlikely murder.'

'That's where you're wrong. It's not unlikely at all. Half the people in Crossways probably knew or could find out when he went out, even his route, which was along deserted country roads. And sorry, but if he was hit hard enough to die from his injuries and then someone left the scene… you cannot possibly be buying that as an accident.'

But where does that leave the attacks on Eliza? And, well, everything, really.

My thoughts are interrupted by an urgent rapping on the front door. I don't think it's a customer in dire need of an emergency book.

'Liv! You are up and about early for a Sunday,' I say, unlocking the door.

Liv Trent arrives in a waft of Dior and barely-contained excitement. 'Have you heard... Oh!' She stops when she sees me and Elliott sitting in the shop first thing in the morning before I've even opened, drinking tea.

'This is very cosy,' Liv says. 'I just wanted to—'

'Talk about Benj's hit and run, yes. But how have you heard about it already?'

Jackson Brodie follows her in, both of them walk in as if they own the place. Jackson trailing mud rather than expensive perfume.

'Elliott wants to hang onto the belief it was an accident. He won't even tell me if Benj was a suspect in the Crossways Killings, so I'm having difficulty processing why someone would want to run him off the road. Tea?'

'But you do have a nasty suspicious mind,' Liv says. 'So I'm sure you'll come up with something. Green if you've got it. I'm not risking your milk.'

I find food for Jackson and fuss his ears while my ancient kettle gives a wheezy objection to being so busy so early on a Sunday.

'Eliza was very reluctant to report the incidents against her to the police. People really need to get talking. Should we start with her? Eliza's got a lot of secrets.'

'Well one of them isn't that she drove Benj off the road last night,' says Liv. 'She was at Isha's party. We all were.'

'No one knows what time it happened,' I say. 'And if everyone was on Isha's gooseberry wine I bet no one can swear who was there, not all evening.'

'Eliza's only got a small car,' says Liv.

'Coincidentally, last night was the first time she'd felt up to driving since her accident,' I say.

'I thought you didn't believe in coincidence.'

'I don't. Not as a rule.'

I check my store of biscuits. Do I have enough biscuits to offer around or should I just keep them for myself?

Liv goes to the window. 'Her car's always sandwiched alongside Grant Michaels' SUV and that four-by-four. Oh. Eliza's small car isn't there. Didn't Benj say Eliza had only take a year's lease on her shop. Was that true?'

'I never got around to checking,' I admit.

'It's not like you to be slow.'

'I can remember the number plate of the four-by-four.'

'I can check any cars you want me to,' says Elliott. 'But do you think Eliza's capable of running someone off the road?'

'Who knows what people can be driven to,' I say. 'Those nasty incidents were getting to Eliza, even though she put a brave face on it.'

'There's a big leap to saying she saw Benj out cycling, a red mist descended, she cracked and she ran him off the road, not so much as looking back,' says Liv.

'True. And we weren't sure it was all Benj. We have to look at everything again now someone rammed Benj off his bike,' I say. 'Someone also shot two people four years ago. I suppose the question has to be whether there's a connection between those deaths. And if those attacks on Eliza are connected. And how it all fits together, exactly.'

We both look at Elliott, who shuffles and makes noises about going.

'I'll put the kettle on again, because you're not leaving without sharing some thoughts. You were kind enough to break the news in person. And your thoughts are always worth hearing. Well, most of them. So what are you going to do next?'

'Sorry to mess with your lovely conspiracy theories. But my thoughts are it most probably was an accident,' says Elliott.

'You'd know if you hit a cyclist. Why wouldn't you stop?' I say. 'Has to be deliberate.'

'The Winters could have been killed by someone following them from the airport,' says Liv. 'But no one believes that either. Didn't we agree ages ago that if we knew the motive for the Crossways Killings we could easily work out who did it. I cannot believe we are still so deep in the dark. It was an impossible crime because there was no motive. Maybe we start with the motive for killing Benj? And what about the motive for the attacks on Eliza? If we start with the assumption it's all connected.'

'I'm not following your logic,' says Elliott. 'If Benj wasn't behind the attacks on Eliza, what, she did the attacks on herself? To get sympathy and support?'

'Now there's some wild thinking and strong imagination you don't show us often enough,' I say.

'Quit the sarcasm,' says Liv. 'What this case needs is a breakthrough. There's still too much we don't know. I'd say the most likely motive for Benj's death might be revenge. Revenge is always a good one. Or cover-up? Covering tracks always gets messy. It can end with a trail of bodies.'

'What this case needs is for Elliott to tell us what Benj told the police at the time,' I say. 'I have found three

Hobnobs from the packet Liv brought and mysteriously disappeared and one bourbon. Elliott, you get first pick if you tell us what Benj said in his original witness statement.'

'You have to tell us,' says Liv. 'Benj was one of only two people in Crossways who spoke to the Winters. The deaths of three people, four years apart, Benj has to be connected. It was an impossible crime because the police failed to find a connection the first time. We're still missing that connection. We have to work together, because how can we be no closer to knowing who is doing this? They must be laughing at us running rings and getting nowhere. And a murderer thinking they are invincible…'

Elliott has resisted my offer of biscuits. I take this as a bad sign.

'You told us insider info about the gun,' I remind him. 'Or at least dropped hints. Please feel free to drop more.'

Elliott says nothing. So I turn to Liv.

'This case! So much people are keeping secret, how do we know what's important? Is it best to think things are connected, or does that just confuse things?'

'Who are you planning on interrogating next?' asks Liv.

'Grant Michaels is always a good place to start.'

'True. He can at least confirm if Benj was telling the truth about Eliza and then I guess someone other than Benj must be behind the attacks?' says Liv. 'That would help.'

'There are others I want to talk to,' I say.

'Are you just ignoring that I keep telling you not to, that this is dangerous. Even though someone's now died?' says Elliott.

'Yes, all of that.'

'Verity,' says Liv. 'Have you noticed our Verity's been

spending a lot of time lately with Belinda, Isha and Margot? I wonder what they're getting Verity involved in. Something her grandmother won't like.'

'If Elliott's refusing to pool resources—'

'Elliott is,' says Elliott.

'You've resisted being bribed by tea and biscuits and that's on you,' I say. 'But you've made a mistake if you think you're leaving. The door's locked. Please don't make me tie you to a chair and wave a gun around. And let's skip another lecture that it's dangerous doing this at all. But you have to tell us something.'

I'm pleased to see Elliott closes his mouth. I hope he's rethinking what he was about to say.

'All right,' said Elliott. 'I have read Benj's statement. 'You were spot on that people are careful what they say in their statements. People may not realise they hold a significant piece of information, because they don't know it's significant. But I can confirm there was really nothing in it.'

'Another dead end? So why did you take so long to tell us nothing?' asks Liv. 'At this rate the worst case scenario comes true. The Crossways Killings get stirred up again, still no answers, but we have one more death.'

'Someone local drove Benj off the road,' I say. 'Someone badly needed to stop Benj doing something. Elliott's right I was going to talk to him again. Mitch talked to him. He was one of only two people who spoke to the Winters. If he knew something, someone made sure he's not talking. If someone's covering their tracks and they keep getting away with it, I'd say the worst case scenario is the Crossways Killer is going to do it again. So the very last thing we have to do is to give up now.'

41

Verity

'Have you heard?' Eliza asked the second Verity arrived at work. 'Benj Beresford got killed last night in a hit and run.'

It was impossible to take in. Verity had such a careful plan. She'd get Eliza talking, find a way to get her to admit she was Carrie Winter's daughter, here in Crossways looking for answers. Find out just how much danger Grandma was in.

But now Benj Beresford was dead. Run off the road and it was impossible to see how it fitted in with anything.

And the day instantly kicked off busy with customers.

Verity tried to focus on serving up portions of salads and olives, all she could think was last night Benj had been killed. And Grandma had been missing again.

Verity was glad she'd snatched Grandma's hoodie from the hatstand in the hall. About the only thing she could think of doing to buy more time was to get rid of that hoodie before Mitch Ravenscroft demanded the video footage. Verity had shoved the hoodie in the bottom of a small rucksack, but had no idea exactly what she was going to do with it. And she suspected any second now Bookgroup Investigates would pounce and she had no idea what to make of anything. Verity kept making mistakes.

She charged someone's credit card for a hundred times the cost of an already expensive jar of tapenade. Eliza gave a profuse apology and an instant refund and insisted Verity take a break.

Now was her chance to at least dispose of the hoodie.

But sure enough, Verity was hardly out of the shop and heading for one of the many footpaths that led from Crossways high street and perfect for disposing of an incriminating hoodie, when Belinda and Isha pounced.

'Benj was knocked off his bike on a country road,' said Isha. 'How are they ever going to catch anyone for that? What's going on? Why do these horrible things keep happening in lovely Crossways? And Benj was behind those attacks on Eliza, wasn't he?'

'Eliza can't drive at the moment,' said Belinda.

Isha turned to her in shock. 'I didn't mean that! Eliza couldn't have got mad enough for *that*.'

'I don't quite know how to say this,' Verity said. 'But Eliza went for a drive last night.'

This was about the only plan open to her. Muddy the waters. Take any chance to create any little diversion. Stop anyone suspecting Grandma could possibly be involved in any of it.

Even if Grandma has killed two people? Or three now, a small voice inside her questioned. She really needed a chance to talk to Grandma. *And what then? Whose side are you on?*

A breathless Margot Latimer scurried up to them.

'I thought you were away on one of your minibreaks, visiting another house and garden,' said Belinda.

'We were, but thanks to Isha, who messaged with the news,' said Margot, struggling to catch her breath. 'We rushed back so as not to miss anything. What's happening?'

'Nothing you needed to rush back for,' said Belinda silkily. 'Although Verity has just said something interesting. Guess who was out driving last night? First time in a while.'

'But we can't be thinking *Eliza* was driving the car that hit Benj,' said Margot. 'And anyway, surely it was an accident. Even though it's been so distressing for Eliza. I'm sure if she was out driving and saw Benj on his bike there's no way she'd have taken her revenge and hit him.'

'You think it's just a coincidence?' said Verity.

'It has to be,' said Isha. 'Doesn't it?'

'Or someone with a very strong motive for running Benj off the road,' said Belinda.

Cal had told Verity something very interesting last night. Now was a perfect time to use it; something that would get fingers pointing anywhere other than Grandma.

'Actually,' Verity coughed and three faces turned to her expectantly. 'There are plenty of people who I can imagine wanting to dump Benj off the road… anyone who'd discovered his secret.'

'Other than his war with Eliza?' said Isha. 'Although we don't know for sure that was him.'

'Well who else?' said Margot.

'What secret?' asked Belinda.

'A secret that would have changed Crossways and would have been deeply unpopular,' said Verity. 'I found out what Benj was really up to.'

'What do you mean, what he was really up to?' asked Isha, who started scratching uncomfortably under her beanie hat.

'Well Isha, I think you might be in the best position to explain,' said Verity coolly.

'What does Verity mean?' asked Margot.

'I'm not sure I know what she's talking about,' said Isha.

'What about all those rumours about Halfway wanting to expand?' said Verity. 'Weren't they put about to cover up that Benj was the one buying up gardens? He wanted to disguise what he was really doing, said he just wanted to expand his cafe. He lied to everyone, because he was buying quietly to sell to a housing developer. And Isha's not the only one who'd already sold the end of her garden.'

'That can't be true,' wailed Margot. 'Our lovely village!'

Isha flushed a brick red under her beanie hat.

Margot rounded on her. 'Isha, you wouldn't! Crossways will soon be under a sea of houses. And you were the first to grab at the chance to cash in? Even if it meant spoiling Crossways forever. You've sold out? You… you traitor!'

'Benj never said any of that…' said Isha.

'And I suppose you're going to tell me it's none of my business that you keep going to see Grant Michaels?' spluttered Margot. 'You've sold out, cashed in and now you're leaving, dropping us all in a mess for us to deal with.'

'That's not true,' said Isha stiffly. 'And you can't tell me you're not even thinking of cashing in, selling your garden and leaving? Or would have done. If Benj hadn't died.'

'Let's not fall out,' said Belinda smoothly. 'It can be tempting when there's a lot of cash on the table. If other people are caving in it can be difficult to resist. There are rumours you're hatching a plan to leave too, Margot.'

'I am not selling to a property developer!' said Margot.

Bookgroup Investigates were very much falling out.

Muddying the waters, getting everyone pointing the finger at everyone else, this was exactly what Verity had to do. She was running out of time to warn Grandma.

Verity slipped away, congratulating herself that she'd done a very good job of distracting any attention from Grandma. Next step was to warn her. More than that, confront Grandma, face to face. She needed to look into her calm, grey eyes. It was the only way she'd feel sure she'd know if Grandma was telling the truth about anything.

But first, she had to find her.

42

Keera

'Grant Michaels has just pulled up in his favourite space right outside Crossways Estates in his expensive motor,' says Liv, staring out the window of Between the Lines in a lull between customers, or browsers today. Not many sales.

Not much through the till beyond a couple of board books. Dire for a Sunday, which is often my second busiest day. I put it down to it being so unseasonably hot. Amazing what a profound effect the weather has on sales. I imagine people are sitting outside or doing the river walk, just in case this isn't so much a spring bonus as our summer. But it's given me plenty of time to think. Unravelling.

'I should go and talk to Grant Michaels,' I say.

'Please take the cat with you. I can't face the way he looks at me if I refuse to give him any more food.'

I find Grant sitting alone at his desk, ready to tuck into a thin sandwich. Jackson Brodie's with me and leaps onto the desk in a loud-miaow greeting and shedding fur.

Grant rubs him under the chin. 'If Jackson Brodie could talk, we'd solve all the mysteries of Crossways.'

'You also get in everywhere, Grant. Exactly like a cat.'

Grant chuckles at this. 'I do! I get into everyone's houses, don't I? But I don't know who shot him. Maybe he's a cat who knows too much and that's why someone shot him?' Grant grins. 'We should learn to speak cat.'

Jackson miaows.

'The rumour going around is Isha shot him.'

'Isha!' Grant chuckles, turning his attention to peeling a tangerine. 'Typical Crossways rumour. Utterly wrong!'

'You sound very sure.'

The air-conditioning unit's whirring white noise again. The air's momentarily full of citrus.

'Isha has difficulty hurting so much as a slug, unlike her father,' says Grant. 'He was ruthless about protecting his vegetables.'

'It wasn't just slugs with him. He shot things. Someone told me shooting feral cats isn't even illegal. Isha looked pretty lethal with that chainsaw.'

Grant chuckles some more. 'The fiercest thing about Isha is that gooseberry wine she makes. Feels like you've been hit over the head. She has a beautiful soul. Have you read her poetry?'

'Maybe more people should write poetry than use guns. Plenty of people around here do have a gun. How many would shoot a cat?' I ask.

'You're saying if we could work out who's cruel enough to take a shot at a cat, we might be closer to answering a lot of questions? Closer to working out who's ruthless enough to ram Benj Beresford off his bike? Or capable of shooting two people.'

'I'd like to get closer to answering a few secrets, and you always know more than you're telling. Being in Eliza and

Isha's gardens last night made me see a few things. Like it's nonsense about Jaxx and Maya buying up gardens. Halfway's the wrong end of the high street. It was Benj buying up gardens. You were helping. You helped him probably because you felt bad about Eliza getting that property he wanted? But why did you help Eliza? I think it's time you told the whole story.' I take a seat.

Grant takes off his glasses to polish them. 'I do like to feel I'm helping. I helped the Winters when they wanted to move here. But that made me feel…'

'Responsible? But Grant, the only person responsible is whoever shot them.'

Grant gave his narrow shoulders a shake. 'They'd still be alive if I hadn't helped them to move here.'

'You couldn't possibly have known what would happen.'

'Then Eliza had that horrible accident. Of course we were all delighted when Ashley secretly smuggled in Verity. Who would have thought it was Benj who needed some sort of guardian angel?'

There's a lot here I need to unravel. Jackson Brodie's nosing in a bin.

'Ashley smuggled in Verity because Eliza needed a guardian angel? You went out of your way to help Eliza. Because you knew she might be in danger? You guessed her accident was no accident.'

'Ashley mentioned she didn't know what to do about her granddaughter. I do what I can for Eliza, of course. I try to drop in most days. Not nearly enough. I didn't want her to do it.'

'Do what? Let's park the thought of Verity being a guardian angel for a moment. What's Eliza really doing here? It was never Benj attacking her was it? She's only on a short lease and will be out within a year.'

'You are very observant, Keera. It's not only me who has to lie and keep secrets. You convinced me you were thinking of buying in Crossways,' Grant counters.

'That wasn't a lie. I think about it all the time. You can't stop me dreaming. I've considered a hammock in the shop. That might be my only hope. I don't need to check my finances to know it's my horrible flat for me. Unless you work some of your property magic?'

'I will see what I can do, of course.'

Jackson Brodie miaows loudly and Grant gets up to shake a bit of dry cat food into a bowl. He looks grateful for the distraction. 'Is he a Six Dinner Sid? If everyone feeds him, why isn't he the size of an elephant?' He bends to pet the cat who purrs without stopping his munching.

'It's time for people to stop keeping things to themselves and start talking. So I'm starting with you, Grant. Crossways has taught me how secrets start to take on a life of their own, even the ones that feel bland and unimportant. But the bland unimportant ones get in the way. Now Benj is dead. No one thinks that's an accident.'

'I didn't want to help Benj with his subterfuge,' says Grant. 'But I was pretty certain of Margot and David holding out. But I think I got that wrong. Verity described Crossways as a cult, but honestly, people like it here.'

'Despite the deaths. But before we get onto those…'

'Isha needed money to finish her renovations.'

Is he going to say he knows Isha was desperate enough for cash she robbed the Winters, thinking it was an empty house? All the time it really was a burglary gone wrong?

'Isha refused point blank to let me loan her the money,' says Grant. 'Selling part of the garden was a way to convince Isha to stay. And it got me back in Benj's good books. I try to help everyone.'

'The reason you went so far to help Isha… the reason you know Isha so well you're certain she didn't shoot Jackson Brodie, even in an accident…'

'Ah. Well yes. I was all for telling people and not keeping it a secret, but Isha wanted to wait until my divorce comes through.' Grant gives Jackson a final pat, sits back down, removes his glasses and polishes them. 'I know you are very sharp, Keera, but I'd appreciate it if the news isn't all around Crossways by noon. Isha seems to think if my wife finds out there will be consequences.'

'So you and Isha are…?'

'I loved Isha even when we were at school together. She went off abroad, I missed my chance, should have had the courage to speak up, but never thought she'd be interested in me. Her dad got sick, she came back. It still took me far too long, but somehow I found the courage to ask if she'd make a go of it with me. I've always been lucky I guess. This business that I love and now the love of my life has come back to me. I must have done something right.'

Jackson Brodie finishes his snack and leaps up onto Grant's desk for a bit of fuss.

'That's the thing with life, it never turns out as you think. Not knowing how our own story will end keeps me going. Take me and Isha. But that poor couple.' His shoulders slump and he strokes the cat.

'When I worked out last night you must have been helping Benj buy up the gardens, it made me go over everything again, making sure I wasn't being distracted by the gossip to look the wrong way. It was only this morning I worked out what brought Eliza here and why you're helping her. And why someone might want to make her feel very unwelcome here. Mitch's chapter mentions Carrie Winter had a daughter by her first marriage.'

'That's not my secret to tell,' Grant says.

'But all these secrets obscure my chance of getting at the truth. I need to unravel which secrets are important and which are getting in the way. Then I'll know which are the right questions to confront people with. And I'll be able to find the right answers. Finally. Or I could say voila! Or I could if I was Liv. Thanks Grant. Now I'm off to confront Eliza.'

43

Verity

She should go back, help Eliza. She couldn't risk trying to dispose of the hoodie, not with a chance Bookgroup Investigates would come breathing down her neck.

She should return with coffee. No chance of Cal and receiving an illicit broken shortbread today. Crossways Cafe was closed. Verity headed for Halfway, but wished she hadn't when she saw Taylor catching an early vape break, puffing out a cloud of sweet-smelling smoke and heading for a quiet place in the car park.

Verity wasn't in the mood for chatting to Taylor, but the girl knew a lot. Grandma's friends had no clue why Grandma kept doing a vanishing act or where she went. Grandma must definitely be avoiding Verity, because the lies on the mini-chalkboard on the fridge kept changing. So Grandma must be popping home.

To get answers it wasn't just asking the right questions, you had to ask the right people. So she followed Taylor towards the low building out back where they roomed overnight guests. Taylor was slouching near the bin-store.

'I'm looking for Grandma. Do you know where she is?'

Instead of answering, Taylor slouched over to one of the guest rooms and knocked on the door. Verity thought she was ignoring her, especially when Taylor called through the door, presumably to the guest inside.

'It's super busy this morning, what with the Crossways being closed'n'all. If you want breakfast in your room again, order soon all right. Or you'll have a long wait.'

The door opened.

Seeing Grandma's head emerge from a room in Halfway was so unexpected, Verity couldn't move, except to widen her eyes in shock. Why was Grandma in a hotel room? Her mind was flooded with questions.

'Thank you Taylor, but I think we may come to the cafe for breakfast,' said Grandma, who was wearing a relaxed vibrant orange summer dress and a big, dreamy smile, her hair was all neatly brushed, orange lipstick in place. She turned to look behind her. 'Yes, we're coming to the cafe.'

We? Who was Grandma speaking to?

Grandma left the room, followed by someone else who Verity knew. Another surprise.

Taylor Messenger sidled up to Verity, one eye closed against a cloud of sweet-smelling vape. 'They're up earlier than I expected. But the big news is it looks like they're coming out in public.' She raised her eyebrows and drew deep on the vape. 'Big step.'

'What's Grandma doing here with Mitch Ravenscroft?' asked Verity. He couldn't be helping her with her obscure chemistry book. 'Is she showing Mitch a secret crime novel?' Verity wondered aloud.

Taylor's eyebrows went up another inch. 'Don't think it's a crime novel she's showing him. From your face I'm reckoning this is news? To be fair they've been working hard to keep it a secret. Guess if they're happy to be seen breakfasting together it'll be all round Crossways before noon.'

'But what are they doing here?'

'At Halfway? Feeling hungry I guess. Or the usual. They gave Mitch a discount to stay after his talk and that includes breakfast and they may as well make the most of it. Halfway do a decent breakfast,' Taylor said sideways out of the corner of her mouth as she released the vape slowly. 'Guess they stayed after the garden party as well. He lives over past Lindford, but he's become quite attached to Crossways.' She quirked an eyebrow and puffed nicotine heavy cloud through her nostrils. 'Or just attached to your Grandma? The main reason people get a hotel room is because they want to get naked and do rude things to each other.'

'Thank you. She is my grandma.'

Verity prided herself on being observant. How had she missed this? Then she remembered Grandma looking a little flirty with Mitch when she surprisingly attended the crime-fiction writing workshop. But Verity had never thought Grandma would actually…

All those times Verity was making her own sad breakfast, or eating a lonely pop and ping lasagne, haunted by owls and creeped out by loathsome countryside sounds. All those times Verity was staring at the mini chalkboard on the fridge. All that worrying. Grandma had never been going to golf lessons, or YogaGals, or spending the evenings entertaining visiting dignitaries. It was all a cover-up. Grandma should just have left the same message every day: *Off having an affair with Mitch Ravenscroft you are totally on your own this summer x*

What a worryingly convincing liar Grandma was.

Was Mitch Ravenscroft's motivation for running all these workshops and events and being in Crossways less to do with being obsessed with solving the Winters murders and more because he was obsessed with being close to Grandma? And unless Verity was ready to confront Grandma right now, in front of Mitch Ravenscroft, she wasn't even going to get a chance to warn her about what Eliza knew. Could things get any more complicated or disastrous?

Taylor had finished her break and went to follow the couple inside. 'Well I guess then you two will have plenty to talk about later.'

44

Keera

I turn Eliza's sign to closed, pleased I don't actually have to kick out customers, although I would have done, I'm in that sort of mood. Ready to kick something. It feels good actually. Like waking up after a long sleep.

'What are you doing, Keera?' asks Eliza.

'I'm doing what I should have done before. I doubted whether going around asking a lot of intrusive questions was the right thing for Crossways, or a great way to fit in. I made a mistake. I haven't asked nearly enough questions. But I'm putting things right and I'm starting with you. So I'm certainly up to ignoring your quizzical, vaguely annoyed look. Vaguely annoyed I can deal with any day of the week.'

'So you have some intrusive questions to ask me? Can we do it quickly so I don't disappoint too many customers?'

'Customers to serve, sales to make. The first question is whether that's really your motivation for being here? Benj Beresford was killed in a hit and run. Things have been festering. The time for keeping secrets is over.'

Eliza does not reply immediately. 'Is your next intrusive question whether I ran him down?'

'Did you?'

'What is this about, Keera? I'm not turning away customers just for you to be rude.'

'Yet I'm not going to stop. You went driving last night. Your car isn't there in its usual place.'

'Arrest me for parking somewhere different. Either that or get out of my shop. I guess Liv is running your shop, but my assistant has vanished. Although perhaps that's partly my fault as she works hard and I really ought to pay her.'

'This isn't about Verity, or even about all the help we all give each other. This is about you. I've done polite small talk and you've never answered truthfully what brought you here to sell overpriced olives.'

'So you've decided being rude is a better idea?'

'I think so, yes. You want to know the truth, so do I, and this is how we get it. I think what brought you here is that the past never goes away does it? In fact, sometimes it just feels like it's a shadow, chasing you.'

'This is all very philosophical, Keera, but—'

'Yes, I'll get to the point as you're clearly not going to be refreshing and own up. Chris and Carrie Winter were your parents, weren't they? There are always more than the obvious victims of serious crime. You came here in search of answers you may never get. Because you couldn't accept it was just a random crime and it would never be solved.'

'Is there a question in there somewhere?'

'Definitely. Very probably more than one. I'm trying to say we all want this solved, so can we work together?'

'With the rude bookseller from next door? The answer might be no.'

'If I'd asked more politely you might have given a different answer? Sorry. But I might get ruder. This isn't just about you any more. Someone killed Benj last night. I actually don't think it was you.'

'Am I supposed to thank you?'

'No, you're supposed to see that things have become urgent. I don't have all the answers, neither do you. But what if together we can get to the answer?'

Eliza sighs. 'I never meant to upset anyone.'

'Well that's a lie. You came here trying to uncover a murderer who's very possibly still living quietly in this village. I'm sure you never meant anyone else to die.'

'Are you blaming me for that?'

'I am trying to stop whatever's going on here and I don't know enough. Grant knows your secret. Does Mitch know who you really are? I haven't seen much evidence of Mitch doing investigating. If anything he seems to be rather distracted.'

'By Ashley Smollett?' says Eliza. 'Yes I spotted those two were close.'

'I think it's up to you and me. I know Crossways better. But you've been doing research, I guess?'

She sighs again. 'All right, if we're really doing this. You're right about the past following me around. This is my last hope the murder of my parents isn't going to be allowed to slide into unsolved case obscurity. I contacted their friends, old colleagues. Trying to find if it really was just awful chance that brought them here.'

Eliza is suddenly wiping away tears. 'Before they disappeared off on this long holiday all I got was an excited message that they weren't really ready to retire and they'd rented a house because she thought Crossways was crying out for a bookshop. Mum taught English, loved reading.'

'Really?' This is a wild thought. Fate really does play a part. 'You mean I might never have moved to Crossways because it nearly already had a bookshop?'

Eliza smiles gently through her tears. 'I kicked myself that you beat me to it. I made my decision a little too late. I came here to look around. I called into Between the Lines, you won't remember. I noticed how you chatted to everyone in the community and they told you things, often about themselves. I thought a shop might help me get answers. People often know more than they're telling.'

'To be fair, olives and salads were the right way to go. You can pack up and be gone in an afternoon. Books aren't dismissed that easily. But they had mentioned their plans to you before they disappeared off on this long holiday? No hint of any reason for picking Crossways?'

'They liked the countryside and that it was close to a city. And it was crying out for a bookshop. Then they went on a trek, wanted to be off-grid, a total break. Next thing was a call from the police. They were dead. I kept believing the police would find out what happened. I kept expecting that call. That time feels like a blank when I look back. I was just going through the motions. I asked myself over and over: what really happened? Why did it happen to them? I couldn't leave it. I realised the police must have given up.'

'You told Grant what you were doing?'

'I had to. Grant was so good to Mum and Dad. I contacted him, and when he said the chance of him finding me a small business premises in Crossways wasn't great, I told him who I was. I know he felt guilty. He wasn't keen. But he could see I wasn't going to change my mind. He's been keeping an eye on me.'

'He keeps an eye on everything. Maybe you asked one too many intrusive questions. Someone worked out what you were up to? Is that why bad things started happening? Grant must have been worried when the attacks started. Guess you were lucky Grant did know and kept an eye on you. Grant suggested to Ashley to get Verity in here.'

I've been trying to ignore Mrs Kinsky tapping on the door for the last few minutes; peering in, wondering why we are inside, but closed. She's gesturing in a way that makes it difficult to ignore.

'You want to pool resources? Fine,' says Eliza. 'It'll take too long to do it now. Do you mind if I open up? Mrs Kinsky is lovely and a good customer.'

'You do get to know people, can't help seeing a lot of customers as friends. We can do this later. One last question before I open the door. Did you suspect it was Benj?'

'Who killed my parents? That's why you asked if I ran him off the road.' Eliza shakes her head as she greets Mrs Kinsky and apologises for being closed. 'No, that's not where my research has taken me. But I have found something, or rather, someone. I'll take you through everything. It's probably time.'

Mrs Kinsky is in a cheerful mood as she places an order for two types of olives. I have to shoo out Jackson Brodie as he tries to follow her in. Cats and bookshops are one thing; cats and food shops less popular.

'Talking of your guardian angel, where is Verity?' I ask.

'Does Eliza need a guardian angel?' asks Mrs Kinsky.

'Yes she does. Keep an eye on her won't you. Eliza, we will talk, the second you stop serving your customers for the day. And please be very, *very* careful.'

45

Verity

Verity meant to go back to help Eliza and try to digest the revelation about Grandma's secret life while serving up colourful salads. But Belinda Messenger and Isha Cheema were hanging around and her feet had minds of their own. They took her a sharp right, away from the high street and onto one of the many footpaths.

She was quickly past the allotments and onto the path that followed the ditch that separated the long gardens on one side of the high street from the field beyond.

Grandma's hoodie was stuffed in the bottom of her bag and she'd get rid of it, toss it into some good thick undergrowth. Any trust of Grandma had utterly vanished. She had no further belief she knew Ashley Smollett at all. Or any idea what Grandma was capable of. Coming to Crossways had dissolved all her belief in herself too, that she was a good observer or could find out anything, or spot lies.

And she'd still failed to warn Grandma of the devastating photograph in Eliza's possession that proved Grandma had lied about knowing the Winters.

Trouble was coming. And Grandma wasn't going to get away with not answering accusations coming her way. Someone in Crossways who had a connection with the dead couple, but who had been overlooked by police, was going to be of interest to a lot of people.

Was this far enough away to toss the incriminating hoodie? Verity paused by some brambles, but was then aware of a sound behind her. Footsteps. Not just walking, but brisk, like someone following. But also quiet. She turned; there was no one there.

She didn't stop to hurl the hoodie but carried on. This path was probably popular with dog-walkers. Although it felt utterly deserted and those footsteps were not going the pace of a dog walker. She turned again. Still no one there. Was she imagining it? Crossways, a place not just of secrets, but of murders, was making her imagine all sorts.

There was a scrubby copse ahead that offered enough cover so she could hide and wait until whoever was behind her went past. She stopped turning around, but concentrated on walking faster. But now the steady sound of footsteps on the cracked earth was unmistakable.

Verity dropped behind the first convenient tree, trying hard not to breathe too loud and alert anyone to her hiding place. She waited, feeling sure someone couldn't be chasing her. Someone would go past. Then she'd double back and head for the safety of the busy high street.

'Grandma!'

'Verity!' Grandma in her bright orange dress, a hand to her chest, stopped. 'Why are you walking so fast? Didn't you see me? I couldn't catch up.'

'You totally weirded me out. Why didn't you call out?'

'It took all my breath just to try to keep up with you. What are you doing here? Should you be leaving Eliza alone? Eliza says you've been very helpful.'

'Wow, I think that was a compliment, Grandma! Careful.'

'Perhaps my summer of instruction is having an effect.'

'Your summer of instruction has been lame since you are never around to give any instruction. And we do really need to talk.'

Verity had the rucksack open and the hoodie half out.

Grandma's eyes narrowed. 'What are you doing with… Is that my favourite golf club hoodie? Verity!'

Verity flung the hoodie as far away from her as possible. Unfortunately it didn't go far as it caught on a bramble and half-landed in a patch of nettles. Grandma moved forward as if considering going to rescue it.

'Just leave it,' said Verity.

'What on earth—'

'It's the right thing to do, Grandma.'

'You are angry with me. But I still don't know why you have to trash my favourite hoodie.'

'People are catching on to what you're up to.'

'Right, right. You have found out things about me. It's not ideal. You've stumbled on things. You were too quick. I was not ready. Can we do this in a civilised way over coffee? And is there no chance for my hoodie?'

'No we really can't! It's much better to do it right here, right now. Best do it where no one is going to hear, because Crossways is awful for gossip. You say you weren't ready to explain, but did you think I wouldn't find out? You put me in there with Eliza.'

'How does this lead to you trashing my hoodie?'

'You need to come clean about everything. You've been lying to me. And your friends are suspicious. Your whole life is a lie. Who are you really? It's like you've become a different person. Even so, I am trying to cover for you and destroy evidence.' Verity indicated the grey hoodie.

'I have been lying. I'm sorry. I'm only human. I thought people wouldn't understand. I thought you wouldn't understand my little predicament.'

'Predicament! You are unbelievable.'

'And it really doesn't explain why you've just thrown my favourite, and rather expensive hoodie, into a patch of nettles. I think I might be able to get it back.'

Verity had to warn her about what Eliza had found out, but there was so much it was difficult to know where to start. Right now, she was mostly too angry to speak.

'You're taking a very harsh way of looking at things.' Grandma drew herself up to her full height. 'But it is my business.'

'How can you say that? It's you who's been lying and living a secret life. I just want to understand why, and you blame me for finding out. What was it all about?'

Verity only just realised this scrubby copse was on the opposite side of the ditch to David's workshop. It felt both a poignant coincidence, but also, a long time since she was there, uncovering silly Crossways secrets with Cal and Taylor. It felt like even longer ago she'd longed for something more significant to investigate than the mystery of David Purkiss's shed.

Verity had wanted to impress Grandma. And she hadn't done bad. She'd worked out who shot Jackson Brodie, the secret of the shed. She'd solved who had been behind that spate of burglaries.

She'd wanted to persuade Grandma that having a certain sort of inquisitive brain was a good thing.

She'd never expected she'd end up using her cleverness to hatch a plan to stop Grandma facing accusations from Eliza and a possible double murder charge. Or triple.

'Help me understand. Was there some big money at stake for you? I heard all the chatter about David Purkiss's windfall, how there was some business spin-off from his science discovery. I know zilch about science business spin-offs. But it sounds like there's a lot of money at stake. David got shafted in the deal. Did something similar happen to you? Something about your long academic career that went horribly wrong? It's the only theory I've come up with to explain it. I want to understand.'

'Verity, I—I have no idea what you are talking about,' said Grandma, twisting her fingers together. 'I do want you to understand. It's nothing to do with feeling unfulfilled in my career. It's just something that happened. I didn't plan it. It will probably take until you are sixty-three to understand how what you look like on the outside is not like what you still feel on the inside. Which is more like thirty-six. People expect you to act a certain way. I've no idea what happens to the forty years in between.'

'Did they come to see you about something? Was that why Chris and Carrie Winter pitched up in Crossways?' said Verity. 'I want to know what happened. When did you become this person? And one who lies very easily to everyone, including me.'

Verity looked into her grandma's grey eyes. More than wanting to know what happened, she wanted to see right inside her. She wanted to look inside her and see Grandma was not lost. The Grandma she remembered was still there, despite the changes, the new clothes and hair, the lying, the secrecy, launching into an affair with someone even though she was in her sixties and should be beyond all that sort of thing. Was Grandma still in there?

'It's been a shock. Of course I was going to introduce you to Mitch, but it's all very new.' Grandma actually blushed. 'I had no idea if he'd even be a proper fixture on the scene.'

Verity took a step closer. 'You do know I'm not talking about you and Mitch, don't you?'

'But I caught sight of you at Halfway and followed you. I guessed you'd seen us coming out of a hotel room together.'

'I'm sure I will be angry about that when I have chance to think about it. But that's not what's important now. I'm warning you Eliza's onto you!'

'Onto me and Mitch?'

'We need a plan, an urgent one. An excuse, an explanation. I have no idea what you are going to do now. But once you worked out who Eliza was and why she was here, it was a genius move to get me to keep an eye on her. You must have guessed I'd find out things. But you need to stop pretending with me. I've found out how much she already knows. So let's put our heads together and work out a plan.'

'You're not angry with me because of Mitch? I'm sure you've every right to be angry with me. I'm sorry about the lying. But… sorry, but you've lost me completely.'

'I'm on your side Grandma. The police focused in on some rubbish burglary theory precisely because the Winters didn't know anyone locally. Now Eliza's found out they knew you. Eliza's onto you and needs answers. She's not going away. We need to decide what we're going to do.'

'What do you mean, Eliza's onto me?' said Grandma.

Verity brought out her phone. 'The irony is Mitch was the one who wanted to stir things up again. But Eliza was already doing it. Your luck is about to run out. You're lucky my investigating means I'm only a few steps behind Eliza. So very few people had any connection at all to the dead couple. Eliza's got evidence. You're her big breakthrough. It looks like she's being trying for years go find a hidden connection. She's their daughter. See this photograph.'

Verity held up her phone.

'There's still a chance we can come up with something. But you need to stop pretending,' said Verity, waiting for the damning evidence that Eliza had painstakingly tracked down to sink in.

Grandma squinted at the phone and muttered she didn't have her glasses. Which was a bit of an anti-climax.

'Eliza ordered an original so she could see the faces clearly. It won't take Eliza long to start demanding answers. You need to be ready.

'What do I need to explain? What are you showing me?'

'You are in a photograph that proves you knew the Winters. There were no other connections here. That's why it was called an impossible crime and the police had no choice but to abandon the case. Eliza refused to believe there wasn't an answer. She's been asking their friends, contacting colleagues, combing their lives for some connection to Crossways. And she stumbled on the fact there is one person who knew the Winters. She knows it was you, Grandma.'

Verity waited. Knowing how very good Grandma was at lying.

'And this photo proves it, does it?' said Grandma, fumbling with the phone. 'That I knew the Winters? Not just a coincidence?'

'Police don't like coincidence. You need an excuse for knowing the dead couple, but never mentioning it. You told me you moved to Crossways after it happened, but I know that's another lie. I wanted to warn you. But you're never around. You didn't want to spend the summer with me, you wanted to spend it with Mitch Ravenscroft.'

'So you are angry about that?'

Grandma just kept fiddling with the phone. Verity had to admit, Grandma was reacting with remarkable cool. She did little more to betray how bothered she was than to chew her bottom lip.

'I'm sure between us we can come up with something plausible,' said Verity.

'I lied about being here at the time, yes. I know you love delving into your mysteries, Verity, and I didn't want to face a barrage of questions. But knew them? That's a bit...'

'You managed to slip under the radar. It's only Eliza, painstakingly going over any possible hidden connections... The case might have gone unsolved forever. Your luck's run out.'

'Hidden connection? This is a group photo of a science award dinner. There are dozens, maybe hundreds of people there. Look, someone called David Purkiss was there too, but that's definitely a mistake.'

'I thought you couldn't see properly without your glasses.'

'Photographs don't always tell the truth you think they do. There's a great list of names here. It shows nothing. It is evidence of nothing.' Grandma passed back the phone.

'But that is you, standing right behind the Winters?'

'Verity, this is nonsense. What happened to my one unbreakable rule about this summer? No investigating and no obsessing over people's lives. What have you been doing? Where did you get this photograph?'

'I told you, Eliza got hold of it. The hidden connection.'

'You have not learned to be interested in people, not in winkling out their secrets, because things are very seldom what they seem. Just exactly what are you accusing me of?'

'It's Eliza,' said Verity weakly. She'd thought Grandma would react by being scared, grateful, ready to plan, but she seemed more… furious. 'Eliza's been here secretly trying to find anyone in Crossways who knew them. She's found the hidden connection everyone's been searching for Eliza's getting close to the truth. I just wanted to warn you.'

Grandma made a sharp turn to start walking back. 'The truth!'

'You could thank me for warning you. Even though you've done nothing but tell lies to me all summer.'

'I need to talk to Eliza. I'm sorry Eliza has got hold of this.'

'And say what?'

'What do you think Verity? Confess that I killed two people?'

'I know it was an accident—'

'I cannot believe—' Grandma turned and levelled Verity with her intelligent gaze and spoke in a very clipped and weary voice. 'This is what you meant when you said we needed to talk? When you accused me of lying to you and having a secret life. Your very famous wild imagination… the conclusion you leaped to was…' She pointed to Verity's phone. 'That I killed two people.'

'It's where Eliza's research had led her to.'

'And what did you believe, Verity? I invited you here because I love you enough to believe you can change. All your intelligence and imagination…' Grandma said in a disappointed tone. 'I cannot believe the conclusion you came to was that I am guilty of murder. Rather than thinking my secret simply being I have been lying to you all summer because a man might be interested in me.'

46

Keera

Ashley Smollett bursts through the door out of breath and agitated just as Liv and I are in the middle of discussing whether we need more biscuits.

'Keera, you have a reputation of getting to the truth of things,' says Ashley. 'I need your help. I was going to talk to Eliza, but I don't think this is something I should rush into, particularly when I'm so very angry. First, I need to ask you how bad things look. Verity took a very dim view.'

'Tea?' says Liv, disappearing into the cubbyhole and climbing over my book buying mistakes to put the kettle on.

I guide Ashley to my comfy reading chair that no one ever uses for reading.

'Do you know what Eliza's been up to? Turns out she's Carrie Winter's daughter. Everyone probably knew this? I've been a little…'

'Distracted,' supplies Liv. 'Plenty of time to talk while Keera's kettle considers if it's still up to the job.'

'Eliza has a photograph of me with her parents.' Ashley scrolls through on her phone.

'Eliza did say she had an important development,' I say. I don't add that it sounded like she had a prime suspect. Was that Ashley?

'I told Verity I needed my glasses to see properly to buy myself time,' says Ashley. 'I sent myself a copy. I don't think dear Verity thought I'd know how to do that.'

She shows us the photo. It's of a huge group of people and it takes her a while to close in.

'Do you know Verity has been digging into people's secrets against my strictest instructions? Apparently Verity's convinced Eliza's fixed on me being some secret Crossways connection. And by association, Verity seems to think Eliza thinks I'm the Crossways Killer. Verity, bless her, came to warn me. Although that photograph does look damning.'

'And are you?' I ask, looking into her grey eyes.

'What? Am I the secret connection? Did I kill them? Know them? Maybe Verity was right to take it so seriously. No, no and no.'

'Yet there has to be a secret Crossways connection,' I say. 'One the police never uncovered at the time. Eliza's been looking for a hidden connection.'

Ashley shows Liv the photo as Liv hands her tea.

'You are there, smiling out of a photo. You were with them not long before they were killed,' says Liv. 'Yet you never mentioned knowing them. It is pretty incriminating because there were so few leads to follow. Maybe test it out on us before you speak to Eliza. What are you going to say?'

'It means nothing. Verity had all sorts on her phone. There are lots of people in this photo because it's what happens—people get brought together to where sponsors are peddling something you have to avoid. You network, celebrate achievements, you get a middling dinner. It's all pretty ghastly, yet I've been to plenty in my time. The fact that Chris Winter was there and so was I, it's just… coincidence. All those photos. Not surprising the photographer made a mistake.'

'It's not a mistake. You are in the photograph,' I say.

'Yes, my being in this photograph, it's not a great look, I get it. But honestly, I get invited, probably for the shameful reason that even in this day and age, I was one of the few who could be bothered to dress up and go. And they got a less all-male photograph. I never won anything.'

Ashley tries to find something else on the phone. 'I caught Verity trying to destroy a lovely hoodie of mine. I've no idea what's going on in her head. She seems to think she's protecting me. Verity's convinced I brought her here as some undercover spy because I suspected Eliza was closing in on me. It's really not the significant deal everyone seems to think it is. Here we go. It looks like David Purkiss was on the invite list as he gets name-checked. But the photographer has named the wrong person, so he or she wasn't that bothered about being accurate. The camera can lie, or at least, not give the whole story.'

Liv squints at the photo on the phone. 'This man here?'

Ashley squints sideways at the phone. 'Exactly. The guy who gets name-checked is not David Purkiss.'

'You're right,' says Liv. 'No one's head changes shape. And not even a beard makes you look twenty years older.'

'Would you like me to talk to Eliza first?' I offer. 'Just to pave the way to accepting all her hard-won research is just a coincidence.'

'It must be tough not having answers,' says Ashley.

Margot arrives to find out if we've chosen the next bookgroup read yet and we all spring apart, doing a shoddy job of not making it look like we are in the middle of something we're being secretive about. We've been lucky to chat for this long. But then Margot does a shoddy job of hiding she only came here in search of gossip anyway.

'If I make everyone a cup of tea can I join in?' says Margot. 'Because I know you're gossiping and I don't want to miss out.'

'All right, as long as you confess what you've roped Verity into,' says Liv as Margot disappears to put on the world's slowest kettle. 'I keep seeing you, Belinda and Isha hanging around with Verity.

'We all just wanted to protect Eliza,' calls Margot.

'You've dragged my granddaughter into doing something dangerous,' Ashley says coldly. 'You're lucky I need to go and sort out an even bigger mess otherwise I would be making it clear how very angry I am.'

'Bigger mess?' Margot asks curiously. 'I'd have been happy if you'd joined us. Verity made us all promise not to tell you, Ashley. Bless. Think she was worried about you. But thanks to Verity we got very good footage of someone in a grey hoodie smashing glass outside Eliza's shop.'

'Right. I've had enough of everyone secretly investigating their friends and gossiping.'

Ashley makes a disgruntled exit, missing Verity by just a few seconds, who arrives with Jackson Brodie in tow.

I think I might ask Margot to make another cup as Verity looks very in need of tea.

'You've just missed your Grandma,' says Liv. 'She's just gone to have a little word with Eliza and tell her everything about that science award dinner photo. It's all coincidence and mistakes. I'm sure all of this is going to be sorted out quite happily.'

My comfy reading chair is working hard as a therapy chair today.

47

Keera

'What did Grandma say?' Verity demands to know.

'You mean how mad was she?' says Liv.

'I think we're safe to call it pretty cross,' I say.

'Your Grandma was just explaining how you accused her of murder,' says Liv. 'Not the best move.'

'But I was trying to protect her,' argues Verity.

'How all very unfortunate,' says Margot, popping her head out from where she's waiting for my very slow kettle to boil again. 'But nothing a nice bunch of flowers and a sincere apology can't fix, I'm sure.'

'She was being secretive. And she's changed since moving to Crossways. Turns out she was being secretive because she's having a relationship with Mitch Ravenscroft. She got mad and said I found it easier to imagine she killed that Winter couple than was having an affair at her age.'

'Yes I can imagine how well that went down,' Liv says.

'Bless! Nice cup of tea on its way,' says Margot. 'Maybe a very large bunch of flowers, a sincere apology and chocolates? Everything looks different after a nice cup of tea.'

'These things blow over,' I tell Verity.

'Keera has *lots* of experience upsetting people,' says Liv.

'Is there a kick-ass goddess who booksellers pray to at a time like this?' Verity asks. 'There's not a bunch of flowers big enough to stop me going home to find my small stash of clothes slung out onto the pavement. I don't think there's anyone left to reach out and offer a second chance. Think I can find a way to make it up to Grandma?'

'I'm surprised you haven't looked it up,' I say. 'The kick-ass goddess who booksellers pray to bit. I really don't know if you can find a way to—'

'Of course we can.' Margot appears with tea. 'Nothing is ever as bad as it seems. There's always a way out.'

Verity sighs. 'I thought I was being clever. But I got things totally wrong.'

'Yes, well don't be too hard on yourself, that happens,' I say. 'So we know you're investigating the Crossways Killings. We know Eliza's also investigating. We all need to stop secretly investigating. We need this to end.'

'She showed us the incriminating photograph,' says Liv.

'What photograph? Don't leave me out!' says Margot. 'Am I supposed to be feeding this cat? It has a hungry face.'

I gesture for Liv to show Margot where we keep a stash of cat treats as my phone goes off. Elliott. 'Let's hope Elliott's calling with some good news,' I say.

'We've been trying to track down any car taken into a garage with damage,' says Elliott. 'You said Eliza's car was missing. And you gave me the numberplate of some big four-by-four that's often parked next to hers. That one's nothing to get excited about because sorry, you've misremembered the number on that one.'

'Sorry to waste your time. But if you're chasing down that lead you must be desperate for things to follow up.'

'That car's not registered to anyone local. Belongs to someone who lives by the coast, name of Millward. Unless it's one of your loyal customers who drives a long way to visit your wonderful shop. First name Royston.'

'Do you know it does ring a bell. And I see that car a lot. I'll have a think,' I say, already with enough to think about. The call ends.

'I need to talk with Elliott,' says Verity. 'If we're sharing.'

'Sounds brilliant,' I say. 'We are definitely sharing.'

'Sounds exciting,' says Margot. 'Anyone want a little biscuit with their tea? I've found a couple.'

'I wish Grandma would see I've been any use at all,' Verity sighs, crunching into a biscuit.

'You've been extraordinary,' says Liv. 'Is it a new lead you want to talk to Elliott about? You could tell us first.'

'All I wanted was something to solve to make my summer a little more fun,' sighs Verity. 'And prove to Grandma I'm not a complete waste of space. I found out who shot Jackson Brodie.'

'That's what you want us to talk to Elliott about?' says Liv. 'The cat? You want me to tell Elliott who shot the cat?'

'No.' Verity shakes her head. 'That's how it started, but things snowballed. It was Isha, by the way. Probably thought Jackson was a rabbit after her vegetables and she's not got great eyesight. Probably still got her dad's gun. But that's not it. It's about those burglaries around the time the Winters were killed.'

'I hate to put a dampener on anything you found out,' I say. 'But this is why sharing is useful. We all get things wrong, all the time. Isha doesn't shoot. Someone else shot Jackson Brodie. Tell me about the burglaries? You really have been doing as much digging as Jackson does.'

'And what was that about a photograph Ashley showed all of you?' asks Margot. 'And went to talk to Eliza about.'

'Grandma was in this photo of a science award dinner that Eliza had gone to a lot of trouble to get hold of,' says Verity. 'I thought Grandma kept quiet about knowing the Winters. But she's right, there were loads of people in the photo. And the photographer wasn't even bothered about being accurate. David got a mention too you know. And that was a case of mistaken identity. He wasn't even in the photo. Probably wasn't even there.'

The cat leaps on Verity's lap and starts kneading her legs like a cushion. 'So who shot you? I can't believe I'm going to get turfed out of Crossways before I even solved that. I'm determined to get to the bottom of something without totally messing up.'

'I'm sure Ashley isn't going to throw you out,' says Margot kindly. 'You are looking very peaky, dear. You worry too much. I'm going to nip along to Halfway to pick up a proper treat. You rather like those caramel shortbread.'

The moment she's gone Verity confesses she's also been looking into the mystery of David's shed. 'I couldn't say it in front of Margot, but Cal, Taylor and I took advantage of the fact Margot and David were away and went to have a look inside.'

'Don't tell me, model railway?' says Liv.

'David's workshop and who shot Jackson Brodie are not important,' I say. 'Verity's discovered something about the burglaries. Let's focus.'

'I'd loved to have found out how much money he got in this science spin-off everyone talks about. I only found out something very dull and David's going to notice someone was in there, we'll probably have to fess up to it anyway. Jackson Brodie followed us in and left dirt all over the shed. Someone's starting digging a big hole next to it and Jackson thought that was the best fun.' Verity crunches into another biscuit. 'Will whoever did those burglaries still be in trouble after all this time?'

'It's difficult for me to make promises on Elliott's behalf,' says Liv. 'But I think the Crossways crimes that need answers have got beyond the small burglaries.'

'I've been doing a lot of unravelling. My guess is it was Cal and Taylor,' I say. 'Everyone said it was just kids and I thought it was just a very Crossways sort of response. How certain are you they didn't kill the Winters? Not even in an accident?'

'I've been pretty poor at judging things,' admits Verity. 'But I believe them. And I believe Grandma's not involved.'

'Elliott will want to talk to them,' Liv says.

'I think they're ready. Especially when I pointed out people already suspected it was them and I think everyone got freaked out once the police started to try to link the burglaries with a double murder.'

'It created a cone of silence,' says Liv.

'No one wanted to land them in trouble,' I say. 'So it all got buried.'

'No one speaks much about the Crossways Killings,' says Liv. 'Verity, you've been invaluable. Keera's right, you mustn't keep all this to yourself. Also Keera's quite wrong about the workshop secret not being important. Come on. What's David Purkiss' secret? Not even a hint of a science lab?'

'It's a writing shed. He's got a whole finished manuscript, a pseudonym and everything. The First Husband by Royston Millward. We couldn't work out if it's some kind of domestic suspense or crime or a romance.'

'Didn't Margot already tell us that's David's pseudonym?' says Liv. 'He must be serious about it.'

'You're absolutely right,' I say. 'She absolutely did.'

'So if you tell Elliott I think two people are ready to confess to those burglaries, but can you get him to promise if they own up they won't get charged?' says Verity. 'I feel I've made enough enemies. Now I have to face Eliza. I hope Grandma's managed to convince her she didn't murder her parents. And then I have to face Grandma. What a complete mess.'

'It absolutely wasn't all your mess,' says Liv. 'A lot of people have been keeping a lot of secrets.'

Verity doesn't look convinced as she leaves to face Eliza and Ashley.

'I can also clear something up,' says Liv. 'That black four-by-four you asked Elliott about is David and Margot's. They've been away on one of their famous minibreaks.'

'Actually no. It belongs to a Royston Millward.'

'That's definitely not right. Isn't that the pseudonym David's used in his writing?' says Liv. 'David surely hasn't started using his pseudonym already?'

'Unless… Unless…'

'You've had an idea. Who are you calling?'

'Unless it being Royston Millward's car explains why David Purkiss wasn't in that science award photo Eliza got interested in. I'm calling Elliott. We've been looking at things so wrong. Everything! You were right and I was wrong, the real mystery of David Purkiss' shed is *very* important. I know who knocked Benj off his bike. Who was behind the attacks on Eliza. And I finally know who shot Jackson Brodie.'

'All very important. You mean it is all connected?'

'Of course it's all connected. Everything in a small place is always connected. Not just connected, but it all explains the Crossways Killings. We said the Crossways Killer would only be found when we found the motive. Well, I finally know the motive.'

'You've solved it?'

'I have. I know who did the Crossways Killings and why.'

48

Verity

The deli was empty of customers. But also, where was Eliza? Verity pushed the door open. No Grandma either. Better than discovering them in the middle of an almighty row, but still…

Eliza would never leave the shop when it was open and the door unlocked. The emptiness felt very wrong. Verity started imagining Grant walking into an empty building and finding dead bodies and blood on the floor. These things happened in Crossways. She called out nervously. No answer.

The discreet white door that led to the flat upstairs was locked. No sign of Eliza stepping outside to enjoy and admire the new garden. She had vanished. Leaving the shop open. And Verity was surprised Eliza and Grandma had resolved their differences so quickly.

Grandma never answered any of Verity's messages and never seemed to use her phone all that much, preferring the mini-chalkboard on the fridge. But she called Grandma's number now, even though Verity didn't know if they were even on speaking terms. Would Grandma pick up?

Then she heard the phone ringing. Here in the shop.

That couldn't be right. Verity traced Grandma's phone, abandoned behind the counter. She stared at it. Grandma's phone was here. But Grandma was not. Verity's heart felt like it did a somersault inside her ribs. Eliza and Grandma were missing. What had happened? Where were they?

So many bad things happened in hateful Crossways and instantly Verity knew something bad had happened here.

But what? And where were they?

She needed to think. But she couldn't think. She'd already moved to panic. Calm down. Grandma had been missing for all of five minutes. Reporting it to the police was hardly going to result in a squad car and a search team. But Verity knew for certain something was terribly wrong. So it was up to her.

If only Verity had arrived a few moments earlier she might have seen them leaving, together? But why not lock the door? And why would Grandma abandon her phone?

There was no way to rewind time and find out what had happened. Verity only had herself to work out where they'd gone. Verity's imagination wanted to go into overdrive, because this felt so wrong, dangerously wrong. She needed her cool investigative side to kick in. Stop panicking. Even though her instincts were to run along Crossways high street, demand of everyone to tell her if they'd seen them.

Then a thought struck. Actually, there was a way to rewind time. If she was lucky. Well, almost rewind time.

Verity fetched the set of steps tucked in behind the garden gate. Her cheap camera would have been recording low-res images of what happened outside the shop for a long time now. There was plenty of chance she'd be unlucky and the card would be full. But she retrieved the camera and for once, Verity was lucky. Among those grainy, flickering images, Verity found there were recent shots.

She watched Grandma leaving the shop, closely followed by Eliza. So they had left together. But that's where Verity's luck ran out.

She was staring at something horrifying.

They were followed by a figure in a familiar grey hoodie. Not Grandma's grey hoodie. Verity had chucked that into a patch of nettles. But the grey hoodie that presumably belonged to whoever had really been attacking Eliza.

But who was it? Actually, lots of people had those Crossways Golf hoodies. Why had Verity ever suspected Grandma?

As she watched again, Verity thought she could detect Grandma and Eliza were being forced out of the shop. It was the way Eliza turned, tried to say something, quite possibly about not abandoning the shop. But she was pushed roughly onward. Eliza and Grandma had left here together, but not because they wanted to.

Surely after all her investigations she should know who was in the grey hoodie. Or could work out the answer. She had to work it out because then there was a chance that would tell Verity where they were now. And she had to find Grandma.

But she did not have answers to any of these important questions and she had run out of time to solve this.

Because even from brief, flickering images Verity watched again, she knew one other terrible thing.

They weren't just being hustled out and threatened by that figure in the grey hoodie. Verity's heart began to pound painfully.

The figure in the grey hoodie had a gun.

49

Verity

She'd wanted to convince Grandma she had useful and important skills. And right now her mind was a blank.

All that obsessive interest, all that gathering information and secrets, all that investigating. Now she had to prove herself. There was a killer in Crossways. They had a gun and it was too easy to let her mind spiral into panic. No way was she letting anything bad happen to Grandma. Think. Answers had to be in her head somewhere. Where would Grandma and Eliza be?

Too risky to walk Eliza and Grandma down the high street. Too much chance they'd see someone they knew. That made sense. This was what Verity needed to do – get inside the mind of a killer and walk in their footsteps.

No she did not need to walk, she needed to run.

With all the certainty she could, Verity thought they'd go for one of the quiet footpaths. The nearest one. Verity left the shop and headed for the path she'd taken earlier. It looped up past the allotments and out into open fields. A good way to go if you wanted to avoid being seen.

Just hang on, she said to Eliza and Grandma in her mind.

It soon felt far away from the high street, away from anywhere. Verity's mind slipped into a methodical run, in time with her footsteps. She increased her pace. She had a hope someone would be at the allotments. Someone who'd seen three figures passing, would tell her she was on the right track, but there was no one.

The path went alongside the ditch that bordered the long Crossways high street gardens. She'd never felt so alone, so unsure, so terrified of making a mistake, getting it all wrong.

She ran past the end of Eliza's garden, passing Isha's, all boarded up; slowed. She had to catch her breath.

The same person had to be behind all the awfulness in Crossways. Whoever had been waging that bitter war against Eliza, the person Verity had captured on that image, smashing glass, whoever had knocked Benj off his bike and killed him. The Crossways Killer. They now had Grandma.

She could be heading in completely the wrong direction, but she couldn't think of that. Focus on the fact they couldn't be too far ahead, she could catch them. But there was no one on the path ahead. Verity's steps got faster despite the tightness in her chest, the aching in her muscles that screamed at her that she had to slow. She ran.

The crow scarer went off and Verity almost had a heart attack. But it wasn't a gun shot.

If she hadn't been quite so ready to believe Grandma's secrets were so terrible, she might have already reached the right answer. She'd got horribly distracted. As she was almost at David's glorified shed she'd broken into with Cal and Taylor, there was still no one. She was running out of time. She could not afford to be wrong. They must have come this way.

Questions jumbled in her mind. Why had Margot been so resolute about not selling when Grant reckoned they wanted to move anyway?

Verity realised there were reasons she'd come this way.

Luckily the ditch was dry as she forced herself across, through branches that snapped noisily, even though Verity moved as quietly as she could.

Margot and David hadn't sold their garden to Benj. Well, Benj wasn't going to be doing any developing now, was he? His dying meant none of the gardens would be dug up.

She had questions tumbling through her mind. But finally, Verity felt they were the right questions.

Why had the photographer at the science business awards dinner identified the wrong person as David Purkiss? David Purkiss who'd made a fortune and then come to Crossways. Why did Chris and Carrie Winter have to die when they moved to Crossways?

She reached the other side and crept towards the workshop.

She, Taylor and Cal had discovered David's secret. Or thought they had. But they'd missed the real significance of when they'd found he'd been writing The First Husband by Royston Millward.

In a repeat of the breaking and entering party of Saturday night, Verity looked through the window. But this time she already knew exactly what she was going to see.

50

Verity

'Dear old motherly Margot, who lost her nice office job,' Verity instantly recognised Margot's voice, even though she kept her head low, beneath the windows. 'Made redundant, thrown on the scrapheap. Forced to take in lodgers.'

'No one ever pitied you,' Grandma said.

'Yes they did,' argued Margot.

Verity risked peeping up over the window ledge, enough so could see Eliza pale and fidgety, Grandma pale, still and terrified, but also ball-fisted enough to look like she wanted to punch someone.

'Women become invisible. Not capable of much, that's what everyone thinks,' went on Margot. 'But you can turn being underestimated into real power.'

Margot had a point. Because even after everything she'd worked out, Verity had been expecting David to be the one holding the gun.

'Good for nothing except cooking dinners, smiling, offering sympathy and cups of tea. Listening to his endless whining. As if I should pity *him*. Me, who had proper worries, fretting if I could even afford to keep my home.'

'That must have been difficult to listen to,' Grandma said, trying, bless her, to say something soothing. But also doing the only thing you could and keeping the person with the gun talking. Until… Until Verity thought of something.

'I still don't see why you had to kill David Purkiss,' said Eliza, rather ruining the calming, sharing atmosphere Grandma was trying to introduce. 'The real David, I mean. That is what happened? The person who you live with is just pretending. Who is he really?'

'The real David stayed with you before?' said Grandma. 'Probably remembered how kind you were.'

'He came back!' said Margot. 'When he wanted someone to listen to him go on and on about how *wasn't his life so terrible.* At the same time, showing off how he'd made all this money, as I cleaned his hair from the bathroom plughole and washed his shirts. What I'd become! He was too traumatised to leave the house, he said. Going on and on, how he'd been shafted in this business launch when he'd made the breakthrough. But it was loads of money! Stupid man talked so big. He was plotting revenge. Typical weak man craving power and thinking it'd been snatched from him. He showed me he'd got himself a gun. As if I thought he'd use it. Horrible, horrible man.'

'So you killed him?' said Eliza abrasively. 'The real David Purkiss. With that gun?'

'It was an accident. And not with his own gun. Not that it wouldn't have been ironic. But no. This whole thing started with an accident. He was killed by fate. And then it felt like it was how things were meant to be.'

Verity couldn't wait much longer while they bought time. If Verity tried to burst in the door, she could surprise Margot. But the gun might go off. In a small space.

Margot was spilling everything and that could only mean one thing. The only thing that was going to stop Margot was if someone hit her over the head with a blunt instrument. And that meant Verity.

A large stick against a gun didn't feel a fair chance, but she had nothing. Verity looked around. In a garden where pretty much everything was plastic, chances of a big stick were zero. She was going to have to go back to the ditch. She didn't think Margot would hear, she was too busy justifying what she'd done.

'So what did happen?' Grandma asked as Verity went back to the ditch for a weapon.

'How did he get killed by fate?' she heard Eliza ask.

'He made a very ungentlemanly move,' said Margot. 'I thought he was limbering up to suggesting he might stay. I was wondering if I could put up with him. For all that money. He didn't ask. Just made a disgusting move.'

'So you shot him?' Eliza asked.

'No!' screamed Margot. 'I told you.'

'So it started with an accident. Now it's got out of hand,' said Grandma calmly. 'The game's up, Margot. You can't possibly think you can keep getting away with things.'

'Oh you'd be surprised what you can get away with if you're patient and no one suspects you. Anyway. I shoved him off me. He stumbled. We were sitting in the garden and his head met one of the sharp corners of my cement borders. Cracked open like a walnut. Blood everywhere. Nothing I could do.'

'It was an accident,' said Grandma.

'I looked at him on the ground, quite dead, and all I could think was that if I reported the accident, I wouldn't even get the rent he owed me. The genius idea did not come immediately. I just transferred the money for the rent he owed because of course his laptop and phone were here. Then I meant to call the police. But I saw how much money he had. What was going to happen to all that money? I knew he had no family.'

Verity was holding the biggest stick she'd been able to find, listening for the right time to do her best and fling open the door, get inside and surprise Margot.

'All this online banking makes it so easy. No one knows if you've died, all you need are passwords. The only difficulty was the amount. You can hardly move anything without people getting suspicious. No one was going to miss him. If I didn't take the money the state would get it. That seemed a shame. It felt like it was meant to be. Fate.'

The way she said it suggested anyone would make the same decisions as she did. And to be honest, Verity could understand why Margot was tempted.

'Do you have any idea how long it takes to take several million from someone's bank account?' Margot asked in a high, squeaky and desperate sounding voice. 'I needed time and I needed help.'

'If you're looking for sympathy,' said Grandma, 'I'd put down that gun.'

'So you called a friend with as few scruples as you?' said Eliza.

Verity had to do it. Now or never. But it was such a risk that if she surprised Margot the gun in her hand would go off. Someone would get hit. She had to storm the door, take Margot by surprise, try to hit her before she even thought to use the gun. Could she be quick enough?

'I presume you buried the body. I guess the remains of the real David Purkiss are under this workshop?' Eliza was now pressing for answers.

All this time Verity had felt she needed to understand Crossways and the things people here obsessed about. But everything had been because Margot had a good old fashioned body buried at the bottom of her garden.

'Royston's a real genius with finances. He has all sorts of clever ideas. I told him the real David had vanished and all he had to do was pretend to be him. But we were trapped here. Fearing discovery.'

'Once you have a secret, you have to keep on covering your tracks,' said Eliza. 'Out of the blue somebody came asking after David?'

'This man was at the door and said how he and his wife by chance were in Crossways, chatter chatter, and did I happen to know a scientist, David Purkiss. Someone had mentioned he was here. Did he have the right address? I found out from Grant with horror they were moving here.'

'So you decided to kill them both,' said Eliza.

Instead of storming in, maybe the smart thing was a distraction. Verity should make a noise, get Margot to open the door and look out. Then hit her as hard as she could.

Yes. Better plan.

But it was Verity who jumped out of her skin when there was an incredibly loud miaowing. Jackson Brodie was at her feet. Verity stared at the cat, then the door was flung open and a gun was pointing right at her.

51

Verity

'Oh Verity,' said Margot, waving Verity inside with a twitch of her gun. 'Very timely. Now you can get answers to all your questions. Just put that stick down, or someone might get hurt.'

Verity joined Eliza and Grandma in a line in the resiny smelling workshop, with Margot holding a gun blocking the door.

Jackson Brodie miaowed as if asking what they were all doing here. Or maybe he was asking the same as Verity was asking herself. What now?

There was no help coming. Margot had killed several people. There was no way this was not going to end badly.

But three against one. They could take her, surely. What other options did they have other than to rush her?

The best chance would be if they could find a way to move altogether. Then Margot wouldn't know which to shoot first. At least that way all three of them weren't going to die and Margot get away with it, which looked the most likely outcome. Even that best chance was going to end in someone getting a bullet.

'I am sorry they were your parents, Eliza,' said Margot. 'I thought if I offered a share of David Purkiss's money…'

'You went over there with a gun.'

'The stress I'd been under. All we'd gone through.'

'I can see you need to convince us everything you've done was reasonable,' said Eliza. 'But you've not even convinced yourself.'

'We had got away with it. Then someone started buying up the gardens.'

'Then suddenly your biggest problem wasn't trying to sluice the remains of the real David Purkiss's money out,' said Verity. 'But you couldn't quietly leave Crossways, not if the end of your garden was developed. Not with that body under the shed. Did you try to move the remains of the real David from under the workshop? Is that why there's so much digging there? Is that why you asked Mitch all those questions about how quickly a body decomposes?'

Jackson miaowed and rubbed around Eliza's legs, wondering why she didn't bend to stroke him.

'You think you're so clever, Verity. Admit it. You weren't even close. I took a cue from you and got a camera fixed up to keep an eye on the place. I heard everything you three said when you broke in here on Saturday.'

Margot's hand holding the gun wasn't even wavering. It was almost as if she was enjoying the chance to show off.

'But I have worked it all out,' said Verity. 'And that means others will too. I even know you took a shot at Jackson because he knew there was something buried under the workshop. Probably wouldn't leave it alone. Some people just never give up, do they.'

'Like you, you mean,' said Margot. 'I think it's time to get this over with.'

'But it won't be over,' said Verity. 'You'll have to keep covering your tracks. Everyone's starting to piece it together. The police are already on their way. In fact they're here. Look!'

Verity pointed behind Margot and out of the window.

Margot looked behind her. Verity could not believe her simple ruse worked. But it was just the distraction Verity wanted.

At that exact moment forensic minded Grandma had reached the exact same conclusion that they needed to move together and they both went at the same time.

Verity planned to rush Margot. Unfortunately, Grandma had other ideas. She kicked up a leg aimed at Margot's hand holding the gun. It was a crisis of bad timing, as Verity rushed Margot, Grandma's kick, instead of knocking the gun out of Margot's hand, landed on Verity's jaw.

Grandma had a hefty kick, possibly owing to all that time at YogaGals.

Verity went down. The gun went off. Someone else fell.

52

Keera

As I arrive at the workshop there is screaming.

There's blood. Took me a moment to work out exactly whose. It took two of us to wrestle the gun from Margot and then somehow Eliza has the gun and is pointing it at Margot. Margot looks as scared as she should be.

I hear myself trying to talk Eliza down, tell her shooting Margot isn't the right thing to do, but I'm only doing it half-heartedly. I'm too focused on Ashley.

I drop to the floor where Verity is trying to press where there is too much blood.

'It's coming out too fast!' screams Verity.

Ashley's face is ashen, sweaty. Her precious blood is leaking onto her clothes and onto the floor.

'Keep that gun on Margot,' I say to Eliza.

'Oh don't worry, I will.'

I take off my t-shirt and press it into the wound. Ashley groans in pain. In the background, Margot has started up pleading, telling us that we can all share the money.

'That's a much better way out of all of this. There's no bringing your parents back. There's no way you are going to shoot, Eliza, you're such a gentle soul.'

'You killed my parents,' Eliza says in a dangerous voice. 'I wouldn't try me.'

'I really wouldn't try her,' I say. 'But our only worry right now is Ashley.'

The cat miaows. Ashley has gone worryingly silent, not so much as a whimper.

Verity looks at me, pleading for me to do something to help her Grandma, but I know there's nothing more that we can do apart from try to stop that blood pumping out. My t-shirt is already soaked.

After what feels like forever, finally, in the distance we hear the sound of sirens. I called Elliott Trent the minute I worked things out, knew there was likely a gun involved, knew I could get here more quickly than he could.

Margot surprises us all by rushing Eliza, barging into her, shoving her aside, aiming for the door. Without a second's thought, Eliza pulls the trigger. Margot screams and falls.

Elliott appears with at least three armed officers, takes the gun from Eliza and ushers in a crew of paramedics.

I cannot look at Verity's face. Margot hasn't stopped screaming, but she's only shot in the leg.

What is much, much worse is that we have completely lost Grandma.

53

Verity

Whatever the ambulance crew did was a miracle. More than a miracle. A few days later, Grandma was actually sitting on the sofa, finally ready to watch all those box sets Verity had been wanting to catch up on.

'I've made student special cheesy pasta for dinner, so sorry, but that means heavy on the onion but no healthy salad,' Verity said as she placed a tray to one side of the sofa. 'Comfort food.'

'Looks very tasty, Verity. You no doubt need the carbs more than I do. A wine would be nice to go with that. You know where I keep the wine as someone's been making their way through all the best bottles. My fault, I shouldn't have left you alone so much.'

'No wine, doctors orders.'

'That means just a small one.'

Verity placed a blanket over Grandma. 'That means you need looking after.'

'It's one of the hottest springs on record. The blanket is too much. Just put the wine to chill. Just in case.'

'What you mean is I annoy you by fussing,' Verity

said, trying again to tuck the blanket around Grandma and plumping up cushions. 'Mitch is probably coming over, so you're not really interested in reruns of old TV shows either. What you mean is you'd like it if I got out the way and left you with Mitch and a bottle of wine.'

'I do not mean that. But I'm recovering quickly and I don't need you as much as Eliza needs you. Everyone's rallying around. I think discovering Eliza's secret identity means Mrs Kinsky and Belinda Messenger have put their differences aside and are covering the shop between them. But they are not experts like you, Verity.'

'Wow a compliment. Things really are changing around here. I suspect Belinda and Mrs Kinsky have made up their differences because Taylor and Cal confessed to their parents about the burglaries and set everyone's minds at rest that they didn't accidentally shoot the poor Winter couple.'

'I wonder how close people got to thinking it was Taylor and Cal and a really terrible mistake,' said Grandma. 'But your priority is to make sure they're doing everything right at the deli.'

'It's putting olives into small containers and making salads. Also I don't think I can order Belinda Messenger around. Can anyone order Belinda Messenger around? Plus I don't suppose it matters that much. I cannot see Eliza hanging around here now.'

There was a ring at the doorbell, which Verity expected would be Mitch, but it was Keera.

'You're not bringing bookgroup I hope?' Verity asked. 'I don't think Grandma's ready for bookgroup.'

'I just brought a little light reading for Ashley. I'm not sure if she's found this series yet, but it's her sort of thing.'

Keera followed Verity into Ashley's cosy front room, where vases of fresh flowers adorned every surface.

'I'm first in line to look after Grandma because I need her to forgive me ever thinking she might have shot those two poor people.'

Grandma crooked an eyebrow at Verity. 'What would you have done if you'd found out I'd done it? Turned me in?'

'Of course not. For a start I really only thought it for a second. Maybe a day. A day or two. At the most. But I was already working on the beginnings of a plan how to sort it all out. Although that might have involved dropping Eliza right in it. I'd have ended up letting someone down.'

'You didn't let anyone down, Verity,' said Grandma. 'You have more than a good imagination. You are very tenacious and thoughtful. I was wrong—you do take a genuine interest in people and you understand them. Actually much better than you think.'

'I don't know. Margot was right. I never suspected she would be capable of killing people and be clever enough to siphon off the real David Purkiss's fortune.'

'It would take more than just being interested in people to spot that,' said Keera. 'I won't stay. Just thought I'd call in as so many people keep dropping into Between the Lines to ask me how you're doing. I'm hoping for a good answer.'

'I'm doing fine, thanks to Verity.' Ashley reached for her granddaughter's hand to give it a squeeze. 'We both misjudged each other.'

'I just wanted to impress you Grandma,' said Verity.

'You always impress me. But impressing people isn't the most important.'

'I think I have worked out what is important.'

Grandma crooked an eyebrow at Verity and waited.

'You are, Grandma.'

'Thank you Verity.'

'Sorry if I caused you a lot of trouble.'

'It's not you who caused the trouble. The trouble was already there. But you do have a nose for seeking it out. And you don't let go—I'm not sure if that's a good thing or a bad one. It can be dangerous to keeping digging when desperate people are involved. You can call me Ashley you know.'

'I know, but I don't think of you as Ashley. I have always known you as Grandma. You will always be Grandma to me, no matter who you are to everyone else. Thank you for taking me in. I was in quite a bad place after that little trouble at university. I thought Crossways was an even worse place to end up.'

'But living here with me hasn't been so awful?'

'Well, except for all the dead bodies.'

These are the favourite books Keera refers to or recommends. They aren't in any particular order, in case of any spoilers! If you want to know more, or read them: uk.bookshop.org/lists/who-shot-jackson-brodie-keera-s-book-recommends

Save the Cat – Blake Snyder
Six Dinner Sid – Inga Moore
A Bear Called Paddington – Michael Bond
Skandar and the Unicorn Thief – AF Steadman
Pride and Prejudice – Jane Austen
Rebecca – Daphne du Maurier
The Adventures of Sherlock Holmes – Sir Arthur Conan Doyle
The Lie of the Land – Guy Shrubsole
Entangled Life – Merlin Sheldrake
Wintering – Katherine May
The Life Impossible – Matt Haig
Here One Moment – Liane Moriarty
The Hometown Bookshop – Jenna Warren
Lessons in Chemistry – Bonnie Garmus
The Impossible Thing – Belinda Bauer
The Twyford Code – Janice Hallett
The Killer Question – Janice Hallett
The Skeleton Key – Erin Kelly
Slow Horses – Mick Herron
Karla's Choice – Nick Harkaway

Nicki Thornton ran her own bookshop for more than ten years, but luckily, none of her customers were ever murdered.

Nicki ran a bookshop to spread the joy of books and reading. She remains enthusiastic about anything to do with bookshops and promoting reading for pleasure.

A bookshop is often the heart of a community. Definitely where people swap gossip! And this is what inspired the Little Bookshop of Murders mysteries.

Nicki has always adored crime fiction and first wrote crime fiction for children as a fun way to introduce young readers to the genre. She writes stories for readers who like mysteries in the golden age tradition, but with a modern edge.

You can get news from Nicki and a peek behind the scenes of her writing life by joining her VIP Club. It's free to join and is part of the Substack community.

And as an exclusive offer to readers of this book, signing up will get you access to a secret page on Nicki's website where she shares many of the locations that inspire her books. nickithornton.substack.com

Also keep updated here:
www.nickithornton.co.uk
instagram.com/nicki_thornton/
facebook.com/nickithorntonauthor
uk.bookshop.org/shop/nicki_thornton

Don't miss the next thrilling instalment in the Little Bookshop of Murders mysteries.

The Game is Murder

Eight suspects. Eight detectives. One body.
A murder party that's no longer a game.

Keera Munroe is dreading playing in a murder mystery evening with an ultra competitive local group as the other players take strategy games way too seriously and are out to win at all costs.

What she's not expecting is when the corpse turns out to be real.

How is it possible someone's killed without any of the clever players seeing a thing? Will Keera be forced to accept this killer is too many moves ahead and will get away with murder?

Have you read the first in the series?

Little Bookshop of Murders

One burnt out lawyer. One shiny new bookshop.
One dead customer.

Former lawyer Keera Munroe wants to put her past behind her with nothing more challenging than selling enough books to pay the bills. But when Keera opens a bookshop in idyllic Crossways, there's a lot she cannot leave behind, like the fact she's hard-wired to seek out truth and justice. Or her nose for trouble - and that's telling her village life is not quite as lovely as it appears. Right about the time the first body turns up.

Nicki Thornton's debut middle-grade fantasy crime thriller The Last Chance Hotel won the Times/Chicken House Children's Fiction Competition and was translated into 15 languages. Her novels have been nominated for awards including the Carnegie Medal, the CrimeFest Best Crime Novel for Children and Specsavers National Book Awards.

The Last Chance Hotel

Hard-working Seth is the kitchen boy in the remote Last Chance Hotel, owned by the nasty Bunn family and their toxic daughter, Tiffany; his only friend is Nightshade, the kitchen cat.

Seth dreams of leaving, and of a future beyond the Last Hope Forest, away from Tiffany's schemes to torment him.

He wonders if his chance for change might finally have arrived when a bunch of strange characters come to stay.

But things go terribly wrong when the dessert Seth carefully made to impress kindly Dr Thallomius, instead poisons him.

Seth finds himself at the heart of a murder investigation with a lot more than Tiffany to worry about when he becomes the main suspect and accused of the crime.